Sins of a Rogue

KAYA AND PAUL

CONRAD CHRONICLES
BOOK TWO

C.K. MACKENZIE

Sins of a Rogue: Kaya and Paul Book 2

Conrad Chronicles Book 2

Contact Information: ckmackenzieauthor@gmail.com

Cover Art by Lynn Andreozzi

Interior Formatting by C.E. Higgins

Publishing History

First Edition, 2021

Digital ISBN 979-8-9850526-1-9

Published in the United States of America

This book has been a journey! Thank you to all who came on it with me. Love you all!

Villa San Giovanni, Italy

JANUARY 1785

Beneath her wide-brimmed hat, Kaya Hartley squinted into the brilliant blue skies of Villa San Giovanni. She watched gulls soar in the distance, beautiful, majestic creatures that glided on the wind. Closing her eyes, she listened to their echoing calls, faint whiffs of sound that lifted her spirits.

Her already sensitive stomach rolled, and she pressed her lips together against the remnants of her seasickness. The air smelled of the sea. Of salt and close bodies and the wonderful scent of people and life and movement.

Kaya whimpered and swallowed hard, trying not to breathe deeply. She stepped onto solid ground and, naturally, her legs gave out and her eyes shot open.

"I've got you." Her husband grasped her arm, and Kaya gratefully leaned against him.

"I hate the water."

"No, you don't," Paul snorted, his humor far too evident for her current liking. Still, he held her securely to his side.

His lips brushed her temple. She barely felt their comforting press through the hijab covering her head and shoulders, but she accepted the solace and relaxed into his touch.

"I do." Her whisper hurt her head. She licked dry, cracked lips.

She wanted to lie down in a dark, quiet room. Out of the sun and away from the blasted sea. She wanted Paul's arms around her and his steady heartbeat beneath her ear. Mostly, she wanted the world to stop moving.

"All my life I wanted to see the water. This is how I'm repaid for my curiosity."

Paul chuckled again, a soft brush of breath over her hot, taut skin. Thankfully, he didn't release his hold on her. Kaya hated her weakness, this unsteadiness that sucked the very life out of her.

Their satchel was filled with only fig rolls, dried dates, and olives, but still its heaviness weighed her down. The tiny bag was nestled between her and Paul, who carried the rest of their things.

"I detest being ill," she grumbled.

"I don't think it's anything personal on the water's part."

Kaya scoffed. Before she could think of a suitable reply, one that would defend herself and disparage the water, a sailor bumped into her. She instantly reached for her dagger with one hand and her bag with the other.

"Oi!" In a smooth step, Paul moved in front of her, blocking any potential attack or theft. "Watch where you're walking!"

"*Mi dispiace!*" The man shouted his apologies but didn't stop.

Grumbling Sicilian obscenities, Paul turned to steady her, his hands warm and firm on her arms.

In the nearly four months since leaving Cairo and her small family, Kaya had learned much of the world. Unfortunately, trusting others was a skill she hadn't yet mastered.

"Paul." She stood straight. Not because she wished to, but because her stiff bodice, and the jewels sewn into it, demanded she do so. Her stomach protested. Violently.

Kaya wished she'd sewn the jewels someplace else, impractical though that might have been. The uneven stones pressing against a stomach that hated the water was about as uncomfortable as anything she'd ever experienced.

Even in her limited experience.

"Come." Paul wrapped his arm around her waist again and took most of her weight, quite the bold move in public "We'll find an inn until you recover your land legs."

"I don't understand." Kaya frowned. "What does the land have to do with my legs and how I recover them?"

He ducked down to see her beneath the hat. His blue-green eyes danced in that way she'd come to recognize meant she'd said something amusing. Or naïve.

"Means until you're steady again on land." Paul shifted and gently took the satchel, slinging it over his own shoulders. He knocked his hat to the side in the process and deftly caught it before it fell.

Kaya marveled at his quick reflexes. The smoothness of them, the grace. She loved the way he moved, could watch him all day. Paul crouched down again to look her in the eye, and he smiled that slightly crooked but utterly authentic grin. Laden with their items, he ignored the added weight and his hat and pressed a kiss to her cheek.

"You'll be fine soon." He brushed his fingers along her cheek. "I'll even buy you fresh coffee."

"Buy, eh?" Closing her eyes and sighing, Kaya leaned her head on his arm.

"Promise." His vow held humor, but if he promised, she believed him. Even if Paul usually erred more on the side of thief than customer. "Come along, you're doing great, sweetheart."

She whimpered and staggered along the wharf, trying very hard to steady her stomach. This was her first voyage on water since leaving Egypt, and she'd discovered how much her body didn't enjoy the sea. "I'm finished with seasickness. No more ships for me. Ever."

The smell of the Strait of Messina, and life and wharves and whatever else clung to the air, churned her stomach.

Fantastic.

"Signora Conrad."

She turned toward the sound of the name Paul had used on their papers—or tried to turn. Paul held her steady, his shoulders stiff with annoyance. Kaya elbowed him, and he grunted. Not one for manners, her Paul.

"Be nice," she mumbled.

Paul grumbled unintelligibly but guided her around so she faced the polite, handsome ferry captain.

A head shorter than she, and with a shock of gray hair, the captain watched her with concerned blue eyes. He'd done so since Kaya warned him of her seasickness when they booked passage.

"Captain Morano." Kaya nodded and instantly stilled.

Her stomach revolted at the simplest things. Like nodding. She grasped Paul's hand, fingers digging into his, and swallowed. Hard.

She detested this sickness.

"The inn at via Brindisi, it stands after the *terremoto.*"

"The *terremoto?*" Kaya couldn't place the new word. Since landing in Sicily, she'd learned much of the language, but not that word. "I don't understand."

Captain Morano frowned. "*Terremoto*...ah." He held his hands up, palms flat, and rocked them back and forth. "Tremor."

"Oh! Tremor. Sì. A ground tremor."

"Wonderful," Paul muttered, entirely too low for the captain to hear. "Just what we need."

"Where is via Brindisi?" she asked.

"Two streets in, on the right." Captain Morano gestured grandly, but Kaya didn't follow his movements.

"*Grazie,* Captain." Kaya smiled at the kindly gentleman, who looked genuinely concerned.

"*Benvenuti.*" The captain tipped his hat, face crinkling with his smile, and turned around to see to whatever ferry captains saw to after they made port.

She patted Paul's hand, warm and firm around her waist. "We'll be fine."

"Plague forty years ago, and now earthquakes," Paul huffed as they walked up the wharf to the main streets. Though he no doubt wanted to move faster, Kaya kept the pace slow until her nausea abated. "I knew we should've sailed for Reggio di Calabria."

Kaya shuddered, shivering in the warm sunlight. "Too far."

Paul grasped her hands and wrapped them in his warm ones. "I know. At least no one knows where we've landed."

He meant that anyone who followed them, either from Egypt or across Sicily, might also assume they'd sailed for the larger city of Reggio di Calabria. Only a fool crossed the Strait of Messina's rough waters if there was another option.

"Plus, we don't know the state of Reggio di Calabria. Ground tremors spread; they are not—" Kaya broke off, searching for the English word. "Not in one place."

"Isolated. Localized." Paul released her hands, moving one of his to the small of her back. Kaya barely resisted stretching into his touch. "Can you walk faster?"

"No." She sighed, body shuddering at the faintest jar, but she forced her legs to carry her more quickly. Each heavy step unsettled her barely settled stomach. "Why?"

"I want you off these wharves." His voice lowered, but she couldn't tell if it was because he'd looked behind them. "I don't want you exposed like this, in the open, where you can't defend yourself."

Kaya started to reply but had no retort. She couldn't fight, not in this condition. If someone threatened her or tried to kidnap her—both of which had happened in the previous four months—she was too vulnerable to protect herself.

"I can walk faster." She uttered only a partial lie.

Her legs trembled, and her head pounded. Despite the monstrosity of a hat she wore over her hijab, her eyes ached in the bright sunlight. However, Paul wanted them in town, where no one remembered them, and she didn't blame him.

She had no desire to repeat their more dangerous adventures in Sicily. Frankly, she wasn't in any position to do so anyway. Right now, she'd be more likely to fall over than wield her khanjar.

They blended in on the wharves, at least, moving easily with the mass of people disembarking and rushing in all directions.

Sailors and wharf workers shouted in several languages. Kaya tensed, waiting for her old fears. Old, unnecessary fears, but they still occasionally shivered up her spine. She waited, but no shout came telling her she'd been discovered.

"Why are we turning right?" Kaya frowned as they rounded a corner.

They passed brightly painted doors and new construction, workers shouting to each other as they hauled large stones into place. She stumbled on the uneven walk, but Paul caught her.

"Easy. Easy, sweetheart. I've got you."

"I know." She licked her lips and tried not to think about how fully she trusted him.

In Mazzarelli, Sicily, they'd agreed to see where their relationship led. They travelled over the island and made love. Grew closer. Being with Paul warmed her. He made her laugh, held her at night, promised with deed and word that he'd take care of her.

The once-spoken words, however, had not been repeated. Paul's confession of love scared and confused her. Her reciprocal *I love you* terrified her. The largeness of that feeling simultaneously crushed and elated her.

Her knees gave out again, whether from seasickness or all-encompassing love, she didn't know. Paul held her firmly. That warmth of security and rightness spread through her, warming her numb fingers and heating her cheeks.

What had she been saying? "Right—why are we turning right?"

When Paul laughed, her heart flipped and her stomach

swooped like the birds she'd earlier admired. Kaya gritted her teeth against that swooping.

She couldn't ignore her answering smile.

"The inn is to the right." He said it as if she were the dense one.

Kaya sniffed haughtily, or as haughtily as she could manage. She closed her eyes and trusted him to guide her along the walk. "This from the man who insisted on traveling *around* Sicily even though Mazzarelli sits on the eastern coast, so much closer to Messina?"

"You wanted to see the island," Paul countered in an equally haughty tone. "I did not wish to disappoint my wife."

She laughed, a soft breath of sound. True. They had seen much of the historic architecture and stunning mountain views.

"Sicily is beautiful," she admitted. "I should have quite liked to settle in Palermo. Or seen Syracuse or Augusta."

"You loved Agrigento." In Agrigento, they explored the ruins, pagan temples, and ancient churches.

"Yes." She sighed happily at the memory of their sheer enjoyment, and she squeezed his hand. "Agrigento was lovely."

"And if we hadn't walked around the island, you wouldn't have seen Palermo." Paul again ducked his head and met her gaze beneath the hat. "Or the Valley of Temples."

The look he gave her stole her breath. That soft, focused look that blanked her mind of anything save Paul. As if none of the people around them existed, and only the two of them mattered.

Kaya returned his smile, her heart skipping and her blood warming, but then quickly averted her gaze. She loved him. It swelled her heart and settled in her soul. That ever-expanding warmth of connection and acceptance.

This wonderful, paranoid, sometimes dishonest, and always concerned for her well-being man.

Scrambling for words that wouldn't convey her inner turmoil, Kaya grasped for the threads of their conversation. "Why are we pretending to stay at the inn?"

Paul slowed their pace. Relieved, Kaya wished for a bed. It'd taken her weeks to recover from her first voyage. Hopefully, a night's rest would restore her from today's short ferry ride.

"I don't want the captain thinking we're not." She heard the grimace in his voice. He stopped and helped her lean against the side of a building. The cool stone, shadowed from the bright noon sun, bit into her back, but it did not move.

"Is that why you used Conrad instead of Hartley?" Kaya leaned her head against the wall, tipping her hat to meet his gaze. No longer moving, her stomach finally settled.

Paul looked around the crowded square, watching everyone who walked past. She knew his back itched, in the open as they were, exposed and vulnerable. She also knew he stood before her to protect her. Kaya's lips curled upward in fondness and trust.

When they sneaked out of Cairo, she hadn't thought she'd learn anything about Sergeant Hartley. It amazed her how well she now knew even his smallest mannerisms. The square of his shoulders, the sparkle in his eyes, the quirk of his lips.

"Our papers say Conrad." Paul's voice was pitched low. "I couldn't find anyone on that entire damn island I trusted to forge a new set."

"You don't trust anyone."

He held her gaze with an intense steadiness that said more than words. It settled over her, the heavy understanding of his wordless look. "I trust you," he whispered.

"Paul." Throat tight, she willed her heart to stop pounding quite so loudly.

He looked away and pulled her upright, steadying her, though he did not look at her. "Can you continue?"

"Yes." She leaned her head against his arm.

He wrapped his arm around her shoulders, and she relaxed. Paul's embrace provided a safety she craved.

"I forgot about our papers," Kaya admitted, accepting his obvious change of subject.

They passed the inn, the sunlight glinting off the stone. Kaya saw what Captain Morano meant about it still standing, though how remained a mystery. Rubble littered the street corners, court-yards, and abandoned lots. This inn, however, stood defiant.

"Where *are* we staying, then?"

"Not sure yet. I'll know it when I see it."

"As long as there's a bed," she sighed. "And coffee, or carob juice."

"I've got you." Paul slipped his arm to her waist and tightened his hold on her. "Just a little further," he promised.

She met his gaze, serious and worried. Kaya smiled; it wobbled, but it was fully formed. "All right."

"Still don't know why you trust me."

Her heart twisted. Paul didn't say those words often. Once, during an argument, when they'd first landed in Sicily, he insisted she'd misplaced her trust in him.

I'm not a nice man.

Kaya had yet to see that side of him. He'd protected her, a stranger, when he could have tossed her body into *en-Nīl* and stolen the jewels for himself. Or abandoned her in the desert, in Damietta, in Mazzarelli.

He'd cared for her when that wretched seasickness took hold.

"You're a very lucky man," Kaya said now. "You're lucky to have me."

Paul laughed, a gentle breath of sound that warmed her heart. His fingers cupped the back of her head, and he pressed his lips to her forehead, his way of agreeing with her when he had no words.

"How about I sit here?" Kaya squeezed his arms and flicked her eyes to a low stone wall beside them. She thought it used to be the side of a building. Now it sat abandoned, its stone stolen for other structures.

"I'm not leaving you."

"Paul." She sighed and sat, too exhausted to move another step.

"*Kaya.*" He raised an eyebrow, and she defiantly met his gaze. "The last time I left you, several villagers thought you were a witch, sent to steal their souls by...I don't even know what." Paul raised his other eyebrow, too, but Kaya steadfastly refused to rise —either to his barb or physically. "You disagree?"

She huffed, annoyed with the memory. "They were clearly mistaken."

"Clearly," he agreed, dryly. "The time before, you were nearly kidnapped by slavers."

She dismissed that with a wave of her hand and an indignant huff. "I fought him off."

His lips thinned, and his eyes hardened. "Kaya, you can't fight anyone off now."

"*I can't.*" Oh, she hated to admit that. The words barely reached her ears, but she knew Paul heard them. Annoyed with her weakness, her body, her aching stomach and head, she looked away from his gaze for a moment then back again. "I'm sure the ginger and turmeric were supposed to help, but I—I can't—"

Frustrated, she broke off. Never had her body betrayed her as it had on the water. She'd trained her entire life to fight, to defend herself from her family's enemies. Once she left her home, Kaya envisioned sailing across the world, exploring every corner of it.

But if she never set foot on a ship again, she'd die a happy woman.

Paul ran a hand down his face. His shoulders tensed beneath his pack, and her own shoulders relaxed at his obvious unease. She knew this mannerism, too. The against-his-better-judgment agreement.

He often looked like that.

"Paul, I'll stay here. I'll be fine. I have my khanjar." She pulled the gold-encrusted, bone-handled dagger from its sheath at her waist.

His lips thinned, and he scowled and pointed a finger at her. "Don't move." He jabbed the finger again. "Don't wander."

"I promise." Kaya refrained from stating the obvious. She was on this wall because her body needed rest. She'd *wander* nowhere. Taking his hand, she squeezed. "I'll stay here."

Paul sighed in resignation. He pressed his lips to her forehead, then turned sharply and disappeared around a corner. Able to move faster without her, Kaya doubted he'd be long.

Clothing rustled near her, and she snapped her eyes open. She gripped her dagger, annoyed at her moment of inattentiveness. Three women walked by, chatting rapidly, a mixture of Sicilian, which Kaya understood, and a dialect she did not recognize. Kaya caught enough to understand they feared something—*oppio*.

Intrigued at this new word, she listened more closely. Their hushed conversation receded as they hurried away. Kaya shivered in the warm sunlight and suddenly wished she'd stayed with Paul.

Alone on the street, isolated despite the freedom of being outside, in another country, Kaya gripped her khanjar and sat up straighter.

Gaze sweeping the via, she thanked her grandfather for teaching her how to protect herself. Gidd, the image of him as she and Paul left her home, burned in her memory, and Kaya blinked to clear tears from her eyes. She needed to remain alert, not succumb to grief.

In Cairo, thousands died from starvation. When she left in September, Gidd had assured her he had enough food and money, resources and connections, to live a very long life. But, with no news from the city and no means to contact him, Kaya worried every day.

Jaw clenched against her grief, Kaya focused on the here and now. Gidd wanted her to explore the world. Perhaps not in *this* sense, but he wished her safely away from Egypt and the long reach of the Ottoman Empire.

Searching the bright square for Paul, Kaya looked for danger as well. People hurried past her, and she didn't think it was because she was sitting on the wall. In the last months, Kaya had learned all too well of the dangers lurking outside her childhood home. Paul, however, had seen only the cruel, dirty world, had fought and killed to survive it.

It hit her in the chest, her love for Paul. Surprised, Kaya

rubbed her fingers where her heart pounded. Of all the people they'd met in Sicily, Kaya had not wished to know any of them as intimately as she did Paul.

She did not want to leave him.

Saying the words *once* had taken more courage than she realized she possessed. More than leaving Cairo with the stranger she married, more than fighting the slavers in the desert or the kidnappers in Damietta's souk.

Shaking herself, Kaya searched for a distraction, as she had for months now. A young girl hurried by with a basket swinging on her arm.

"*Perdono*, what's in the basket?" Kaya used her careful Sicilian, pleased when the girl stopped.

The girl halted but didn't approach. Her head swiveled left and right, and she looked down at her basket in surprise, as if she'd forgotten she carried it. She moved toward Kaya with measured steps, keeping the basket between her body and Kaya, a move Kaya heartedly approved. "*Bergamotto*."

In small increments, so as not to startle the child, Kaya leaned forward and peered at the fruit the girl held up. "They look like lemons. May I purchase one?"

"They are special." The girl shuffled closer, clearly warming to Kaya. She glanced over her shoulder and took another step. "They grow in the winter. They are very good to rid yourself of *pidocchi*."

Frowning at the unfamiliar word, Kaya asked, "*Ripeta prego*."

"*Pidocchi*." The girl frowned, clearly trying to think of another way to convey her meaning. Finally, she reached to her head, hand hovering over her tightly bound braids, and pretended to scratch violently. Kaya brightened. Lice! *Pidocchi* had to mean lice, and if it didn't, anything that soothed an itchy scalp was worth the purchase price.

"*Sì, sì. Quanto?*" Kaya reached into the small pouch on her waist, pushed her dagger further up on her lap, and offered the girl a few coins.

Eyes wide at the sight of the dagger, the girl pocketed the coins. As she did so, Kaya sensed Paul. She turned and spotted him casually strolling from the opposite direction he'd left in. She narrowed her eyes at his relaxed stroll. Did she need to run? Or had his inn-scouting gone better than anticipated?

His tight grin worried her. Standing, Kaya gripped her khanjar and braced to fight.

"What's your name?" Kaya calmly asked the girl.

"Teresa." Teresa followed Kaya's gaze. "Is he your *marito*?"

She jerked. Kaya often introduced Paul as her husband. He was, after all, and she had grown used to being referred to as his wife. The way Teresa asked, however, brought home that very real fact.

"*Sì*." Her smile widened. Her fingers loosened on her dagger, and warmth flooded her bones, easing her weariness and exhaustion. "*Sì*, Teresa, he is."

"He comes from the dens. Be careful, signora." Teresa's voice shook. Her eyes, wide now and scared, darted over the street again. "He walks from a bad place."

Two

ens? Bad place? Perhaps she didn't understand the Calabrian words correctly.

Kaya frowned and looked back to Paul. He walked faster now, lips pursed, jaw set, body rigid beneath the pack and satchels he carried. Hand gripping her khanjar, she stood in front of Teresa.

"Stay behind me," she snapped. "What bad place? What are the dens?"

Paul took Kaya's elbow and turned for the opposite direction before Teresa had the chance to answer. "Can you walk?"

A chill ran down her spine. Paul spoke in English, alarming Kaya more than the abruptness with which he'd touched her.

"*Sì.* What happened?" Kaya fell into step beside him, grabbing Teresa as she did so.

Her eyes slid from Teresa to the empty street. No one walked it. It looked darker, more sinister than the rest of the area. Kaya shuddered and met Paul's hooded gaze.

"Let's go." He jerked his head toward a nearby street and tugged her arm, pulling her with him. His gaze landed on Teresa, and he switched to Sicilian. "We'll find an inn, one far from the wharves."

"Paul!" Kaya stopped and looked to Teresa. The poor girl looked equal parts frightened and intrigued. Torn, confused, Kaya stepped from him. She deliberately spoke to Teresa. "What is it? What is that place?"

"It's the *oppio*, signora." Teresa's voice, young and thin, trembled. "Don't go there. Listen to your man."

"*Oppio*?" Kaya repeated, careful to keep her own voice low. "What is that?"

"Opium." Paul flinched but continued in quick English, "She means opium, Kaya. The street is filled with opium dens."

His voice carried a heaviness that squeezed her heart. Kaya wanted to ask what he meant. She did not know what opium was or why Paul sounded as panicked as Teresa. Paul, who had seen and done things Kaya never wanted to.

"Marco is there." Teresa's tone was firm, and Kaya looked to the girl. She was holding her basket more firmly. Clearly still terrified, she stepped for the street. "I need to find him."

"No." Paul's command shot along the street as if he'd shouted it. Teresa flinched. She looked from Paul to Kaya with her chin jutted out. "Teresa, you know what's down there." He swallowed hard.

Kaya didn't understand. Paul's reluctance and his frantic urgency sent chills over her skin.

"Kaya." His voice trembled. "We need to leave. Teresa, we'll walk you home. Where do you live?" Paul met her gaze. His normal calm disappeared, and he now looked wild.

Even as she opened her mouth to question him, Kaya thought better of it. His agitation terrified her. "Teresa." She tore her gaze from Paul's and looked to the girl. Teresa looked mutinous but scared. "Who is Marco?"

That wasn't what Kaya had meant to ask, but she recognized Teresa's stubbornness all too well. Stubbornness had helped her perfect everything her grandfather taught her. Had pushed her out of Cairo with a stranger.

Glancing around the square, Kaya noticed they were alone. Oh, people walked past them, but they gave the trio a wide berth, eyeing them as if they suspected them of a most heinous crime.

Something else leaving Cairo and sneaking from city to city had taught her: when the populace turns on you, run.

"My brother." Teresa whispered the words so low Kaya almost didn't hear her. "Mama says he is lost to the dens, but—but—" She broke off with a sob.

Helpless, Kaya looked to Paul. Jaw rigid, eyes flat, he opened his mouth only to snap it closed. He didn't want to get involved, she could tell. But Teresa's tenaciousness, and her very real fear just beneath, urged Kaya to help.

Stranger or not, and as out of place as she might have been, Kaya needed to help. She knew nothing about children or opium dens, but she knew her heart. If she didn't help, she'd never forgive herself.

"Teresa!"

The girl flinched. The shout forcibly reminded Kaya of her aching head and unsettled stomach. Knuckles white around her khanjar, she shifted and stood next to Paul.

A woman not much taller than Teresa barreled toward them. The fire in her dark eyes and her rapid pace did not detract from her obvious fear. From the resemblance between them, Kaya guessed this woman to be Teresa's mother.

"Mama." Teresa sighed and confirmed Kaya's assessment. "She'll be angry."

"I told you not to come here." The woman, seemingly oblivious to Kaya and Paul, grabbed Teresa's arm and shook her. "I told you—to the market and straight home. Stay away from this end of town."

"*Sì*, Mama." Teresa hung her head, her basket drooping. "But the signora, she—"

"Teresa warned us," Paul interrupted. He bowed as deeply as possible given his pack, her satchel, and the stiffness in his body.

"My wife"—he gestured to her, and Kaya nodded—"and I were unaware what the street held."

Teresa's mum didn't look convinced. Her gaze darted between them and the street where, apparently, her son now resided. Her fingers still clenched Teresa's arm, but the girl didn't squirm, merely stepped closer to her mother.

"If you'd be so kind as to direct us to an inn," Kaya said in the stifling awkwardness. "We've only just disembarked and need a place to sleep."

Her tiredness abruptly returned, and she blindly reached for Paul's arm.

"Mama." Teresa stood straighter, holding her basket higher. "They can stay with us."

Paul snorted. Wonderful. Just what they needed. A family with at least one child lost to the dens inviting strangers into their home. But he understood. Generosity toward strangers, travelers such as they, was a way of life here.

In Bombay, even the poorest families offered food and shelter to traveling strangers. He'd seen it and scoffed at their naïvety, their stupidity. They hadn't even been able to feed themselves.

But he'd never been so grateful to generous strangers as he was now.

"Paul?"

He looked down at Kaya, and she tugged his arm. Only then did he realize he'd turned toward the street and the siren's call of opium. The damned scent already clung to him, clogging his airways. Grinding his teeth, Paul held Kaya tighter.

His lifeline, his salvation.

"What's wrong?" Her voice, low and concerned, barely carried past the roaring in his ears.

Protect Kaya. Keep Kaya safe.

"Nothing." He swallowed around the lie. "Everything's all right."

"Don't lie to me," she snapped.

He opened his mouth again, but no words came.

They had not traveled so far as to be completely free of either the Ottoman Empire's reach or the East India Company. They might never. To keep her safe, Paul vowed to do everything in his power—however illegal, immoral, or dishonest—to stay clear-headed and protect his beloved wife.

The simple fact was he couldn't live without her.

"My wife," he heard himself say to Teresa and her mother. "She needs rest. The ferry crossing made her ill."

"You may stay with us." Teresa's mum nodded as if she offered such hospitality to every couple arriving in their city.

He hadn't the energy to argue and merely gestured for the woman to lead the way. Far, far from this street with its remembered temptations. Paul hurried Kaya after the woman, his legs itching to run—to or away from the dens, he didn't know. He held Kaya tighter, though she seemed able to walk much better than when he'd left her.

Had it only been moments ago?

Felt like a lifetime.

After they turned a second corner, Paul realized he hadn't paid attention to where they headed. Cursing, he forced his focus on the streets, the turns, their surroundings. He needed to keep alert, wary.

The scent of it followed him. That rich, flowery smell, as if someone had immersed the poppy seeds in a pot of boiling water to release their aroma.

"Paul." Kaya forcibly slowed and tilted her head, meeting his gaze. "What's wrong?"

He wanted to tell her. Wanted to let the words spill from within and confess his past. But he locked his jaw tight against the words. How could he tell her his deepest shame?

"Just a memory." Paul looked to his wife. His love. The vise around his throat eased, and he tried again. It didn't surprise him that Kaya didn't know about opium. He very much doubted Tahir had spoken to her about the ills plaguing Cairo—every city, any city in the world.

Kaya snorted. "You are a terrible liar."

"Only to you," he muttered.

He'd have to tell her. He hadn't been able to control his reaction to walking down that street. If he'd had more time—if he'd been even a little prepared.

He barely heard Teresa's mum welcome them into her home or direct them toward a small room with a bed. He watched Kaya sink gratefully onto it but didn't move. Frozen to the spot, Paul floundered.

"Paul." Kaya rose and crossed the short distance between them. "Come. Here, let me help you."

He caught her hand. She already had; she'd already saved him. The words stopped in his throat—the vise had returned.

"Give me the satchel." Her voice gentled, and he felt more like the child, Teresa, than Kaya's husband. Nonetheless, he did as she ordered and pulled her satchel over his head.

His hat fell to the ground, but nether made an attempt to pick it up. Eyes trained on it, Paul felt Kaya move around him.

"I need your help, Paul." Her hands brushed over his shoulders, and he automatically reached up to release the pack. She caught it, and he wordlessly took it from her, leaning it against the wall.

He shucked his coat and waistcoat and sat on the bed. Paul pulled Kaya down with him and held her. His fingers, numb since discovering the dens, warmed against her skin.

He wanted to make love to her, wanted to feel her skin beneath his, to taste her, feel her shudder around him as she climaxed.

"It calls to me." The words ripped from his throat. "I hear it like a siren's song. A gentle wave of smell, the heavy temptation of smoke."

Part of him wondered if Kaya knew what a siren was, but then he realized she'd read widely and in many languages. Surely, she'd read the ancient stories. The other part of him wondered if he made any sense. He doubted it.

"John and Oliver dragged me out of the dens. I don't remember that. Don't remember them finding me." He snorted, shuddered. "I don't even remember how I found my way in. They said I'd disappeared a week before and the provost was after me. They lied to him, bribed the surgeon, and searched Bombay for me."

For his worthless hide.

"They are good friends." Her lips brushed his neck, soft and warm. "How did they find you?"

Paul laughed, a short, humorless sound. "No idea. I never asked. By the time I was coherent enough to...well, then Tahir's letter arrived. And then—"

And then the massacre. The desertion. What did Kaya insist on calling it? His righteous protest of the cruel and unjust order against innocents. The East India Company would *not* see it as such. The more time passed, the more Paul wondered if she was right.

"Opium, it is like alcohol, then? You crave it, believe you need it?" Kaya shifted and unwound her arms from his waist.

Paul immediately missed her touch, the warmth of her understanding and love. He watched her straighten, remove her hijab, and unlace her bodice. Upon loosening the constraints of boning and the jewels sewn into the material, she breathed deeply. Paul lay on the bed. The fresh cleanness of the bedding struck him, and he pulled Kaya close.

"When Teresa said her brother was lost in the dens, she meant that he doesn't know he's there."

She shifted onto an elbow and ran her fingertips over his

brow, along his cheek. "You knew what she meant. That's why you wanted us away from there."

"I want us away from this entire city." Paul closed his eyes and captured her hand, holding it to his lips. "It doesn't matter that I know what they're going through. Well. What the son... I doubt he even remembers he has a family."

"Signora Spanò—"

"Who?"

Kaya huffed and splayed her hand over his chest. "Teresa's mum. She seems determined not to mention Marco."

"Ah. Yes, I'm sure." Paul looked from her to the plain stone wall, the small, high window.

He blinked several times. Instead of the warm, clean room in Villa San Giovanni, he lay in that stifling filth in Bombay. The room Oliver and John dragged him to once they found him. Where the surgeon tied him to the bed and force-fed him.

"Paul!"

"What?" He jerked. "Yes."

Kaya frowned, troubled. He didn't know how to speak the rest, how to tell her about the pain of withdraw, the cramping, the cravings so strong he nearly scratched his arms off. How did he tell her such things when she didn't see him as that sort of man?

"You're not that person anymore." Kaya kissed him. Damn it, how did she always know what he was thinking, what to say? "You're not, Paul. Whatever happened then, however it happened, you're not that person."

She rested her head on his chest, and he tightened his arm around her. How could he let her go?

"Rest, Kaya. You're not recovered from the ferry."

"I'm fine. The walk restored me greatly."

Paul laughed. He tilted her chin and kissed her, a soft, slow kiss that probably did more to steady him than it did her. Kaya was strong, but the water undid her. He ran his fingers along the scoop of her chemise. He undid her, too, and, like the new addiction she was, her taste obliterated the remembered touch of the opium smoke.

"Kaya." *I love you.*

He didn't say the words. He wanted to, but they terrified him as much as the lure of the dens. She pulled back and framed his face, her dark eyes blazing with the love she didn't speak, either.

"I won't let you fall."

"Will you catch me?" His voice cracked, fingers clenching around the base of her neck.

"Always."

Paul kissed her again, rough now, hard and bruising, and, though he wanted to be gentle, he couldn't stop himself. Kaya whimpered, returning his kiss with all the passion he'd grown to expect from his lovely wife.

Eventually, he eased her head back to his chest, where she rested against his pounding heart. Her hand flattened over his belly, and she turned onto her side and pressed against him.

"Sleep, Kaya. Please."

Within moments, her breathing evened out and she slept. Paul kissed the top of her head and carefully slipped from underneath, reluctant to leave her. After brushing long tendrils of hair off her face, he stood and grabbed his coat.

Small as the room looked, that the Spanòs' house had at least two separate bedrooms told him the family's status. No sharing a bed, no single room for a half dozen people. This family had money.

Enough for Marco to afford opium. At least in the beginning. What the boy did now to fund the craving, Paul all too easily guessed.

He slipped out the bedroom door and eased it closed behind him. No matter what Kaya said, the ferry ride had drained her. She'd fallen asleep too quickly to be as restored as she claimed. Paul didn't want to disturb her, but the justice she sought for others now beat within him.

One way, a small way, to atone for his past sins.

"Do you want your son back?"

Signora Spanò, standing at the long wooden table kneading dough, jerked. Grimacing, she rubbed her knee and eyed him warily, fingers clenched. Her lips thinned, and her gaze darted from him to where he presumed Teresa stood. Paul didn't look away from the woman.

"You cannot return him to me. He is lost to the opium."

"I can. Are you willing to do what it takes to keep him?"

Three

Kaya jerked awake. Disoriented and thirsty, she reached for Paul.

No, he'd left. She'd vaguely felt him slip from beside her, heard the soft thunk of the door closing. He'd taken his coat and hat. Stretching upright, she rolled her shoulders and eased her neck from side to side.

On a small bedside table sat a bowl of fresh cut fruit. Kaya didn't recognize it but reached for a slice anyway. Her stomach had finally settled, and her head no longer ached. Rubbing her tender belly where their jewels rested, she slowly chewed the fruit.

Delighted at the fresh taste, an oddly sweet burst of flavor, she took another piece. Their items lay in a heap of disorganization that surprised her, given Paul's usual meticulousness. Kaya ignored her untied bodice. Enjoying the freedom entirely too much to worry, she bent to righten the pack and satchel.

Beyond the door, the house remained silent. Kaya frowned, then quickly tied the laces of her bodice and draped her hijab around her. She grabbed the bowl of fruit and stepped out the door. The house was larger than she expected, the stone walls cool to her touch even in the heat of the day. She walked down the short hallway toward the main rooms.

Teresa stood there, kneading dough, but her mother was nowhere to be found. More suspiciously, Kaya did not see Paul anywhere.

"Hello." She smiled at Teresa and only then heard clanking from a separate room off the kitchen. Signora Spanò emerged, face bright with sweat. "Thank you for allowing us to stay," Kaya said suddenly.

Awkward in this new situation, Kaya wondered how one thanked people for their hospitality. Derya often told her about the ritual of helping those who need it. But she and Derya, who had raised her, had never done so in their Cairo home. They'd never entertained anyone.

It'd been far too dangerous to accept strangers into the house.

Traveling these last months as she and Paul had, they'd stayed in inns along the base of Sicily's many mountains. Deep in the woods, where no bandits or overzealous villagers could find them. Other than with Letizia in Mazzarelli, Kaya had never stayed in someone's *home*.

"Your husband, he is mad," Signora Spanò spat.

"Ah, yes."

This probably hadn't been what Derya meant by opening one's home to strangers in need. Derya also probably hadn't meant *Paul*. Would she have approved of him? Kaya hoped so— Tahir did, and usually that had been enough for Derya. But for Kaya's husband?

She had no idea, and the upswell of grief at knowing Derya would never meet Paul made her throat ache.

"*Sì*, Signora Spanò." Kaya repeated before she thought it through. "He often is."

"Signora Conrad—"

"Kaya," she interrupted.

Strangers or not, Kaya was staying in their house. She wished them to call her by her proper name. So few ever had.

"Kaya." Signora Spanò nodded and offered a slight smile. "I am Antoinette."

"Pleased to meet you, Antionette." Nodding, at a loss for further words, she ate the last bite of fruit. What had Paul done to earn him such a pronouncement so early in their stay? "What is this fruit?"

When in doubt, change the subject. Paul had taught her that.

"Bergamot." Teresa offered that bright smile she'd first bestowed Kaya on the street. "It has many uses. But you must go far into the mountains to find enough."

Before Kaya responded, Paul walked in without so much as knocking. His eyes, wild and wide, met hers and softened. He ignored their hosts and crossed the room, taking her hands.

"How are you feeling?" His fingers brushed the insides of her wrist, and Kaya shivered. He frowned and bent to look her in the eye. "Still queasy?"

"No." She licked her lips. His touch alone had that effect on her. "Where were you?"

They spoke in Sicilian, though Kaya didn't know how much Teresa and her mum understood. She supposed they'd need to learn Calabrian now that they were here. On the other hand, Teresa had heard them speak in English.

Paul's paranoia had rubbed off on her. More so than normal. Kaya pushed languages aside. One problem at a time.

"I know where the boy is." Paul grimaced. His hands tightened around hers, and he breathed far too shallowly. Only then did Kaya smell the sickeningly sweet smoke clinging to his clothing. "I need—" He squeezed his eyes closed, hands clenching and unclenching. "I need to get this stench off."

"Antoinette." Kaya didn't tear her gaze from Paul's pale face. "We need a bucket of water, *pi fauri*. And Teresa, more bergamot."

Kaya didn't pay attention as they raced to fill her request. Antoinette spoke rapidly to Teresa, but Kaya only understood every few words. Rigid and breathing shallowly, Paul looked—she didn't know. Kaya had never seen him like this, so stern and yet open, in a way.

He normally didn't show outsiders this much emotion.

It terrified her.

"Paul." She pressed her hands to his cheeks and willed him to open his eyes. "Paul, talk to me. Tell me what's wrong. What can I do?"

He wrapped his arms around her and crushed her to his chest. Surprised and out of her depth at such a vulnerable and obvious display of affection, Kaya hugged him back. She let him hold onto her and muttered soothing nonsense. She didn't know if it helped or not, but she refused to let him go.

How could she when he desperately clung to her?

Paul buried his face in the crook of her neck and heaved in great breaths. Finally, finally he released her, stepping back. He didn't drop his arms from her waist.

"Don't leave me." He sucked in a deep breath and shuddered. "Help me bathe. I have to get the smell off me."

"Come into the room." Kaya caught Antoinette's gaze and titled her head toward the rear. Far from the mistrustful, suspicious look heir host had offered earlier, now her face was pained. Stricken. Sad.

"Teresa." Kaya forced her voice to remain calm and polite despite the panic rising in her throat. "Please take Signore Conrad's clothing and give it away. We'll find something else."

"Kaya." Her name on his lips, a strangled word of helplessness, tore at her, and she guided him toward their room.

Kaya kept her gaze on Paul though he closed his eyes, his hands clenched at his sides. She tapped her toe while Teresa and her mother set a pair of water-filled wooden buckets on the floor and a bowl with three or four of the fruits on the table. She didn't watch them leave.

She'd have to thank them later, not only for their hospitality but for this extra kindness.

"Give me your coat, Paul." She walked behind him, her hands running over his taut shoulders, his rigid spine. She didn't wait for him to move but slid the material down his arms. He shifted just enough to let the coat fall to the ground.

"Now your shirt. Paul, I need your help. You have to undress."

He snorted. "This is *not* how I want to hear those words from you."

The fist around her lungs eased. If he could joke about their private life, he wasn't as far gone as she feared. The opium dens hadn't taken him.

"You have to undress first." Kaya walked in front of him and winked.

This she also understood, the passion between them, the desire to touch him, to taste him, always bubbling beneath the surface. She ran her hand over his cock, gratified when he hardened beneath her touch. That fist closing around her chest slipped further open.

"Sit"—she glanced at the scarce furniture in the room—"on the stool. I'll find a linen."

The three-legged stool, far too low for a man of Paul's height, groaned ominously under his weight.

"Take your shoes off and untie your trousers."

Gaze on hers, Paul did as she commanded, dropping his clothing in an undignified heap. He sat back on the stool and waited for her.

Kaya scooped up the clothing, averting her face from the cloying smell, and opened the door. Teresa shifted from foot to foot just outside.

"Thank you, Teresa." Nodding to the girl, Kaya handed her the clothing and stepped back into the room.

She brushed her hands down her skirts, hoping to rid her skin of the stench. Turning to Paul, she pressed her lips together and braced for this next, uncertain step. His intense gaze unsettled her.

Suddenly, her limbs stiffened, and her fingers forgot how to function. Graceless, uncoordinated, unwieldly, Kaya knelt before him. Her knees slammed against the wooden floor, and her dress caught awkwardly beneath her.

Ill at ease, a feeling quite unfamiliar, Kaya tore her gaze from his. Staring at her hands, useless against what troubled him, her mind raced for something to say. Anything to break the storm brewing in his gaze.

The Paul who stared at her was a stranger.

Deeply inhaling the scent of the fruit, she squeezed it into the water, which was lukewarm to her touch, and swirled it with her hand. She dipped a rag into the bucket and wrung it out.

"What did you find?" The words, whispered as they were, shattered the silence.

Paul jerked beneath her gentle touch. Kaya closed her eyes, praying she hadn't set him off, broken something. She didn't understand. She wanted to shove those words back in, but the damage had been done.

"Marco is—he wasn't in the dens I searched."

Kaya frowned. "There are more than one?"

She looked down at the bucket of water. Wonderful. She needed to control her tongue. Her questions normally made Paul chuckle, at the very least smile. Now he continued to watch her as if she were the stranger. Or his only salvation.

"What—" She scrambled for words, for understanding. "What did you find?"

"Hell."

Paul didn't elaborate.

Kaya didn't know how to ask him to. Instead, she ran the linen over his shoulders, along his scars and rigid muscles. She kissed down his back as she washed away the clinging stench of the opium.

He didn't relax, not as she expected him to. Slowly, painfully, his hands unclenched. When she knelt before him again, the lines bracketing his mouth eased. Kaya kissed him, a light brush of her lips. When Paul kissed her back, she nearly wept.

Uncertain, floundering, scared, Kaya swallowed her questions.

Paul's hand cupped the back of her head, and his mouth opened to hers. Letting all her love and passion for this amazing man pour into the kiss, Kaya felt his desperation beat through her.

Whatever happened in those dens terrified him.

Paul carefully undid her hijab and pressed his mouth to the base of her throat, nipping the skin there. He breathed in and sighed her name. His fingers combed through her hair, and he groaned against her mouth, his breath still shallow.

She took him in hand, fingers playing over his hardness with the assured skill that had come from months of learning him. Enjoying him, tasting him. Kaya moaned as she pulled back. She caught his gaze, darker now with passion, and widened his legs.

Settled between them, she licked his cock, his taste exploding over her tongue. Kaya stretched up, arousal shivering through her as she closed her lips over him. He groaned, and she knew he was close. A surge of power shot through her. She moved her mouth over him, taking him as deep as she could, running her tongue over his tip.

Paul's fingers tangled in her hair, danced through her curly tendrils. Kaya's body throbbed for his. His hips jerked, and she moaned around his cock. Paul growled her name, his hand tightening in her hair. She reveled in it.

He stiffened beneath her, and Kaya pulled back so that only the tip of him stayed in her mouth. When he came undone, she swallowed, kissing his softening length until he relaxed.

Pulling back, she licked her lips. She still knelt before him, perfectly still. Panting and exhausted and quite unsure how her world had changed in the space of only a few hours, but still she felt powerful.

Paul grinned lazily, fingers combing gently through her tangled length of hair. The pleasure blurring his blue-green eyes told Kaya everything she needed to know. She smiled back.

"I love you," he said against her mouth. The admission surprised her and warmed her. "So damn much."

"And I you." Kaya moved toward him and rested her head on

his shoulder. Her breathing had finally begun to even out, though her body still begged for his touch. "I do, Paul." Kaya pulled back and brushed her fingertips over his brow, combing his curls off his forehead. "Very much."

"Thank you." Paul took the forgotten linen. "I can finish."

She looked at him askance. "I'll do it." Kaya cleared her throat. "Let me."

Kissing him again, Kaya dipped the rag in the water and continued to wash him. She wanted the smell off of him as much as he did, wanted him clean and hers once more.

The silence that settled between them didn't have the same prick as earlier, that jab of nervous disquiet.

Questions danced around her mind, and she debated the best way to ask. Settling back on her ankles, Kaya focused on her breathing. When she looked up at Paul again, she knew what she wanted to ask.

His looked quietly amused, braced for her questions, but calm.

"When did you first hear of opium?" She still had no idea what either he or Antoinette meant by it, but she knew the smell turned her stomach.

"Oh, London, I suppose." His words, an easy answer for anyone other than her, held a thread of strain she heard all too clearly. "We all knew someone caught in the dens."

That cleared nothing up, but Kaya nodded anyway. "And in Bombay?"

"The Company held control over it. But everyone drinks it. I heard even the Raj enjoyed it." Paul cleared his throat. "It's everywhere," he whispered, eyes focused over her shoulder. "From the emperor to the elephants, from the lowest peasant to the Company's army."

"What—" Kaya hesitated and dipped her linen in the water. "What is its purpose?"

Paul snorted and tilted her chin up. "I'm sorry. You—I never wanted you to know. It's not anything I'm proud of. I wanted to let this part of me die in Bombay." The laugh that broke free sounded as rough as his words. "You deserve a stronger man than me."

Kaya caught his hands. "What about you is not strong? I don't mean physically. You showed patience and kindness to a stranger you were forced to marry." Her lips curled slightly, and her heart thudded when he returned the small grin. "Though you are suspicious of everyone, and charm them needlessly, you help. Do you not see that?"

Paul shook his head. "I help to protect you. Not because they need it, but to ensure your safety."

She didn't believe him, but she dropped the matter. They could argue about this day and night. At the moment, all Kaya wanted was his peace. All right, and answers.

Squeezing the linen, she held Paul's gaze. "I think you under-estimate yourself, Paul Hartley. I never would've stayed with the man you described."

Kaya ran the cloth over him again and again, but he remained silent. She hoped she'd made her point. But there was a sickening churning in her stomach that told her she knew nothing at all.

"Once you have a taste of opium, you're never rid of it. It calls you, more seductive than your kiss, more intense than your taste, Kaya. It runs in your veins and holds onto you like a brace—locked and immovable."

"And you still feel its call?" The entire concept remained foreign to her, but Kaya strived to understand.

"Every day. Every hour. As much as I long for a bottle of wine, that sweet splash of liquid in my throat, I crave the opium." His eyes turned hazy, and his jaw clenched.

"Paul?"

"Don't let me fall, Kaya." His gaze, bright and haunted, met hers. "Please. Don't let me fall."

Unmindful of the wet linen, the buckets, even Paul's damp skin, Kaya stood and hugged him close. She pressed his head to her belly and kissed the top of his head. Paul's arms wrapped around her, and she swore she heard a broken sob.

"I won't. I'm here, Paul. I promise. Always."

Kaya hoped her promise was enough. For both of them. She had a queasy feeling it was not. Whatever this opium was, however it affected him, she promised she'd stay by his side.

Four

Kaya kissed Paul's forehead and slipped from the room. New determination burned within her, and she stalked down the short hall to the main living area.

Paul had gone into that street, the dens, to find Marco because Kaya—naïvely—believed she could help. It had taken a toll on him, and she never wanted to be the cause of that again. But Teresa had clearly walked to that area of town to find her brother, even against her mother's wishes.

Kaya admired that resolve. Breathing deeply, she stepped into the main room of the house, determined to find Marco so neither Teresa nor Paul ever set foot in that street again.

Teresa continued to knead dough, her small hands digging into it with extreme force. Kaya eyed the poor dough.

"Where's your mother?" The question came out harsher than she'd intended. "Sorry." Kaya cleared her throat awkwardly. "Sorry," she repeated with a rueful smile. "I wish to speak with her about Marco."

She honestly had no idea how to handle her fear for Paul or a conversation with the women who'd welcomed them into their home. Perhaps it was she, not Paul, who needed to practice polite conversation.

"Trading signore's clothing." Teresa eyed the front door. "I brushed his boots. They sit by the back door."

"*Grazii*"

"*Grazie*," Teresa corrected.

"*Grazie*." Kaya nodded her thanks. She so disliked being wrong when she prided herself on her education. Her logic. Right now, with the new life she'd crafted these last months hanging by a thread, she took a much-needed moment.

Logic.

She grasped it with both hands.

She noted the room—bare but clean, and larger than she'd expected, given all she'd seen of peasant homes in Sicily. The Spanòs' home was no peasant dwelling. However Teresa's father earned money, he provided well for his family.

How had their son been caught in opium's grip?

Through the open shutters, a strong breeze cooled the interior and banished the flies that hung heavy in the air. The sun cast shadows along the floor, long stretches of claws that ticked away the minutes.

They had arrived in the city shortly before luncheon. Kaya's stomach lurched, and she suddenly remembered she hadn't eaten since before dawn, hours before the ferry sailed.

Eyes frozen on the expanding shadows, she heard Paul's call in her mind. Braced for any sound from their room, a hint he needed her, Kaya smoothed her hands down her bodice and stepped to the long wooden table Teresa used.

"I'm sorry," she said in slow, deliberate Sicilian. "It's been a long day. We appreciate your hospitality and any food you might share." Kaya paused and chose her next words with as much determination as she'd used to study her sword fighting.

Folding her arms over her stomach, hands cradling her bare elbows, Kaya titled her head. For as much as she teased Paul about his frequent slips of manners, she had no idea how to proceed with any sort of politeness.

"We thank you for your hospitality and shall help you retrieve your brother. Are you strong enough to help him recover from the opium?"

Wide-eyed, Teresa nodded. It occurred to Kaya that she should be speaking with Antoinette, or at the very least meet Signore Spanò. The shadows grew longer, the breeze blew harder. What kind of omen it portended, she didn't know, but she felt it deep in her bones.

Time ran out in a wholly unfamiliar way. Kaya used to count down the days, knew the hours between study and sleep. She had once wished away the night, dreaming about adventures she longed to have.

But never had she felt time slip from her fingers as she did now.

She needed to get Paul out of Villa San Giovanni.

Teresa, the brave, young girl who first wandered toward the dens, possessed more strength than her mother. That internal strength Kaya understood—physical stamina aside, one did not deliberately walk into danger unprepared.

She hoped.

Unprepared as *she* was, Kaya called on all her learning, her experiences from these last months. Her love for Paul. Even now, as she was scared and uncertain, that love warmed her.

"I do not know what happens after we retrieve him. You must keep him here until he is sober. I don't know how long that might take or what you'll need to do to keep him here." Kaya floundered and stepped back. Toward Paul. "If you are willing to do that, I'll find Marco."

"Mama thinks he's lost." Teresa's voice trembled, and Kaya wanted to soothe her. She had no idea how to do that, what to do or say or promise. "Papa thinks he's dead."

Neither Derya nor Gidd had been affectionate. Her grandfather had often taken her hands in his, his own way of telling her he cared. Derya had occasionally hugged her; Kaya remembered those embraces clearly. When she'd had a nightmare, or after she returned from her one illicit foray into Cairo.

She knew what hugs were, of course. She found herself touching Paul more frequently than she had any other in her life. A child? Kaya had never met a child until Sicily. Still, Teresa's large brown eyes glittered with tears. Following her instincts, Kaya did what she'd have done if Paul needed her.

Crossing the room, she gathered Teresa in her arms and hugged her tight.

"I don't know, Teresa." It pained her to admit she did not know something so obviously important to the girl. "I promise to look everywhere in the city and bring him home if I can find him."

"Can you?" Antoinette stood in the doorway between the main kitchen and the room with the fire roaring beneath a large pot. "Your husband, he did not."

Furious with the woman's disparaging of Paul, and so, so protective of him, Kaya glared. "Neither did you," she spat. "You left him. Your own son."

Antoinette flushed and dropped her gaze.

Stricken by her outburst, Kaya pressed her lips tight against her anger. She cleared her throat but didn't know what to say to ease the awkward tension filling the room.

"I traded clothes. Roberto's, his are far too small for the signore."

"That is most kind of you." Kaya released Teresa to gather the clothing from her. Antoinette reminded her of Derya, but she could not say why. Perhaps because Kaya missed Derya with a longing even four months of adventures couldn't lessen.

"*Grazie*." She stepped for the hall. "We are grateful for your hospitality, but I'm afraid we're not up to sharing supper with you." She paused again, searching for the right words. "If you would please bring supper to the room. No meat, please."

"You want only noodles and bread?" Antoinette eyed her suspiciously, no doubt taking note of her hijab. "No meat? What of fish? We have tuna with eggplants and zucchini."

"No meat," Kaya repeated then nodded. "The tuna would be delicious, however. Thank you."

She wanted to promise she'd search for Marco immediately, but Paul's state scared her. With the unfamiliar streets and alleyways of the city, she did not wish to venture into such a yawning unknown so close to sunset.

"I'll leave at first light and search for Marco." Glancing at Teresa, Kaya willed the girl to understand and not leave the house. "I promise."

In the silence that followed, Kaya retreated to their room. She knocked to alert Paul. She knew better than to simply open the door and step in. Most others followed the rules of polite society she so often teased him about.

He stood there completely naked, arms folded over his chest, glowering at her.

Kaya valiantly swallowed a laugh. Almost.

"I—" She cleared her throat but sensed it was a hopeless task. A giggle broke free despite the situation. "I brought you new clothes. Antoinette traded your other ones for these."

Paul stood there, curls riotous over his shoulders and dripping wet, legs braced as if he expected a fight, beard neatly trimmed. He did not hold his dagger, which spoke volumes.

Kaya hummed and tried to suppress her smile. She failed. Letting her gaze roam lazily over him, all too appreciative of his body, she closed the distance between them.

His scars didn't bother her; they added to her respect for him. Even the small point where he'd stumbled over his bayonet as a new recruit, though she teased him about that mercilessly. Under her stare, his cock twitched, and her laugh broke free.

"Did you expect an attack?" She hoped this easy freedom between them lasted and that the horrible, suffocating fear from earlier had been relegated to the past.

Paul sniffed and dropped his hands. "One does not know when one might need to defend oneself."

Kaya laughed again, breathing effortlessly for the first time since arriving in this house. The Paul before her, she knew. Understood. Wanted. Protected. "Were you going to fight them off with your bare hands?"

He lunged and caught her shoulders, drawing her close. She laughed again and dropped the clothing, bracing her hands on his chest. Paul nuzzled just beneath her jaw, his hands gentle along her back. He lifted his head and stared at her, so close, so hers.

"If need be," he murmured.

Paul dipped his head and kissed her, settling his hands on her hips. Kaya sighed and slid her fingers over his muscles, enjoying the jump and movement of them, the steady beat of his heart, the even in and out of his breathing.

This normalcy relieved her.

"Thank you." He breathed the words against her mouth and leaned back to watch her.

His gaze, clear now and so crystalline blue, stole her breath. It rushed from her, that warmth of emotion, and she grabbed it with both hands. He looked at her with that unwavering strength she'd grown accustomed to. It burned her, his passion, and Kaya willingly stepped into the fire. Embraced it.

"What happened?"

Paul watched her for another moment, a long beat that stretched between them. He wasn't going to tell her. That realization settled within her, but it didn't anger her.

"You—" *scared me,* she wanted to admit. But she also didn't want Paul to worry. "I didn't understand what happened. What alarmed you."

No matter what she did or didn't understand about Paul's reaction to opium, the dens, or Marco's plight, she knew they'd make it through. Confident in their love, in their trust in one another, she knew, whatever happened, they'd be all right.

Oh.

She grinned and wrapped her arms about his neck, pulling him to her. "Do you trust me?"

"Yes." Quick, confident, bold.

"Do you love me?"

"Yes." Strangled now, torn from him.

"Good. Then let me in. Let me help."

"Kaya." He pulled back, his gaze troubled, but she knew him. She *knew* him. "Why?"

"Why do I want to help? Why do I want to protect you? Why do I want to save Marco and help the Spanòs? So many questions, Paul." She caught his face between her hands. "Because I love you." She pressed her lips to his on the rush of relief that saying the words brought. "And I trust you, too."

As if the proclamation stunned him, Paul stumbled from her. His hands dropped from her waist and his eyes widened, almost comically. Confident, full of love and trust in this contrary man, and assured she could help him through whatever troubled him, Kaya merely grinned.

"Talk to me, Paul." Even to her own ears the plea came through clearly. "I want to help. I need to understand." Kaya held up a hand. "I don't mean just because I don't know what this opium is. I want to understand why you're so frightened of returning."

"It's—I—" Paul shook his head, helpless. His gaze flew around the room like a trapped bee. "Where are my boots?"

He stooped to pick up the forgotten clothing and started to dress. Kaya opened her mouth, then closed it. She scrambled, frantic to find the words that would get him to talk to her. Eventually she lifted her skirts and crossed to the bed.

They would get through this. They *would*.

"Teresa cleaned them." Kaya watched him tug up the long trousers with no buttons at the bottom and cocked her head to the side. "Antoinette traded your clothes for these. They are far different than the clothes you procured in Damietta."

She stood, nervous energy now tingling through her hands, along her spine. Kaya strode the few steps to their items and picked up her satchel, though she had no idea what she wanted with it. Just as Paul slipped the shirt over his head, a knock startled them.

Kaya paused and lifted her head high. She crossed to the door and opened it to find Teresa carrying a large wooden tray filled with still-warm bread and the same pasta and sauce they'd eaten in Sicily. In addition were two plates of the fish and zucchini Antionette had promised and a small bowl of stew. She saw not one bit of meat.

"*Grazie*," she whispered. Then, because she felt guilty for abandoning the girl and her short words from earlier, Kaya added, "Later, perhaps tomorrow, you'll teach me Calabrian?"

"*Sì, sì*, signora!" Teresa grinned. The happiness dispelled her lingering melancholy, brightening her eyes and making her bounce in place.

Kaya returned the girl's smile. She'd never bounced in place. Had never been so excited over so mundane a task. Frowning, she closed the door with her foot and pushed those glum thoughts aside.

"I specifically asked for no meat." She set the tray on the small table and poked in the stew. "I'm sure Antoinette suspects me already."

Shirt untucked, looking deliciously unkempt, Paul dug a spoon into the bowl, sniffing. "I doubt she'll kick us out. Not after inviting us into her home." He chewed and shrugged. "I taste no meat. Here." He handed her the other spoon and broke off a chunk of warm bread. "I'll speak with Antoinette. Explain you do not eat meat at all. Less suspicious that way." He looked up and winked. "She might not understand, but, as a good hostess, she'll prepare you something else. If here is anything like Sicily, there's plenty of fish."

"She'll think me a heathen." Kaya scowled and picked up a cup, sniffing carefully. In Sicily, most people drank wine. She'd fully expected wine with this meal and berated herself for not asking earlier. However, the fresh scent of oranges greeted her, and she sipped it. "Every village we crossed in Sicily thought me so."

Paul grunted. "Most people think anyone who doesn't do as they do are heathens. They don't understand. Don't want to understand."

Kaya hummed and passed him a cup. "I'm sure they'd embrace me with warm, open arms if they knew I was Egyptian."

He met her gaze, that same blue-green fire flickering. "I won't let anyone hurt you. Ever."

Reaching for him, she placed her hand on his now-rigid arm. "I know. Thank you."

Gingerly scooping out the noodles, Kaya cautiously chewed a bite and debated her next question.

"Tahir never struck me as a devout Muslim." Paul scooped up a bite of fish and zucchini. "I watched him pray, and he never drank with the Company, but—" He broke off and shrugged.

Standing, he handed her the rest of the bread. "Eat. The bread will help settle your stomach."

"I suppose everyone has certain edicts they follow, no matter the religion. Gidd did not drink, and I know he went to mosque regularly and followed the pillars. Derya, on the other hand..." Kaya sighed, a soft smile on her face. "She taught me but was far from strict." Kaya cleared her throat and broke off a chunk of bread. "What of you?"

"What about me?" He tilted his head to the side. "The only pillars I know are what you've taught me."

"No." She laughed and ate another bite. "I mean your religion. England is a Christian country; surely you've gone to church? Believe—or believed—in God?"

"I...yes. The local vicar, the man in charge of my education, believed in daily mass." Paul flinched and poked at his nearly empty bowl. "Haven't stepped inside a church since joining the Company."

"Do they not require it?" Kaya sipped her drink, grateful for this thread of conversation, though it had little to do with what she really wanted to ask Paul.

"The Company?" He snorted. "More interested in profit than their army's souls. No, it wasn't required. There were a few vicars there, Company chaplains, but they weren't the missionary type."

"Do you believe?" Kaya frowned at the remnants of her bread. "What do you believe?"

"I believe—" Paul floundered, a rarity. She looked up and caught his gaze. "I believe in you, Kaya."

Her smile stretched over her face, and she set the rest of her fish aside. Leaning over, she kissed him softly. "I believe in you, too."

"You shouldn't," he whispered. "You know it's dangerous."

"Many things in this world are. Walking the souk is dangerous. Exploring Sicily is dangerous. Crossing the Mediterranean is dangerous." She shuddered at her recent sickness.

Paul caught her hand and kissed the inside of her wrist. "I'm glad you're here with me, sweetheart. I—I couldn't go through this alone."

"You're never alone, Paul." She hoped he understood, willed him to do so. "I'm here. I won't let you face the dens alone."

Silent, his gaze heavy with the memory of opium and Bombay and she didn't know what else, Paul gathered their dishes and set them on the tray. He moved it to the door, returned to the bed, and gathered her in his arms.

Despite the relatively early hour, Kaya loosened her bodice and slipped off her hijab. Shifting in his embrace so her lips just reached the base of his neck, she closed her eyes.

They lay there, his heart beating steady beneath her ear, his hand cupping the back of her neck. She heard the sounds of supper outside their door, the shouted greeting of, presumably, Signore Spanò. No one bothered them, though Kaya felt an obstinate tugging to greet their host and thank him for their hospitality. She pushed up, but Paul caught her to him.

"Stay. You can thank them again later."

"How did you know what I was going to do?" she huffed.

"As you're so fond of reminding me, your manners are far nicer than mine."

Kaya snorted. "And you call yourself a charmer."

"I am!" His head jerked up, and he looked down his nose at her. "I am excellent at charming men out of their wine and coin, and women out of their virtue." He paused. "Their coin, too."

She huffed again. "So long as you don't try to charm any women now."

"No." His voice softened, and he leaned awkwardly down to kiss her forehead. "Now I have you." He lay back on the bed, and she heard his smile. "Besides, you'd probably castrate me if I even tried."

Kaya leaned up on her elbow and looked at him seriously. That uneasy wrench of uncertainty remained, drumming through her in time to her heart. She didn't know how to quell it, nor did she understand why it thrummed so dreadfully.

Unable to completely ignore it, she nonetheless grasped the lightness Paul offered.

"Yes." She nodded seriously. "Yes, I would. Don't forget that. I shan't warn you before it happens."

Hand tangled in her hair, he drew her forward. "Never. No matter what I wanted when I first marched into Cairo, meeting you changed that. Changed everything," he grumbled rucfully. "You told me you didn't want to marry me, and I'd never heard such conviction from anyone."

Paul kissed her, softly at first, then deeper, until she braced her hands on his chest and slid her leg up over his.

"You've changed me into a one-woman man, Kaya." Paul rested his forehead against hers then rolled on top of her. Nestled between her legs, he leaned on his elbows and cupped her cheeks. "I'll protect you with my dying breath."

Cold seeped into her bones. It was as if he had uttered a portent, not a vow. She ran her hands up his back, beneath his shirt, to feel his warmth.

"I won't leave you alone, Paul. I swear to you."

Kaya drew him down and kissed him again, her body arching into his. Despite her waning desire to thank the Spanòs and her stifling fear about what lay ahead of them, she needed Paul. The feel of his body moving against hers, the touch of his fingers gliding over her wetness.

"I love you," he whispered, fingers slipping into her heat. "I love you more than I think you realize."

He quickly brought her to orgasm, and she cried out. Gasping, she opened her eyes and met his just as he slipped into her.

"I know, Paul. I know."

Five

"Planning to sneak out?" Paul asked conversationally.

He didn't need to see in the dark. He knew Kaya froze, fingers around the door handle or close to it. He rolled from the bed, crossing the room in his bare feet until he stood right behind her. With one hand on her shoulder, he gently turned her to face him.

A single window graced the room, and no light slipped between the cracks of the shutters. His gaze, far too used to such darkness, easily watched Kaya's chin tilt, her lips purse. Stubborn woman, his wife.

He loved that about her. It terrified him, but he did admire her stubbornness. Even when it was directed at him.

"Yes." Kaya didn't step from his grasp or offer excuses. She never did. "You don't want to return to the dens. I don't want you to, either. Therefore, I shall fetch Marco on my own."

Hell. That was not what he wanted to hear. Part of Paul already knew Kaya's intentions, but he hated them. Hated the very idea of her anywhere near those filthy, horrid places.

His hand moved to her wrist and tightened. "No."

"Why not?" She pulled from his grasp. He wanted to apologize for his roughness, but the words caught behind a lump of fear. "It is a sound plan."

Furious—fury born of terror—Paul dragged her from the door and searched for his clothing. She didn't turn for the exit again but listened to him. He had no idea why. Once Kaya made up her mind, that was that, and very little could change it.

"You wish to join me?" Her voice softened. "Paul, you—please don't. I don't want you near that street again."

In the darkness, she shuddered, a movement she couldn't hide, and his heart turned over. He had no desire to be anywhere near that street either, but here they were. At an impasse.

"You don't know what you're walking into," Paul spat.

"I don't," she agreed, clearly frustrated. "However, I do know it's a stinking business, and it frightens you."

"Because of that, because it frightens me, you think it's a good idea to walk into those rooms?" Incredulous, he stopped dressing and stared at her. "*Alone?*"

"No." Kaya huffed a helplessly annoyed sigh and waved her hand at him. "I much prefer to walk into the unknown with *you*. I always wish to face danger with you at my side. But I have seen what that place does to you, and I don't want you to experience that again."

"Kaya—"

"I love you, Paul. And I shall protect you."

So saying, Kaya turned and walked for the door. She didn't bother to move quietly, and she certainly didn't hesitate. She simply opened the door and strode into the darkness. Cursing, Paul tugged on his boots. *Damn stubborn woman!*

Right foot jammed awkwardly in slightly too-small boots, he ignored the discomfort and stalked down the hall after her. She seemed hellbent on putting herself in danger. Walk into a damn opium den? Sure, why the hell not. She had no idea what the smoke did to a person, let alone what the dens looked like.

The filth, the stench, the desperation that even the opium smoke couldn't cover.

Yet here she was, dressed in her fancy blue gown, scarf covering her head, facing this as if it were simply another obstacle to overcome.

"You're not going alone." He raced around her, desperate to block her exit. Folding his arms over his chest, he glared.

She easily met his gaze in the quickly brightening day. "Stand aside, Paul," she said, as calmly as if she wished to stop and sketch the view.

Paul used every means at his disposal—height, folded arms across his chest, literally blocking the front door—but Kaya refused to back down. That in itself did not surprise him. Nor did her trying to sneak out of the house to find Marco.

Little she did surprised him, and yet Paul constantly found himself surprised. He rubbed a hand down his face and tried to work out a logical argument. Logic truly was the only way to win any argument with her.

"I don't want you near the dens," she hissed.

She looked over her shoulder to the rest of the house, clearly concerned about waking their hosts. Paul didn't care. They left their son to die. He'd only searched for Marco for Teresa. For Kaya.

Her stubborn sense of justice had rubbed off on him, it seemed. Tahir had taught her well, though perhaps in a more simplistic way than was practical in the real world. She'd seen injustice and charged in. He admired that about her.

But her lack of self-preservation terrified him.

Paul closed his eyes against the temper that wanted to explode. The house barely stirred. A gentle breeze blew through the front door, where the faint stirrings of morning life reached them.

"Believe me, I don't want *you* anywhere near them, either." He reached out and caught her wrist, again harder than he meant to.

Jaw clenched, he gentled his fingers over her skin. He pulled her into his arms, partly to impress upon her the importance of keeping her from that street of hell.

But mostly because he knew it was the best way to keep her out of trouble.

"Kaya." He ran his fingers over her cheeks, rested them on her temples, pressed his lips to her forehead.

To keep her from bolting out the doors. To ground him.

"You don't know what to expect, what—the dens are called that for a reason."

Kaya cocked her head to the side, as if deciphering his sentence. In the faint strands of predawn light, he couldn't clearly see her, but he knew she hadn't accepted his reason. That also didn't surprise him.

"I know." The seriousness in her voice hung heavy between them. "I don't understand any of it." She huffed a long breath. "There are many things I don't understand in this world, more than I expected. But I know two things, Paul." She took his hands, holding them tight. "We promised to find Marco. And I don't want you anywhere near those streets."

All the breath rushed out of him. "Kaya." What else could he say? What else was there to say? "You don't know what danger you're putting yourself in."

"I know I'm protecting you. That's enough."

Paul crushed her against him, holding her close as he struggled to breathe. "Why?"

"Paul." She pushed back and looked up at him. "You're a fool if you don't know."

That surprised a chuckle from him. "Knew I was a fool from the moment we met."

"How so?" She tilted her head again, and Paul's heart flipped in his chest. He brushed his fingers down her cheek.

Beneath his rough fingertips, her soft skin tempted him. A balm to the jagged edges of his soul. A lure to keep him in place.

"Come on." He changed the subject and took her hand. "Before the household wakes and Teresa wishes to join us."

She squeezed his hand, and he stepped backward, out of the house.

*And this is how men fall. Lost between a determined woman
and her infuriating logic.*

Paul almost smiled, almost chuckled at his own, all too true,
thoughts. Squeezing his eyes shut, he waited while Kaya quietly
closed the door, then retook her hand. He didn't want to lose her.

Or himself.

The darkened street reminded him, absurdly, of Cairo. They'd
sneaked out of there, too. As they hurried around corners and
across streets, Paul couldn't help but compare the two.

In Cairo, he'd wanted to smuggle Kaya from the city before
anyone she feared found her. Now, he wanted to meet their destination head-on and, with any sort of luck, escape without
drowning.

Paul slowed as they neared the stone wall he'd left Kaya on
yesterday. Yesterday? Less than a full day? Seemed a lifetime. Yet
Kaya easily kept up with him, rushing beside him as if she planned
to do so always.

He tried not to think about that, the implications of her love
for him. They terrified him.

"Kaya." He slowed beside the wall, the entrance to the street
straight ahead. "Marco might not know himself. He might not
answer to his name."

Pausing, he turned to face her. From the corner of his eye,
Paul caught the yawning alley, the endless abyss that both beckoned like a siren's song and disgusted him.

The horizon pinkened with the dawn of a new day, and
already he heard shouts from the wharves. A warm breeze
brought the fresh scent of the water with it, the dawn of another
beautiful winter's day here. Overhead, the birds called to each
other in an excited chatter of noise. He glanced up at them and
wondered if they were warning him.

Roberto, Teresa's father, would wake soon and begin his work
at the offices. Teresa, probably already awake, might try to follow
them despite their sneaking out. Antoinette might not let them
back into the house, even if they did discover her son.

"We can't save everyone in there. There are—" He swallowed. Did he remember his own time in the dens or the images from yesterday's rash visit? Paul had no idea; his memory was a haze of smoke and longing, loathing and disgust. "There are dozens. Hundreds. They crowd the beds and fall to the floor, unwashed, uncaring about anything but their opium as they lay in their own filth."

"They cannot even move?" she asked in surprise. "How is that living if they do not know their surroundings?"

He snorted. "It's not. It's—the opium is all that matters."

Paul licked his lips, rubbing his fingers over the inside of her elbow. She grounded him, steadied him. Even as the scent called to him, its thick smoke a temptation he thought he'd never heed to again. How could he ever explain to her that hopelessness? Kaya craved life, wanted to see everything.

Not too long ago, he'd craved darkness. An end to a miserable existence.

"They don't eat." His voice cracked, and Paul swallowed and shook himself. "Nothing else matters."

"I don't understand." She frowned, her voice low despite the empty street. "Why immerse yourself in a haze when there is so much to see and do? You cannot experience life on the floor in your own filth."

"No." He clenched his teeth against the erratic thumping of his heart. Each breath was painful. "That's the point. Once you're in the opium haze, everything you once worried about is gone. Food doesn't matter, but neither do your troubles."

She tilted her head but slowly nodded. "All right."

Her sudden capitulation startled him. "All right? You understand?"

"No. I do not. But I understand why a person"—and by that, Paul assumed Kaya meant him—"might want to forget. Not everyone wishes to experience the world as I do."

He snorted and kissed her gently. "No. No, they don't. But you're Kaya."

"What do you mean?"

Standing on an increasingly daylit street, steps from the opium dens, with the few people who hurried by staring at them as if they brought dreaded disease, Paul merely smiled. He didn't know how to tell her she'd changed his entire life, brightened it, made it worth living again.

"Let's find Marco."

Kaya snorted, that annoyed, amused sound he often equated with impatience, but she let him lead the way.

"Don't wander from my side."

She met his gaze, her own hard and steady. Far steadier than his. "Do not wander from mine."

The moment he stepped from the main street into the darkened alleyway, Paul wanted to vomit. The stench crowded over him, thick and cloying, as if the smoke had drifted in on a lead rope and wrapped itself around him. As if it waited to pull him in.

One foot in front of the other.

Deeper into the half-remembered mist of his time in Bombay. Basu and Harry beside him. At least, they'd been beside him when he willingly walked into the dens. Curious, eager to inhale the sweet aroma of opium.

Basu, killed in the massacre mere months after Oliver and John pulled him from the dens. He never figured out what happened to Basu between entering the dens and that day. Never had the chance to ask, and now would never be able to.

Paul never knew what happened to Harry.

Dead, most likely. Oliver hadn't been able to find him. Then again, Paul doubted anyone had looked very hard. Harry wasn't a man anyone, even his supposed friends, went to great lengths to help. Even afterward, free from the opium, if once more immersed in alcohol, Paul hadn't searched for the man.

Another mark against him. Another blemish on his soul he needed to atone for.

Kaya's hand tightened around his. Paul focused on that. Even as he breathed in the smoke, even as his mind went hazy. Gloriously blank.

"Paul." Kaya's sharp voice cut through the smoke like Moses parting the Red Sea. "Paul, look at me."

He turned his head and met her gaze. She covered her mouth and nose with the edges of her hijab. "I checked the first two doors yesterday." His own voice sounded distant.

"All right." Her voice was calm but sharp.

How did she stand strong against the thick haze? He gratefully, if metaphorically, leaned against her.

Paul knew they'd entered several doors. Knew he stayed at Kaya's side as they looked for the young boy among hundreds of young boys. Among old men and young women. They asked every child about Marco's age their name. Many were named Marco, but none answered to any mention of Teresa.

Door after door, room after room. The deeper they walked down the street, the more labyrinthine rooms they checked in each dilapidated house, the foggier his mind. Paul drifted, caught in a nightmare of memories and pain.

Harry, the pair of them running from home at fourteen. Meeting John with Oliver on that crowded, stinking ship bound for Bombay. Drinking with them, gambling in the backstreets. Befriending Basu. The bloody streets, covered with the dead, all reaching for him.

"Paul!" Kaya's frantic call spurred him forward, and before he knew it he stood at her side.

Protect Kaya. Save Kaya.

Only Kaya mattered.

His mind cleared in that instant, though a part of him understood that it didn't, not really. Paul licked his lips, tasting the thick smoke. His stomach cramped, and he breathed deeply. He watched his hand reach for a discarded pipe, the bowl.

"I found him."

Paul blinked down at Kaya, who was crouched beside a scrawny child no more than twenty, barely old enough to shave.

He looked as if he hadn't eaten in weeks, and when he blinked lazily up at Paul, his eyes were as vacant as the ocean.

"Help me get him up." Kaya didn't wait for him and tried to lift the boy alone. Strong as she was, malnourished as Marco was, she struggled beneath his dead weight.

Kaya muttered in Egyptian even as Paul crouched down.

"I'll get him."

Easily lifting Marco from the floor, Paul knocked the pipe from his hands. Away from the boy. Away from him. It hit the young boy next to Marco, smacked him in the face, but he didn't so much as blink. Paul closed his eyes and turned for the door. Sickness rose within him—the second boy lay dead.

Paul strode for the door, ignoring both the remaining inhabitants and Marco's feeble attempts to free himself. Kaya hurried beside him, silent as she skirted bodies and opium lamps, pipes and pipe bowls.

She shoved open the door, and Paul breathed in fresh air—and promptly choked on it. Kaya, hand resting on his, led him out of the alley, toward the glaring light of the main street and a new day.

Away from the dens, the choking smoke, Paul breathed. He dropped to his knees, Marco still cradled in his arms, and simply breathed. Retching, the sun blinding him, Marco slipped from his grasp and tumbled, boneless, to the ground.

Paul stared at him. The street dug into his knees and palms. His muscles ached to turn around and retreat to the blissful darkness of the dens.

"I'll—Paul. Paul, look at me." Her hands cupped his face and turned it toward her. "Breathe in, yes that's it."

"Kaya."

He blinked in the morning sun and looked at his beautiful wife. The cloud of opium dissipated, and he saw her clearly. She crouched before him, dark eyes wide and worried, dress stained with things he didn't want to imagine.

He never wanted her to see that side of life. To know he'd

once been a part of that. Had, indeed, enjoyed it there, on that unknown Bombay floor.

"Let's get back." Paul struggled to his feet, Marco's listless body still draped in his arms. "Then let's get the hell out of this city."

They walked slowly, Kaya's hand on his arm, Marco's body hanging limply from Paul's hold. People stared and whispered as they walked past. Paul ignored them all.

Kaya hadn't let him go. She hadn't lost him in the sickly sweet darkness.

"We'll wash," she said as they navigated busy streets and the crowds that stared at them. "Wash the stench and—I'll need a new gown. We'll, *I'll*, take care of this one and give it to Antoinette."

"All right."

"Then we'll leave. Yes?"

One step. Paul felt her gaze on him but feared moving his own from the street ahead. One step. Another. "If you—yes, that's for the best."

"We'll walk the mountains, yes?" Kaya's voice washed over him, a balm to his troubles. "They are different than the Eastern Mountains of Egypt, colder, I suspect. Certainly contain more vegetation than—"

Kaya continued to talk about the mountains and their walk. About the creatures they might see and the flowers sure to line the mountain paths. She insisted on drawing each of them and vowed to find a stationary store for more supplies.

"Perhaps I shall practice my portraiture. Will you sit for me again? I promise not to draw your nose quite so round this time." Her voice, light and nearly prattling, as prattling as Kaya could ever sound, loosened the ropes binding his chest.

Paul relaxed his jaw and his punishing grip on Marco. They neared the Spanòs' modest home, and each step brought him closer to leaving here. If he wasn't in Villa San Giovanni, he couldn't be tempted.

"I especially liked the way you drew my chin." His voice

sounded hoarse, rasping. Foreign to his own ears. Paul plowed on. "Very handsome."

They both knew by the time she'd filled in the shadows of his chin that she'd been playing. Once she overestimated his nose, she'd lost her seriousness. Even now, caught as he was in the opium trap, Paul knew she'd have never laughed over a mistake before leaving Cairo.

Tahir wouldn't have allowed it, and Kaya demanded perfection from herself in every new activity.

Suddenly, they stood before the Spanòs' front door. Kaya slipped around him, eyes still wide and far too observant for his liking.

"Paul, look at me."

He did. How could he not? "I'm all right, Kaya."

"No." She snorted and wrinkled her nose. "You're not, and you promised never to lie to me."

His lips twitched, and he nodded. "Let's get inside."

She observed him for another moment before banging on the door. When Antoinette opened it, Paul barely saw her. He focused on Kaya.

"Antoinette," Kaya said, voice louder now that they had entered the house.

Kaya greeted the Spanòs in Calabrian. Only then did Paul realize they'd been speaking English in the street. So much for keeping a low profile.

"You—you found him."

"I'm afraid that is not the hardest part of his recovery." Paul laid the boy on the floor beside the kitchen table. Unconscious now and unresponsive, he breathed evenly but shallowly.

"He won't thank you." Straightening, he didn't look at anyone save Marco. "He'll curse you and hate you. It won't be easy, won't be short. It takes—he'll always want to taste it again. Someone must stay with him at all times, possibly for months."

"He is home!" Antoinette cried and knelt beside her son. "That is what matters."

Six

Later, scrubbed clean of the stench of opium and well fed, Kaya slipped from their room and into the main house. She was dressed only in her hijab, stockings, and chemise. She didn't worry about anyone seeing her. Paul had seen her in far less, and Roberto left for work hours before she and Paul returned with Marco.

More importantly, she never, ever, wanted to wear that dress again.

Kaya watched Teresa race around the home, grabbing blankets and water, food and linens for washing.

"*Perdono*, Antoinette?"

"Anything, Mrs. Kaya. Anything." Antoinette cupped Kaya's cheeks and kissed each one. "How can I repay you for finding my son?"

"Teresa." Kaya smiled at the girl, who grinned widely back. "She deserves the thanks. She is a strong and determined girl. Don't stifle that."

"*Sì, sì.*" Antoinette looked to where Teresa crouched beside Marco, bathing him. Her fond, soft look belied her wringing hands and constant movement. "She is stronger than the rest of us." Eyes glistening, she grinned. "What do you need? Anything!"

"I need to fit the new gown. May I borrow a needle and thread?" Paul also needed another set of new clothing. He flatly refused to even look at what he wore after exiting the dens. "And I'm afraid I must ask you again to find additional clothing for my husband."

"*Sì, sì.*" Antoinette bustled around the rooms, humming and smiling as if she'd been granted a sultan's commission. Her gaze drifted to Marco, who now twitched on the floor, but her smile never dimmed.

Kaya took the sewing items and fled to their room. Pushing open the door, she sought Paul. Naked, and quite uncaring, he crouched before their items, packing and repacking what few possessions they carried. She settled on the bed with her old gown's bodice spread over her lap. With a sigh, she began the tedious process of ripping the seams and stitching their jewels into her new gown.

Anything, Antionette promised. Anything Kaya desired.

Kaya stared at the jewels littering the bed beside her. Jewels she possessed. A life outside her home in Cairo lay within her grasp. Paul, ominously silent, set aside her sketchbook, the one he'd purchased for her in Palermo.

She had him, too. A man she loved and respected despite his past. Or because of, perhaps. He would not have been the man she married without that past. The man she'd fallen in love with. Paul stood strong against those who'd tried to kidnap her, he protected her and showed her a world beyond her walls. He explored with her and made her laugh and never deserted her.

Even now, as she stood in a haboob of uncertainty, at a loss as to how to help this beautiful, brave man, Kaya knew she had him.

The only thing she wanted, which escaped Antionette's grasp, was a chance to speak to Gidd again. Once more, just once. She wished to tell her grandfather of her happiness. To admit he'd make a sound choice in Paul. Mostly, she wanted him to know she'd left Cairo, escaped Egypt, and even now steadily walked as far as possible from the long reach of the Ottoman Empire.

Kaya closed her eyes. Or maybe she wanted to talk to Derya, the woman who raised her, one more time. But Derya had died in a food riot before she married Paul.

One more day.

"What are you thinking?"

Kaya jerked and stabbed herself with the needle. Paul chuckled and knelt before her. He took her hand, kissing the small, bleeding wound. Curling her fingers around his, she tugged him between her legs. Still naked, and seemingly comfortable as such, he settled his hands on her hips.

Warm through the thin linen of her chemise, his fingers brushed along her hips, up her sides, down her back and the curve of her bum. Far more relaxed with him than she'd imagined she could be, Kaya dropped the needle and rested her hands on his shoulders.

His muscles bunched beneath her touch, but they weren't as rigid as they had been when they returned from the alleyway. She dug her fingers into them, hoping to chase away his memories.

"If you had one more day with anyone, who would it be?" The moment she uttered the words, Kaya knew he'd brush them off.

Paul didn't talk about his past. The little she knew of it she'd pulled from him, or he'd let slip. He disliked the man he used to be and insisted the only man she needed to know walked beside her.

Tangling her fingers in the curls at the base of his neck, she massaged his scalp. Paul hummed, and his eyes closed as he leaned into her touch. From the tone alone she knew he was thinking of changing the subject.

"Or anywhere," she added. "Maybe not a person, but a place?"

He frowned, his fingers pressing the small of her back. "What brought this on? Why ask? You're not one to look back—ah." He opened his eyes and met hers, nodding in understanding. "You miss Tahir. I'm sorry, Kaya."

"I—I do, yes, but Antionette offered us anything for the return of Marco." Kaya held Paul's gaze. His shadowed, hunted look had not diminished.

His lips twitched. "I'm sure she didn't mean *anything*. It's a saying."

"Yes, I know." Kaya impatiently waved that away. "That's not important. I do not need anything. What more do we need?"

Paul took her hands, gentle now. "You thought of Tahir. You want to see him again."

"Of course I do." She snapped the words, but they sounded thick and sad to her own ears. Swallowing against the tightness in her throat, she looked down at their joined hands.

"I'll work to send him a note. Return to the wharves and speak to Captain Morano." Fervent, Paul's gaze blazed with a new kind of fire. A distraction from the dens, from his past. Kaya smiled and, for once, accepted his change of subject with both hands. "Perhaps Roberto knows of a ship sailing to Damietta or Alexandria or Rashid. Someone can be bribed to deliver the letter."

"What if—" She blinked back tears.

"Tahir is a strong, wily old codger. He's alive. Trust me."

Kaya didn't know what an "old codger" was, but Paul's tone and smile told her enough. She hugged him tightly, even if she only half believed him. She believed *he* believed his words. She also knew he'd do his best to see someone delivered a letter to her grandfather.

"Thank you."

Paul snorted. "Don't thank me. Haven't done anything yet."

"You're willing to try. Not many are."

He frowned at her and sat on his heels. "I hate that you know that now."

Kaya picked up her needle and stared at it. "It is the world. The real world. And I wanted to learn all about it. You haven't shown me anything that wasn't there."

"I've shown you far too much ugliness."

"Paul." She grabbed his hand and squeezed until he met her gaze. "You've shown me beauty. Truth. More than I've seen my entire life. Sicily was stunning."

"We had to keep moving." His frown deepened into an angry scowl. "And they tried to kill you."

Conversely, Kaya smiled. "You showed me people. Life. I can't, and won't, fault you for others' actions."

"Everywhere we go, I put you in danger."

Ah. He meant here, in Villa San Giovanni. Pressing her fingers around the thin needle, Kaya struggled for the words that might ease his guilt. "Paul, you couldn't have known. You wanted to help Teresa; so did I. What I saw, what we found in that alley, wasn't your fault."

"Maybe not, but if you hadn't been with me, you wouldn't have had to see it."

"Paul, if I wasn't with you, I'd either still be in that house in Cairo, or I'd be dead." She hadn't meant to speak so bluntly, but it was the truth and they both knew it. "What happens to us here, wherever we walk, is on both of us. We agreed, yes?"

His eyes, hollow and haunted, met hers. "Yes," he whispered.

"We leave tomorrow."

"Good. I don't want to spend any more time here than I have to."

Kaya didn't either, despite its beauty and the kindness of the Spanòs. She had had quite enough of this place. She certainly didn't want Paul to remain here. Kissing him softly, Kaya returned to her sewing.

But her attention was only half focused on her work. Her mind raced for a way to ask the question that worried her most—then Antionette knocked and called through the door. Opening it, Kaya smiled at the other woman, who was still grinning and thanking them and was now carrying Paul's new clothing.

Marco's recovery lay in his family's hands. Kaya had no idea how to close down the dens, or if that would stem the use of opium.

She wanted to discover just how pervasive the drug was.

Nearly finished sewing their jewels and gold into her new bodice, Kaya looked to Paul. He'd put on the new clothes and now sat on the floor, back against the door, head tilted, eyes closed, hands limp between his knees.

"You're staring."

"How do you always know?"

Paul opened his eyes, clearer now, and raised an eyebrow. "Survival." His bluntness surprised her. Usually he shrugged off such questions. "What do you want to know?"

She sighed and set aside her sewing. "Where did Marco obtain the opium?"

Paul shrugged but didn't move. His eyes met hers, but his fingers curled into fists. "Who knows. It's everywhere, easy enough to buy. Once you're in the dens, it's just there, you don't have to worry about it anymore."

"This—it's free?"

He snorted but didn't move; she didn't think he even blinked. "No. Once your coin runs out, they toss you into the street. Marco paid for his place on the floor, he paid for weeks' worth of the drug. No doubt stole the family's savings and ran off."

"And where—" She licked her lips and pressed her fingertips to the tops of her thighs. "You said you smoked opium in Bombay. Is it everywhere?"

"Probably. The Company has a trade monopoly on it, so it wouldn't surprise me. I'm sure even in the Americas they have a steady supply."

"I don't understand. This trade is legal? It is legal for people to profit off a drug that destroys those who take it?"

"Oh, yes." His words quieted, mocking and angry and self-loathing. "It's a big moneymaker for the Company. And, I'm sure, anyone else who smuggles it on the side."

"I want to stop it." Fury stiffened her spine, and she bunched her hands in her new gown. "I don't care who's involved, this has to stop."

"Kaya." Paul pushed off the floor and appeared at her side so quickly she wondered if he'd flown. "You can't. It's everywhere. I mean that literally. *Everywhere.* I'm sure it's in the Russian court, the slums of Prussia, and every household in Calabria."

He grabbed her hands and tried to soothe them, to unfurl her angry fists. "Kaya, look at me."

"It comes from someplace."

"Yes." His voice was strangled. "And it always will."

"I do not care." She seethed. Not at Paul's reluctance to help. That she understood. At the East India Company's flagrant disregard for what opium did to people, to families. All for profit. "I want to stop it here and now. So it doesn't tempt Marco again." She unclenched her jaw and looked to the closed bedroom door. "Or Teresa," she whispered.

"Kaya." Paul's hands tightened on hers. "I don't speak lightly when I say it's everywhere. You can't stop it. Not while the Company continues to trade in it."

She knew he was right. She had no idea how to stop the East India Company. Yet. "For now, I'll stop it here." Her voice came out in a harsh whisper. A vow. "I don't want Teresa to be touched by this ever again."

Paul scraped his hand through his hair but didn't look away from her. He sighed and shook his head. "I'll talk to Roberto, see if he's heard anything about smuggling."

Kaya leaned forward and kissed him softly. "Thank you."

"I haven't done anything."

"But you're willing to try."

They left early the next morning. Paul waited in the doorway while Kaya hugged Teresa and Antionette. He had no idea when they'd grown so close. Perhaps it wasn't the time they'd spent together so much as it was the presence and the spirit of Kaya.

When she made a promise, she kept it.

Antionette Spanò hugged Paul as well, and he patted her gently on the back. He tried not to grimace, but he didn't like accepting her gratitude when he knew what lay ahead for them.

No matter how he tried to impress upon them how difficult these next weeks would be, Antionette didn't seem to hear. He didn't know how else to tell her that returning Marco might not have been the blessing she believed it to be. He looked to Teresa and hoped she understood.

But that was a lot of responsibility to place upon the thin shoulders of a child.

He'd spoken to Roberto about the possibility of sending a letter to Cairo. Roberto, who hadn't looked at all suspicious when Paul mentioned it, had readily agreed. Perhaps he, much like his wife, was willing to do anything to thank them for returning Marco.

The coins they'd left in their room would more than cover their stay. Kaya had insisted on leaving them in secret. She'd been afraid the family wouldn't accept them, that they'd see Marco's return as payment enough.

Now, standing outside in the warm afternoon sunlight, Paul smiled and nodded. Mentally, he urged Kaya to hurry. He wanted away from this house.

Turning into the sunlight, he hoped the warm brightness would burn away his own memories. The half-forgotten haze of clawing pain and desperate agony.

"Ready?" Kaya asked, curling her hand around his elbow and tugging him from the doorway.

More than you know. He didn't look back at the Spanòs' doorway, though Kaya did. Paul didn't want any reminder. Not of poor Marco, lashing out while the opium seeped from his veins. Thrashing and moaning on the floor, begging and crying. Not of his own painful memories.

His failings.

"Teresa cut up oranges and bergamot for us," Kaya said as they hurried down the street. They spoke in English, though he knew Kaya wanted to practice her Calabrian. "And Antionette packed cooked fish."

She easily kept pace with him, saying nothing about the speed with which he walked the direct route from the Spanòs' to the mountain road. He didn't want to walk near the dens. Couldn't. He only wanted out of this town.

Grinning up at him, Kaya's hand slipped from his arm to his palm. Paul blinked away the house in which they'd found an odd measure of peace and upheaval. More chaos than anything, perhaps. The thick loathing of his past choked him as surely as the dens.

Yet he would miss Kaya's enjoyment of being there. Of simply speaking with Teresa and Antionette. Of staying still for even a short time.

In the brightness of the Calabrian morning, Paul watched her stretch toward the sunlight like a blossoming flower. He walked beside her in the warm January breeze, the scent of citrus fruit heavy in the air.

The serene calm of her face. Her dark eyes now closed against the sun, her lips curved upward, soft and lush. The warm sunlight glinted off her skin, healthy again after their rest in Villa San Giovanni.

Rest. Bah! Paul's hand tightened around hers as they trudged up a hill. Still, with every step, everything around him faded until only Kaya remained. Her joy and beauty, her excitement in her surroundings, her simple love of exploring.

The image of the two of them walking through the green mountains eased around his heart, loosening that fist of memory. For the first time, probably ever, Paul took a moment to breathe in the day. Birds soared overhead, calling to each other. Nameless animals scurried in the underbrush. And Kaya smiled up at him as if she only saw him.

Her beauty stunned him. Her sheer joy in the simplest things. His love for her slammed into him, stealing his breath. Paul wanted to stop, kiss her. Make love to her under this perfect day.

Kaya turned that radiant smile toward him, and once again everything else vanished.

One good deed, ten years and a lifetime ago, had changed everything.

He adjusted the beam, that bane of his existence, along his back and grimaced, an overly exaggerated scowl. "I'd prefer walking without this tent."

"Where did Roberto find one?" Kaya looked curiously at him as they continued their walk along the base of the mountains.

"I've no idea. When I asked, he simply nodded and wrote himself a note. Next thing I knew, he'd returned with this."

Head tilted, she examined the beam and nodded. "You offered quite exact measurements."

"I think he had one fashioned from wood from the docks." Paul hated carrying the heavy beam, but it meant they wouldn't need to sleep in the open now that they had a means to keep their tent upright.

Kaya laughed as she was meant to.

"The desert tribes have traveled with their tents for centuries. They don't complain." Kaya shot him a mischievous look, one full of delight and sass and lust.

Lust, Paul knew how to handle. Those other emotions made him nervous, uncertain. They wound through him, tight around his heart and sparking through his veins.

"The desert tribes," he shot back in a tone that matched hers, "don't carry them on their backs. The have camels for that purpose."

Kaya held out her hand, as if to acknowledge a minor point. The plain linen fabric of her dress gleamed in the sunlight. For a moment, Paul mourned the blue gown he'd bartered for in Damietta. That bodice had hugged her breasts and accentuated her generous hips.

He loved her hips.

"I doubt Captain Morano would've allowed a camel on his ship." She sniffed. "And I'm certain Captain George would've kept her when we landed in Mazzarelli."

"Probably would've charged us triple for the camel." Paul scowled. "Damn thief."

He felt Kaya's eyes on him and turned to meet her gaze. "Do you think part of his cargo was opium?" she asked.

Gut clenching, Paul forced words from his ever-tightening throat. "Morano? George?"

"Both. Either."

He tilted his head from side to side. "Possibly. I wouldn't put it past Captain George. Wiley sod, him, and not worried about following the law. Morano?" Paul paused to seriously consider that.

They walked several more steps up the steepening mountain path, away from the well-traveled road. Kaya didn't interrupt his silence; she often didn't. She let him think, didn't rush or push.

"I don't know. But then, it's always the quiet ones."

"What do you mean?" Kaya, gaze steady on his, stopped. She tugged him off the path, though he heard no one in the surrounding area. "How does being quiet affect what they do or do not accomplish?"

Paul snorted. He lifted her hand and kissed the inside of her wrist. He loved watching her eyes flutter closed when he did that.

"Take you. One would never know how skilled you are with your khanjar simply by looking at you. All they see is a woman." He gestured to her bow, quiver, satchel, and dagger. "You carry men's items, but when others look at you, they don't see what I do. They see a woman carrying her man's weapons."

Her eyes narrowed, and he worked hard to curb his smile. She sniffed and raised her chin, as haughty and regal as ever. "Touch my weapons, and I'll break your fingers."

His laughter echoed over the mountains, and Paul didn't even care.

Seven

His laughter broke free, and the constant weight on his chest loosened. In a gesture he didn't think through until he'd already moved, Paul leaned down and pressed his lips to hers. The kiss was chaste, easy. A testament not only to the closeness that had formed between them, but the change in him.

Her fingers played along the back of his neck, and Kaya deepened the kiss. Paul groaned. One simple touch from her made him want to forget his concerns.

Kaya filled him with such life, such feeling, he nearly forgot all else.

Wanted to know only her.

She pulled back, eyes alight, and grinned. Shadows continued to haunt her gaze, but her lips curved in a real smile, and some of her joy in the day returned.

"What did Roberto say about Vibo Valentia?"

"He'd heard more than one worker talk about it." Paul retook her hand, tugging her along the rocky, uneven surface. Before the sun set in the mountains, he wanted to walk as far as possible from Villa San Giovanni. "Hushed tones of fear as they rushed past his offices."

She frowned, no doubt at the lack of specifics. "How odd, to be so frightened of an entire town."

"Perhaps," he agreed. But Roberto's suspicions alone had convinced Kaya to look into the town, made her certain that it was the origin of Marco's opium habit.

"How far?"

"In a rush already?" Paul listened for sounds of pursuit, the quick march of enforcers or the sneakier steps of thieves. But he only heard unfamiliar birds and the rustle of leaves in the wind. Still, better alert than caught off guard. That happened far too many times with Kaya for his comfort.

"Paul."

Jaw clenched, he nodded. "Two, three days' walk. Depending on the terrain." He stopped and pushed all thoughts of pursuers to the side. "More if you want to walk the mountains." He pulled her against him. "Or if you want to spend the day sketching everything we pass."

She laughed and kissed him, a soft kiss full of promise and love. It wound through Paul. A balm to these last days.

"Teresa said the harbor there is full of exotic fish." Kaya's voice was free from the weight of their mission.

She stopped and peered at the side of the road, "road" being a generous term for the bare path they traversed.

"Everyone says that about places they've never seen." Grateful for this change in subject, Paul grasped it with both hands.

Kaya's wish to stop the opium supply had everything to do with how the mere mention of the drug hurt him. Paul knew that. But it wasn't her desire to help that cut him clean through. It was his own weakness.

She crouched at the side of the road and brushed her finger over the petal of a bright purple flower. She hummed at the touch and leaned in further to sniff it.

"Oh, you're beautiful." She looked over her shoulder. "Do you know this flower?"

"No, I'm unfamiliar with it." Paul frowned at the cone-shaped purple petals. "It's not one Letizia taught me. Probably has no medicinal properties."

"It does not have to." She folded herself into the dirt and rummaged in her satchel for the pencils and sketchpad they'd bought in Palermo. "A flower can be beautiful all on its own."

He watched Kaya work and did not disagree. Not when she found such joy in exploring her surroundings. Her pencil raced over the page in long strokes that transformed the blank slate into a nearly perfect replica of the purple flower beside her.

She sketched quickly, noting along the side of the paper the color of the petals and leaves. She counted the darker purple irregular circles inside the cone petal and made a note of them, too. Paul patiently waited for her to finish, listening for anyone who might be following.

Standing, Kaya held the pad at arm's length and studied her drawing. Tilting her head one way and then the other, she looked between her rendition and the flower itself. A crease deepened between her brows, and she frowned at her work.

Without thinking, Paul rubbed his thumb between her eyebrows, smoothing the lines away. She relaxed at his touch but continued to study her drawing. What had he done to deserve her?

"Ready?" he asked quietly.

She met his gaze and smiled. "With you? Always."

<hr>

They made camp near a waterfall, a stunning cascade over rocks and greenery that drew her eye. Captivated by the scene, one she'd heard of only in stories, Kaya stared at the constant flow of clear water along the mountainside.

How had they not seen a waterfall in Sicily?

Kaya shivered in the shadows of the mountain, but she was unable to look away from the sight.

In the morning, when the sunlight hit the water, she'd sketch it before Paul dragged her back to the path.

"Hold the end. Kaya!" Paul's frustrated voice snapped her back into the present.

"Sorry!" She rushed to comply.

He hated erecting the desert tribe tent Gidd had given them before they left Cairo. Kaya hadn't the heart to point out that a true tent was huge and able to house entire families, much larger than this small, single-post one. Still, it had kept the desert sun from them in *aṣ-ṣaḥrā' al-kubrāthe* on their walk from Cairo to the coast.

Kaya tied her end to the post and didn't say a word. She understood Paul's frustration, that it wasn't with her. Ever since discovering the dens, he'd been short, abrupt.

Scared.

So, rather than telling him, *again*, that they could find one of the small villages that dotted the mountains and stay at an inn, Kaya gathered their things and carried them beneath the tent.

Then again, if they'd stayed at an inn, she wouldn't be standing next to her first waterfall.

Once the tent was secure in the rocky soil, Paul collapsed beneath it. He ran a hand over his face, his frustration and exhaustion evident in the lines bracketing his lips. Legs stretched before him, he dropped his hand and looked up at her.

Her heart twisted, and she hiked up her dress and knelt beside him. On her knees, she crawled awkwardly behind him and helped him out of the ill-fitting coat. The thin material, far better suited to walking in warmer climes, felt flimsy beneath her touch.

"What are you doing?" Paul didn't resist when she folded the coat over a boulder and dug her thumbs into his shoulders. "Oh," he moaned. "Whatever it is, don't stop."

Kaya kissed the back of his neck, just below where his hair curled along his linen shirt. He shivered and sighed. She remained silent for several long moments, kneading his shoulders and back, the base of his neck.

"When was the last time you slept?"

He was boneless in her arms, and it surprised her when he didn't jerk away. *Progress.* Instead, Paul captured one of her hands and turned his head to kiss her fingers. He sighed and rested against her chest.

"Tell me. Please."

"Kaya." The way he said her name sounded both tortured and intimate. No one spoke her name like he did, as if it was more to him than a simple form of address.

Paul's hands tightened on her hips and drew her back against him. His hands slipped up her back and held her close. Even through her bunched-up skirts, Kaya felt the hardness of his cock. She shivered, her hips rocking against his without her permission.

Her need for him burned in her veins, hot and insistent as it singed her.

She let herself be distracted. Wanted to be, not because she didn't want answers, but because she knew Paul. Arguing would do her no good. He'd close up and stop talking if she pushed him for answers.

Making love distracted them both.

Later, when he didn't expect it, when he was relaxed and, hopefully, dozing in her arms, she'd ask again. He might be the sultan of distraction, but she was the sultana of persistence. Paul knew it, too.

Kaya quickly untied his trousers and cupped his cock. His fingers, cooler than she was used to, slid up her inner thighs. She shivered at his touch, her hips arching against him. He brushed over her wetness, parting her sex and slipping in.

"Christ, Kaya." Paul pressed his lips to the hollow of her throat, traced his tongue along her collarbone. "Why do I always want you?"

She had no answer. A flippant retort died before it had fully formed. She felt the same way. Her fingers ached to touch him, and her skin yearned for his kiss, for his body against hers. Her hips rolled against his fingers, silently begging.

Paul teased her, shallowly thrusting, his thumb pressing her clit. He pulled her closer, grasping the lovely curve of her bum. Kaya shivered, arching her hips in silent plea.

"I want you always, too." Kaya didn't know what else to say. "We've met many on our travels." She dug her nails into his shoulders. "Handsome men, but none compare to you." She forced her eyes open and met his gaze, pleasure tightening through her, though not enough. "None made me feel like you do."

Kaya reached between them and ran her fingertips over his cock. Paul shuddered, and a surge of power ran through her.

"I love touching you." She dragged her fingers up his cock. "I love the way you feel in my hand."

His hand tangled in her hair, anchoring her to his insistent kiss. Kaya opened herself to him. She ground down, her hips jerking against his touch.

He chuckled against her mouth, his hand now cradling her head, fingers slipping from her.

Kaya whimpered, "No." Her fingers tightened on his cock, her teeth sinking into his lower lip. "Don't tease, Paul."

Leaning back slightly, Paul trailed his fingers down her spine. "Not tonight." His hand once more pressed to the small of her back, urging her closer. "No teasing tonight."

His fingers wrapped around hers, and together they guided him into her. Kaya sighed at the feeling, rocking her hips to bring him deeper. The ground dug into her bare knees and the breeze cooled, brushing over her in featherlight touches.

She rose up, the delicious glide of him moving in her. His fingers lazily touched her, winding her pleasure higher and higher, like a bird soaring on the wind. Kaya sank over him, and he filled her.

Her head fell back. Paul's teeth nipped just below her jaw. Kaya tangled her fingers in his hair, urged him on and moved faster over him. Close, she was so close now. Her orgasm tightened through her belly, and she strained for climax against his touch.

"Harder." Her fingers dug into his arms, and she ground against his touch. "Harder, please."

Her orgasm shot through her, a bolt of lightning. Her fingers dug into his scalp, tingling with her release as she rode him.

"That's it," he whispered against her neck. "Come for me again, Kaya."

His fingers continued their relentless touch. Though her clit was sensitive, her body reached for another orgasm. Kaya whimpered, ground down hard on his hand, his fingers. Quick as lightning, that pleasure tightened through her, and she moved faster. Suddenly, she came again, a hot, clenching need that shook her to her soul. Her climax rushed through her, hard and fast.

"Kaya." Paul shifted, rolled them to the side. He slipped out, and she whimpered again at the loss. "Kaya."

He thrust hard into her. She bent her knees, opening for him. His lips pressed to her skin, breath coming fast as he moved. Skirts bunched around her waist, Kaya locked her ankles around Paul's hips, her hands tangled in the curls at the base of his neck.

She felt him falter, groaning unintelligible words against her skin. He was close, his thrusts harder and uneven. His teeth sank into the linen covering her shoulder. She arched her hips, wanting more.

Suddenly, he pulled out as he climaxed. Kaya gasped, her fingers pressed hard to his scalp, and held him. Her breathing slowed, finally, her senses focusing back on their surroundings. She didn't move, not to clean herself nor to release Paul.

"Kaya." Paul moved, his lips kissing up her neck to find hers. "All right?"

"Hmm." She stretched her feet and ankles, moved her arms above her head even as she kissed him back.

Once more, her fingers found his hair, a favorite place of hers. Gently kneading his scalp, she waited for his sigh. A sign that told her how at ease he felt, calm and relaxed and at peace. She wanted that for him always but didn't know how to give it to him.

Demons haunted him, threatened to drown him. Kaya caught

glimpses of that past, snippets of stories he let loose. Another piece of the man she married.

The man she loved.

In the darkness, Paul reached for their bags and a handkerchief. He cleaned her, his touch gentle and lingering, and Kaya sighed. When she moved to sit up, he helped her with a tender hand to her shoulder.

His shadow moved toward the small pool of water. He wrung out the handkerchief and returned to her. The shock of the cold linen on her skin had her instinctually jerking away, but Kaya didn't protest. Paul kissed her belly, down her thighs, his fingers smoothing her dress over her legs.

Only then, his ritual complete, did she move.

He lay next to her in the dark, sheltered by their desert tent, legs tangled together, his arms securely around her. She adjusted her hijab so it lay properly, even though they were the only ones here. His lips pressed to the top of her head, and Kaya closed her eyes. Much as she loved sex with Paul, lying with him afterward warmed her in a way no number of climaxes ever could.

They needed to move, unpack the bedroll, eat. But Kaya couldn't bring herself to shift. Not yet. Not with her body still loose and sated from his, with his arms around her and the steady beat of his heart beneath her ear.

She wondered, in these quiet, tender moments, if this was what love felt like. It moved through her, content and so very trusting in Paul's arms.

"I don't know," she whispered into the dark.

His fingers combed through her hair, dislodging the braids she wove this morning and pushing her hijab askew. "Don't know what?"

"Why you always want me. Why this—this passion between us has not yet cooled." Kaya pressed her lips to his chest, breathed in the scent of their day's walk, of sweat and of Paul. "But I always want you, too."

Eight

Paul patiently sat on a boulder and waited for Kaya to complete her morning prayers.

"Fig roll?"

Startled, he tore his gaze from her hands and met the warm brown of her eyes. Head tilted slightly, Kaya held one of the rolls Antionette had packed. He silently crossed the short distance between the boulder and where she was patiently kneeling by the pool of water.

"Before Cairo, I never had a fig." Paul frowned. "I don't think I did in Bombay." He chewed a bite and grinned at her startled look. "They don't have figs in England."

Kaya blinked, her dark eyes wide. "What did you eat there?"

He shrugged. "Fish. Sausage. Meat pies."

"And in Bombay?" She tilted her head again, that inquisitive look he adored. Brushing wisps of hair off her cheek with the back of her hand, Kaya sat on her heels and chewed the roll.

The mist from the waterfall clung to her hair, dewdrops sparkling in the rising sun peeking between the thick trees. They weren't so high yet, and despite the cool morning and the sun just rising over the mountains, the rays warmed his face.

Paul reached over and touched the drops, which were shining

like gems. It continued to amaze him how this naïve, curious, strong, amazing woman could captivate him so thoroughly.

"Oh, the same." He shook his head and gave her a wry smile. "The Company is not one for change. Even in a country that eats little meat. Anyway, Indian food was too spicy for them."

Paul stopped. They'd shared several stories over the previous months. Surely one about his food sampling would not sour their morning with talk of nightmares and death. Or opium.

"There's a dish there, I've had it several times. I don't know what's in it, but it's everywhere. The locals ate it, and when we ventured past the garrison—" Paul cut himself off. Best he didn't think on exactly why they'd ventured beyond the garrison and wandered the streets.

"Then it is just as well we aren't going to England." Kaya brushed her fingers on her gown.

"Anyway, it was chicken marinated with spices and a thick sauce poured over it."

"Sounds delicious. I should quite like to try this mysterious chicken meal."

Paul met her gaze, surprised she hadn't pushed. She looked calmly back at him and waited. *Damn it*. Sighing, he stood, dislodging his own dagger and the half-packed bedroll, both resting on his knees. He bent over and offered her a hand. Kaya's eyes danced, and she let him pull her upright, as easily as if he always had.

Kaya stepped back and shook her dress. Dirt clung to the hem and streaked across the skirts. Because of him. A flash of arousal stole his breath, choked him.

He loved this woman.

Tugging her to him, he kissed her. She tasted of fig and stale bread, of cool water and fresh mint. Of Kaya. Paul deepened the kiss, seeking her taste and hers alone. His fingers tangled in her freshly braided hair and held her close.

"Paul," she whimpered.

Her short nails scraped through his hair, and he groaned.

Until Kaya, he never realized how arousing fingers on his scalp could feel. He grasped her arse, pulled her closer. Wanted to stay in this secluded area forever.

"Come on." He finally pulled away, fingers lingering on her cheek. "Let's get moving; we have a lot of ground to cover before nightfall. You still wish to walk into the mountains?"

"Yes." She hesitated, eyes troubled, that line once more between her brows. Paul traced the arch of her eyebrow and smoothed it, eliciting a slight upturn to her lips. Her eyes remained on his, troubled, dark, assessing. He smiled and pulled back before he touched her again.

After packing the rest of their things, he watched her as she settled her hijab over her head and shoulders. Adjusting her satchel, bow, and quiver, she turned to him. "Do you truly believe the smugglers are in Vibo Valentina?"

Paul absolutely did not want to step foot in Vibo Valentina. He didn't want Kaya anywhere near smugglers, opium, dens, or other people. "I don't know. If Roberto thinks they are, it's a good enough place to start."

"How does one find smugglers?" Kaya tilted her head, her eyes still shadowed as they met his.

"Never thought about it." He frowned. It was a good question, but he had no good answer. Since he'd lived his life on the edge, men like that were always around. They were all he'd known. "I've never searched for them, always just knew."

"You don't want to find them."

He snorted and turned for the path, such as it was. "Of course not. I don't want you anywhere near them. I don't care what they're smuggling."

"We promised."

Swift anger rose up and choked him. He wanted to yell at her. Clenching his fists, he shouldered the pack and banged the wooden beam across his shoulders. Cursing, he stalked forward.

She'd promised. *She* wanted to find the source. *She* wanted to stop the supply into Calabria.

Paul clamped down on his anger and listened to make sure Kaya was following him. He could've said no. Could've kept quiet about Roberto's suspicions. Yet he hadn't, hadn't even thought to, until this moment.

Kaya had slipped into his heart, and he didn't know how to stop her, how to rid himself of this emotion.

This love for her.

Didn't want to.

"You confuse me, Paul." Perhaps relationships constantly required blind faith. Trust. "How I feel for you, not just during sex, which I enjoy very much, but in all aspects." Kaya frowned. "I have no words for—I don't know what to say, how to help you. I want to. I want to be strong for you, to understand this." She stopped, swallowed. "I don't know how to do that."

Paul stood a single step from her, hands curled tightly around hers as, yet the distance between them felt like the entirety of their trek from Cairo to this point. As if she were shouting at him from atop the mountain to the valley below. A cloud passed over the sun, partially obscuring its setting rays. Kaya shivered and hoped it wasn't an omen.

She scoffed. She didn't believe in omens.

"You—every day, you help me." He offered a rueful smile. "Don't you know that? You are strong for me."

"Is that what love is supposed to be?" Her voice tentative, Kaya drew on internal strength she didn't know she possessed. She had never needed to voice such things, love and promises. "You promised, in Cairo, that we'd figure things out. You never said how."

He snorted and dropped her hands. "You think *I know*? You think admitting I love you has been *easy*?"

Paul looked so furious, so hurt, Kaya nearly stepped back. Instead, she calmly stood in the face of his anger. She thought her own temper might spark again, but his words surprised her into speechlessness.

"You think I've ever been in love before?"

"Oh. I thought—I mean, I assumed... You have not?" Kaya curled her fingers into her skirts. For all their talking over the previous months, she still knew so little about him.

The tension in his shoulders released and sagged all at once. Paul ran a hand over his face and shook his head. He made an odd choking laugh in the back of his throat. When he tilted his head back to look at the darkening sky, his lips quirked at the corners.

"Kaya." He shook his head again. "I don't know what to do with you."

She had several answers to that but swallowed them all down. "If you—you haven't... I mean, if you haven't been in love before, then how do you know what to do?"

Paul looked as if he was going to answer, but he stopped. Then he kissed. It warmed her more surely than any fire. Kaya wrapped her arms around his waist, her fingers grazing his bum. He shuddered against her, and she pressed closer to him, mindful of the beam. She wondered if he felt that stinging numbness of fear as well, or if there was something else behind his quiet, shuddering tension.

"I don't know." He said the words against her mouth, his lips brushing along her jaw, her cheek. "It is terrifying. I'm not sure it's supposed to be. But it is."

"You're scared, too?"

"Kaya, before you, I used the word 'love' to seduce whomever I wanted."

"Oh." She swallowed but the question burst forth: "Did you—did you seduce many women?"

"Yes." She heard the flatness in his tone, the one that told her he did not wish to speak of it. "Love wasn't an emotion. It was a word, nothing more. I used it to get what I wanted when I wanted it."

"And now?" Kaya let the "many women" comment pass.

Perhaps the ugly, stabbing twist in her stomach was hunger, not jealousy. But she knew better. She *knew* jealousy. It had been an intimate friend all her life. Oh, yes, she knew that all too well.

"I think you know." He brushed his fingers over her lips.

She nodded, warm and happy and content. "I do." She tilted her head to the side as he kissed down her throat. "I love you." Saying the words still sent a tingle through her, shivering up her spine even as the vastness of that admission tightened her stomach.

Paul pulled back and retook her hand. "I love you, too, Kaya." His lips caressed the inside of her wrist, a chaste kiss that nonetheless shook her to her core. "Now let's find someplace to sleep tonight."

They walked along the uneven path, deeper into the mountains. They didn't speak much, simply enjoyed the rapidly cooling day and the simple silence between them. By now, they should've already found a place to make camp. Walking through the mountains at night was far more dangerous than walking through the desert.

"Tell me about those women."

Paul snorted. "What do you want to know? *Why* do you want to know?"

Kaya moved her shoulders, restless. "I want to know everything about you." She wanted to ask if a woman introduced him to opium, if there were women in the dens. She still didn't understand Paul's need to smoke it, his shaking after they walked out with Marco, but she wanted to. "I want to know who you were before I met you. You say so little of yourself, Paul."

"You wouldn't have liked me then. I wasn't a nice man." His words, so clipped and angry and final, were a repeat of things he'd said to her since the beginning.

"So you've said." She squeezed his hand and hoped her touch conveyed understanding and acceptance. "Tell me of your first lover."

"Do you really want to hear about her?" His question was full of skepticism and disbelieving laughter.

"No," Kaya huffed. "I certainly do not."

Paul's laughter echoed over the mountains, even as they moved deeper into the brush off the main path. The low bushes caught her skirts, but Kaya ignored them. Shivering again, she stepped closer to Paul.

She tripped over a branch or bush or rock and yelped.

"I got you, sweetheart." Paul's strong arms wrapped around her and steadied her on her feet.

"Thank you." Just as they found a clearing, she asked, "Did you seduce so many women because you could? Or because they let you? Or maybe you had nothing else to do?"

Paul laughed again, but she heard the difference in this sound. It was more like the hard, faraway memory of Before. The pack dropped to the ground, and they fumbled with setting up the tent.

"I don't want to set up the tent in the dark again." Kaya tried not to grumble, but she was shaking from the cold.

"We'll set up camp earlier tomorrow," Paul promised. "Or maybe spend the day resting. You can sketch."

He used a small spade to dig in the hard, rocky ground, and together they pushed the pole into the hole. They'd set up this tent so often, Kaya knew which end went where and, despite the lack of light, secured her end with relative ease.

"Her name was Mary." Paul spoke so suddenly, Kaya almost asked who Mary was. *Oh. His first lover.* "She worked in the tavern down the street from the house we lived in."

"We" being him and his mother. He never spoke of her, and the one or two references he had made were not complimentary.

"Nice lass. We grew up together, she, Harry, a few others. Always around each other." He stopped, and Kaya watched his shadow in the moonless night. "She never yelled at any of the boys who hung around the tavern her dad owned. Always had a smile."

He stared at the tent as if it were this Mary and the tavern he frequented. "Always had a spare bit of bread for me, too."

Before he joined the Company, then. So fourteen, maybe fifteen. Kaya waited, but he didn't say more. He looked so distant, so close yet so far. As silently as possible, and careful not to trip and ruin the moment, she closed the distance between them and took his hand. She held onto him and waited until he snapped back to the present.

"I don't know what happened to her." Paul coughed a little and met her gaze in the cold, dark night. "I like to think she had a good life, married a good man who looked after her, took care of her. The last time I saw her was when the recruits marched out."

Paul dropped her hand and stooped beneath their shelter, pulling their pack toward him. He focused all his concentration on unrolling their bed and sweeping stray stones out of the way.

Kaya knelt beside him. She had questions about Mary, many, *many* questions. But she swallowed them down. Her expected jealously was conspicuously absent. In its place lay a hollow pain for the young Paul Hartley. For Paul, yes, but also for the faceless Mary, who worked in a tavern and had most likely never, ever, left that neighborhood. Who had never had the chance to explore as Kaya did.

"I'm glad you had her." Kaya reached into the pack and pulled out the last of their fig rolls. "I'm glad you had someone then."

"I never really had her." His voice cracked.

"You had someone." Kaya refrained from mentioning his mother, who sounded as though she ignored and neglected her only child.

Kaya didn't understand that. Not that she understood children or what one did with them. Or mothers, even. However, to have a child then neglect it? Her own mother died in childbirth, but Derya never mistreated or ignored her.

She pivoted and sat beside him, leaning her head on his arm. "You have me."

His lips brushed over the top of her head, and she heard the long breath he let out. His shoulders sagged enough to tell her that the strain of remembering his past had somewhat dissipated.

"Yes." He wrapped an arm around her and pulled her tight against his warm body. "Yes, I do. But I think you only use me to keep you warm at night."

Kaya laughed and pressed her lips to the underside of his jaw. "Yes, I use you for your body. I'm glad you finally realized that."

The next morning, birds chirping, the sun cresting over the mountaintops, Paul packed their things and took Kaya's hand. His nightmares had kept him awake far later than normal.

Talking about the past always made the nightmares worse.

Last night, they choked him. The stink of that house, the clinging mist that did nothing to hide the derelict, crumbling buildings, the crowded tavern and reek of unwashed bodies pressed close together. Memories that made him restless, even after making love with Kaya and holding her close throughout the night.

This morning, those memories banished. With her sleepy "I love you" and the soft press of her mouth against his, Kaya reminded him how far he had traveled from the boy who joined the Company's army and ran away from life. She reminded him of the man he'd become.

Maybe the poets had it right. Maybe love wasn't so awful.

The sun over the mountaintops shone blindingly bright in a clear blue sky. Kaya stopped to quickly sketch the clouds clinging to the mountain, careful to note the colors in the margins.

He wanted to buy her paints and wax pencils for coloring her sketches. She never asked; it was impractical to carry so much. Still —still. He wanted to buy her anything she wanted.

Love might not be terrible, but it did make one do foolish things.

Paul shook his head and pulled her along the path. "If I let you, you'd spend weeks drawing every single thing we see."

Kaya laughed, a happy, carefree sound that warmed his heart. "Perhaps." She observed him from the corner of her eye, a mischievous tilt to her lips.

"Let's buy food in the next village." Kaya deepened the kiss, her tongue teasing his. "And make camp early today."

"I do like the way you think, sweetheart."

"I know you do." She grinned against his mouth, took his hand, and tugged him eagerly along the trail.

They walked the short distance to the next hamlet, another nameless dot nestled high in the mountainside. A stiff breeze blew cold over the path, sending a shiver down Paul's spine. They'd have to find real shelter soon or move down the mountains, closer to the coast.

"Let's cross the mountains today, toward the coast." Kaya looked up at him with that same happy tilt to her lips. How did she always know what he was thinking? "I want to see the water." She shuddered. "Just see. I want to sketch it. I've no desire to actually set foot in it."

He snickered. "You can watch it from the beach. Stay—"

He heard it. A sound Paul had buried deep in his past, where the sounds of gunshots and trampling horses waited. The slick memory of wine. The cling of opium.

"Paul?" Her voice called him, distant, faint against the roaring in his ears. "*Paul?*"

Standing in the center of that nameless hamlet, head thrown back in laughter—an oily, sickening sound—stood Private Harry Appleby.

The most despicable human Paul knew.

Nine

Wind roared in Paul's ears, a monsoon of sound that blocked all else. Hands numb, feet rooted to the ground, he stood in his own private hell. It hurt to breathe. His vision dimmed, narrowing to a pinpoint of distant light.

Those days in Bombay, hazy with opium smoke and wine. Appleby's laughter echoed, a throbbing staccato of drunken, hollow merriment. The blood and screams and grayness of death.

"Paul? Paul!"

Kaya.

Paul blinked. The world refocused, rushing around him in a cyclone of memories. He jerked his head to look at her. Her large, dark eyes searched his. Her fingers tightened in his grip, and only then did Paul realize he was holding her hand far too tightly.

He dropped it as if her touch burned.

"What's wrong?"

Voice frozen, Paul opened his mouth. *Run. Turn around and run. Run, Kaya, and leave. Now.*

"Paul?" Kaya's voice softened, a gentle, questioning sound.

She gripped her dagger as if to protect him. He almost

laughed but couldn't. His fierce wife looked around the path leading into the small hamlet as if able to discern the danger.

"You should've left me in Mazzarelli."

Kaya's eyebrows shot up. "That's not how I remember our conversation." She stepped in front of him, blocking his view of the village—of Appleby. Still holding her dagger, she cupped his cheek as if physical contact might help.

"I love you." Desperate words tumbling over each other, but he had to tell her just how important she was to him, how precious. How cherished.

Appleby's laughter echoed in his head. Paul cursed his hesitation but couldn't make himself move. No matter how strongly he willed his legs to carry him away from here, they refused.

"What?"

"Remember that, Kaya. Only you." Paul gripped her arms, held her tight. Too tight, he vaguely realized, but his fingers refused to cooperate. He didn't know how to let her go. "I meant what I said. Everything I said. Each and every word."

"I believe you." Kaya's hand wrapped around his elbow, and she stepped into him. "Paul, I believe you."

He nodded, words failing him once again.

"What's wrong?" Kaya's voice softened. "Paul, what happened?"

"Hartley!"

Appleby's voice drowned out all else, an icy cascade of a past Paul hoped never to revisit. He was not that lucky. Never had been. Now he'd dragged Kaya into that murky filth.

"Appleby." Paul's fingers tightened on Kaya's arms, or maybe the numbness he felt only made him think so. She easily stepped from his hold. Slipped from his fingers.

Please don't let that be a portent.

Appleby, ruddy face alight with dark joy, crossed the distance with his arms wide. He ignored the woman he'd been talking to, and Kaya, and hugged Paul. He smelled long-unwashed and of stale wine. Standing rigid in the friendly looking embrace, Paul swallowed bile.

Karma was a very real thing.

Each and every one of his past actions now had an effect on his present. What was it Basu always recited? *Happiness comes due to good actions, suffering results from evil actions.* Yes, karma now bit him in the arse.

"I thought you died in that den!" Appleby's voice, loud, pretentious, fake, scraped over him like a dagger over his bones. He tried not to breathe in the sour waft of decay.

"Sorry I managed to survive." Paul stepped back, his eyes meeting Appleby's bleary gaze. His voice hardened, took on that smooth façade Appleby knew too well. He didn't know the man Paul had become, and Paul planned to keep it that way. "I thought *you* died in the dens. Oliver never found you."

"No, no, left there." Appleby waved a dismissive hand.

Paul's eyes narrowed. No one walked out of the dens on their own. "How'd you leave Bombay?"

"Not enough opportunity there."

He either boarded the wrong ship in a drunken, drugged haze or stowed away onto one bound elsewhere in an effort to hide from the authorities. Unfortunately, Paul knew both tactics all too well.

Curling his hands into fits, Paul resisted the pounding urge to punch Appleby. Repeatedly. Punch his past, pound Appleby into the ground as if he were the sole reason for Paul's self-loathing and hatred.

He also wanted to grab Kaya's hand and run and never look back. Maybe that was what caused this trouble in the first place. Running without making amends.

Wasn't that what second chances were all about? Wasn't that what he was trying to do now? Atone?

Basu, a good man for quoting a sacred text and defying it in the next breath, had also repeatedly told him, *As a man himself sows, so he himself reaps.*

It sounded very much like what Kaya taught him.

"And who is this lovely lady?" Appleby eyed Kaya like a prize.

Nausea churned Paul's stomach. Growling low in his throat, he stepped between Appleby and his wife. "Don't."

Head high, eyes cold, Kaya stepped to Paul's side, standing proud in the face of Appleby's lecherous leer. "Kaya."

"A beautiful name for a lovely lady." Appleby took her hand, but Kaya jerked it out of his grip.

"I have not given you leave to touch me," she snapped. From the corner of his eye, Paul saw her hand tighten on her khanjar.

Appleby's eyes darkened for a beat, his face thunderous. He took a half step forward and Paul shifted again, keeping his body between his wife and a man he had never wanted to see again. Appleby's eyes slid to where Paul stood, coiled and angry.

"Harry," Paul snapped. Ready to drop his pack and defend Kaya, he snarled, "I warned you."

Appleby laughed. "Feisty! I like it."

"You are?" Kaya demanded.

"Harry Appleby, at your service." Appleby bowed, adding far more flourish than necessary. "Paul's oldest and closest friend."

"Harry and I joined up at the same time." Paul consciously unclenched his jaw but didn't have as much luck with unclenching his fists.

He tore his gaze from Harry and met Kaya's.

She slowly nodded, one long move. Whatever she heard in his voice or sensed in his stance, burning anger or discomfort or embarrassment, she kept her cool and remained silent. For so trusting a woman, Kaya was no fool.

Paul loved her all the more.

Once more, Harry's obnoxious laugh scraped down Paul's spine, jerking his attention to the matter at hand. With his hands on his hips, Harry looked as if he posed for a painting or a newspaper sketch. Or maybe he was waiting to take his bow on stage. Unfortunately, as horrible and detestable as Harry was, it was no act.

"Oh, we did more than that!" Harry clapped Paul on the shoulder, eyeing the tent's beam. Paul shrugged off his touch. It didn't seem to deter the other man, but Paul knew better. Harry Appleby remembered every slight, every embarrassment real or perceived. "Didn't we, Paul?"

Paul met Harry's gaze, the soulless brown eyes. "Yes. A long time ago."

"Who is your friend, Harry?" The woman, a pretty brunette with wide, dark eyes, her long hair tied back in a single braid, stood at Harry's side.

Slinging his arm around her shoulders in a move far too familiar to be proper, Harry yanked the woman against him. Kaya growled, but the other woman didn't seem to notice. Or care. Her face remained smooth and blank. Paul supposed that could've been an act, too.

"This is my old friend, Paul Hartley." Paul flinched. Did Appleby have to use his *real* last name? Damn the man. "And his woman." Harry nodded to Kaya, a disturbing look in his eyes, his gaze drifting down her body.

"Wife." The word slipped out before he realized it. Too late to take it back. Or chop off his tongue.

Damn it! Telling Harry seemed wrong. As if he'd just given the man leverage against them. As if he'd endangered Kaya.

"*Wife?*" Harry's eyebrows shot up, and his grin widened. "A wife! Come, my friend. We must celebrate! You've been busy this last year."

By now, the entire village had congregated by the fountain, watching this less-than-friendly interaction in rapt interest.

Perfect. Bloody perfect.

"We're just passing through." Paul wanted to refuse, but Kaya rested her hand on his arm.

To curious eyes, it looked like a wife pleading with her husband. But Paul knew better. Her fingers tightened slightly on his arm, a subtle sign he'd grown used to since Damietta.

"It's late." Kaya's voice held an aloofness he almost forgot. "We can stay the night."

Narrowing his gaze, Paul met hers. She tilted her head to the side, chin jerking up incrementally. She had seen or heard something he had not. Something she didn't like.

"One night." Paul nodded in easy agreement. Hand on the small of her back, he guided her into the village. "Of course, one night can't hurt."

"Excellent!" Harry's voice echoed over the eerily silent square. "We shall celebrate tonight."

"The inn." The woman gestured in the direction of the tavern. "You will be most comfortable there."

"Thank you." Unable to stop them, Paul's fingers dug into the back of Kaya's neck. Her head jerked to the side, and he winced, dropping his hand altogether. "Sorry."

"What's your name?" Kaya asked in English, and Paul nearly smiled.

Brilliant woman.

"Marta." She smiled over her shoulder, a short, thin smile, but she didn't step from Harry's restrictive hold. "My family, we own the inn."

"Thank you, Marta."

"Oh, Paul, wait until you try their wine." Harry kissed the tips of his fingers. "Excellent, truly. You'll love the local vintage."

"I'm sure it's delicious."

He hadn't had wine since—since Bombay. Avoiding it hadn't been the least bit easy. The Spanòs had looked at both he and Kaya as if they were heathens from the pits of hell when they'd refused their offer.

Gut clenching, fingers aching, shaking with want—*one sip, just one*—Paul licked his lips. First the opium dens, that sickly sweet smell of heaven, now wine. Calabria was trying to kill him.

"This visit isn't going to end well," he muttered in Egyptian as they entered the dimly lit tavern.

"I'm sure it's not."

The inn was much larger than it looked from the courtyard outside. Long tables flanked two of the four walls, with smaller round ones toward the front. A bar ran along a third wall, and stairs led to the upper floors along the fourth wall. The center of the inn, a cleanly swept wooden floor, looked well-trodden.

Marta immediately walked behind the worn wooden bar and poured wine from the large barrels into a bottle. Her smile remained in place, but her eyes flicked from Paul to the open doorway and back to Appleby. She seemed to ignore Kaya.

Who or what did she search for?

Appleby slid against the high bar. His shoulders hunched as he leaned against it. Beside her, Paul stood stiffly, shoulders tense, face set, fingers curled loosely at his side. From the corner of her eye, Kaya watched him open and close his hands, press his fingers to his thighs, then curl them into his trousers, only to start the process over again.

She wanted to demand answers, but an angry tenseness settled over Paul and set her teeth on edge.

His confession of love was not the balm she'd expected. Kaya never thought hearing him say those words would knot her stomach the way these last minutes had.

"As we're staying for the night, may we secure a room?" Kaya eyed Harry, who drank down the wooden mug of wine in one swallow.

Paul took her hand again. It comforted her, even as questions swirled in her mind like a haboob, fast and frantic and relentless.

"Only for one night." Paul squeezed her fingers, that genial, fake smile tugging his lips.

She hated that smile.

She had seen that detested smile on Paul's face numerous times since Cairo, usually when he lied to people about their origins or destination. But Paul no longer directed that smile at her.

"*Sì*," she heard herself say and met Marta's gaze. "If you have any available?"

Appleby's caustic laugh startled Kaya. Her fingers grasped Paul's more tightly.

"No one actually visits here!" Appleby swallowed another mouthful of wine. "Not in this provincial little nothing place."

Marta's eyes narrowed for the briefest moment before she returned to pouring wine. Appleby drank it so quickly, Kaya wondered why the other woman bothered pouring at all. Clearly, handing him the bottle would be much faster.

"Then why are you here, Harry?" Paul's voice, that misleading cordial tone, made Kaya frown. She quickly covered it with a smile. "I doubt there's much here for you to enjoy."

Every word out of Paul's mouth only created more questions. She didn't miss his emphasis on "enjoy," nor did she miss the sly smile on Appleby's lips. It made her skin crawl.

Despite the wooden beam he still carried, Kaya stepped closer to Paul and studied the room. Few people inhabited the inn at this time of day, and those who did sat as far from Appleby as possible. They looked at her and Paul with such mistrust, Kaya wondered how anyone could miss their hostility.

They should've turned around and left. Kaya hadn't been able to, however, when she noticed Marta's wince or her faint and all-too-quick scowl when Appleby yanked her close. This was not a willing woman.

"Oh, there's plenty here to enjoy. Depends on how you look at it."

"You'll have to share." Paul's fingers tightened harshly around hers, but their hands lay hidden in her skirts, where neither Marta nor Appleby might see. "Perhaps over dinner?"

"Yes, yes." Harry downed another mugful of wine. He couldn't enjoy it, swallowing so quickly. "Marta here makes the best pasta."

Marta smiled, nodded, and met Kaya's gaze. "I'll show you

your room." She paused and repeated in halting English, "I show you the room."

Kaya bit her lip to keep from answering in Calabrian. Paul's sharp tug on her hand, an unnecessary reminder, told her what she'd already guessed: he didn't trust Harry Appleby and, for whatever reason, didn't want him knowing they spoke the language.

"Thank you, Marta." Kaya paused and deliberately said, "*Grazie,*" in a truly abhorrent accent that made her toes curl distastefully.

Marta nodded and lifted the bottle of wine, presumably to return beneath the counter. But Harry's hand shot out faster than Kaya believed possible with the amount of alcohol he had already consumed.

"Leave it," he growled.

For the first time since meeting her, Kaya watched Marta's eyes visibly widen and her lips thin. Appleby could not have missed it, though the change lasted a fraction of a heartbeat. When she spoke, it was calm and soothing. "Of course. Forgive my forget."

"That's fine, luv." Appleby's hand curled tightly around Marta's. Then he suddenly smiled and released her. "Now go show my friend and his"—again he eyed her, and again Kaya resisted the physical need to remove that look from his face—"wife to their room."

Paul growled, low and dangerous. "Do not." He dropped Kaya's hand and turned to glare at Appleby. "Be careful, Harry."

Face carefully blank, Kaya stepped around the end of the beam and stood beside Paul. She didn't retake his hand, had no wish to diminish his stance against Appleby.

She saw the fear flicker in his eyes, but he merely laughed and threw back the rest of his wine, slamming the mug on the table when he'd finished.

Turning back to Marta, she nodded. "*Grazie,* Marta."

Marta, eyes wide, face pale, didn't speak as she led the way up the stairs and pushed open the first door at the top. Several doors along the long hall stood closed against prying eyes. Kaya wondered if Appleby slept in one or if they were unoccupied. Appleby said no one came to this village. Had he lied? Why have an inn if no one needed rooms?

Kaya thanked Marta again and waited as she left, closing the door softly behind her.

Anxious to have a moment alone with Paul, Kaya slowly removed her bow and quiver and rolled her shoulders. She hadn't realized her own tension until now, in the stifling quiet of their private room.

"Who is he?" Her question, not louder than a whisper, startled him.

Paul jerked and turned from the door. The long wooden pole smacked one shoulder, and he winced. Blinking as if waking from a vivid dream, Paul lifted his hands to the pack's straps. He methodically loosened them, his entire focus on that single, mindless task.

Kaya waited. She'd never seen him like this, so distant he looked lost. Or trapped. It terrified her, ran cold down her spine, settling like a rock in her stomach. More so than even his daze in the dens, this vacant stare settled deep in her bones.

"We joined the Company together." Paul's voice broke, but he didn't seem to notice. "Two boys from the neighborhood with nothing better to do and nowhere else to run."

Paul looked at her then, the pack sliding loosely from his grasp. His blue-green eyes bleak, his face stunned, he met her gaze. He looked so adrift it broke her heart.

"The Company. They don't much care who they have in their army. Long as you follow orders. We didn't follow orders, but we didn't stop anyone, either. Wasn't my business."

Kaya crossed the room and stood helplessly in front of Paul. He held her hand, his own shaking. Whatever seeing Harry Appleby meant to him, none of it made him happy.

"You said you conned people." Kaya kept her voice soft. She

didn't know if anyone was listening outside the door, and, more importantly, she didn't want to scare Paul.

"Conned, scammed, stole, seduced. All of it." Paul shuddered. "Christ, I thought I left all this in Bombay."

She stepped into his embrace and wrapped her arms around his waist. Leaning back, she waited until he looked at her again and nodded for him to continue.

"Harry, he made friends with some of the officers. Whatever they wanted, he found. No questions asked, just took their money or wine and left, conscience clear."

"Found?" The word tasted like ash in her mouth.

"Found and *delivered*. Anything they wanted. Everything." Paul closed his eyes. "Even women."

The way he said that made Kaya swallow her next question. Suddenly, she had a startlingly vivid image of that woman in the desert, bound, bloody, beaten. How she'd been at peace in the end, in those final moments Kaya had sat with her, happy to die and escape a life of misery.

"Oh."

"I didn't." He hissed the words so fiercely, she jerked. "I never. Slavery—" He shook his head just as fiercely, his eyes blazing. "Some women went to the officers willingly. They, the officers, kept them as mistresses. Others, the ones their families sold—"

"Not you." Kaya didn't know if it was a question or a statement.

"Never." His hand cupped her face, his normally warm fingers now cold and stiff against her cheek. "Kaya, I swear to you, I never, *never*, forced anyone into that kind of life. I stole and I scammed people—*rich people*, people who could afford it. I'm not proud of my past. But never that. *Never*."

"I believe you."

Paul stared at her for a long, taut moment.

Suddenly, he collapsed into her arms, his breath rushing out in relief. He pressed his forehead to hers, his body shuddering.

Kaya turned her head and met his lips, and he kissed her in frantic desperation, his fingers flexing on her neck.

"Why?"

"Why?" she repeated.

"Why do you always believe me?"

"You promised never to lie to me." Kaya held him tighter, as if that might keep him with her forever.

But she had a sickening feeling that no matter how tightly she held onto him, it wasn't enough.

Paul kissed her again—hard, rough—and backed her toward the bed. Kaya let him. She welcomed him into her body. It was fast and frantic, and before long she cried out her own orgasm and held him as he shuddered through his.

"Thank you." He turned his head and kissed her stomach, his arms tight around her.

Kaya wanted to tell him she'd always believe him, always hold him, but something stayed the words, caught them in her throat. Instead, she kissed the top of his head and held tighter, terrified to let him go.

Ten

Paul paced the length of the room. Three strides by four strides—three all-too-short strides along the wall overlooking the hamlet, four down the other side of the room. The shutters stood open to the cold breeze, but he barely felt it against his numbness.

He wanted to return to bed, to lie there with Kaya wrapped in his arms. Her head resting on his chest, his fingers tangled in her hair. The softness of her skin beneath his touch, the scent of her a balm to his screaming soul.

His fingers ached to touch her. He wanted to return to yesterday when they'd made love by the water. When she'd welcomed him into her body, holding him tight. Her kiss a promise, every touch an assurance.

Yesterday, when she'd embraced this new man. Not today, when all his secrets—his transgressions, his shame—came to light and spilled out before him.

Now, she sat on the bed, back ramrod straight, following his every move with the slightest turn of her head.

Paul's hands opened and closed at his sides, and he paced faster. He didn't want to think about Harry Appleby, so of course Harry was all he thought of. Memories he had buried for decades suddenly resurfaced, suffocating him. Choking him. Disgusting him.

"The room is not going to widen."

Paul snorted and whirled back around. Kaya tilted her head and gave him that inquisitive look, silently asking what the hell he was doing.

He had no idea.

Though Paul didn't want to sit, he forced himself to. He needed Kaya in his arms more than he needed to expel the energy pumping through him. The raw, nervous energy of having one's past catch up to them.

It yawned before him, a pit of laughing despair. Mocking him for his past deeds. For thinking, even for a moment, that he might ever escape the consequences.

He hoped his past didn't swallow him whole.

"I'm restless." After that unnecessary admission, Paul tugged Kaya into his arms.

"I can see that," she said.

Stretching out on the bed, he did his best to quiet his body, subdue his impatience. Lying still, with Kaya in his arms, pulled him back from that yawning abyss he'd been treading along.

She anchored him. Steadied him.

"Is that why you left?" Kaya leaned only far enough to meet his gaze. "You said you deserted when the Company finally went too far, when they ordered the massacre. Did—did Appleby have anything to do with that?"

"No." His shoulders twitched, an odd combination of restless and immobile.

Paul pulled her back against him, snug against his side. Her hand slid beneath his shirt and traced over his chest, down his belly and up again. Random patterns that showed her own uncertainty more clearly than her calm words. Her body warmed his soul, the only possible warmth he could imagine right now.

He grasped it with both hands and held tight.

"That was—no. Harry was long gone by then. I don't even

know where he was, to tell the truth. In the dens or...well, I thought he'd died." Paul shuddered and squeezed his eyes shut. He'd thought Harry dead and hadn't even thought to mourn. Hadn't searched or, frankly, cared all that much.

Selfish bastard that he was.

"The—what happened, that was the officers. They gave the orders from high atop their horses, and we idiots below obeyed."

Her hand stilled on his chest, her fingers splayed over his heart, and she pushed herself up. Her lips brushed the underside of his jaw, along his neck. Not in passion, but comfort. Paul didn't know how to take that, how to feel about her consolation. No one had ever comforted him, not like this. Not with quiet kindness.

He opened his eyes and met her serious, dark ones. Warmth and kindness shone there, yes. Steely determination, too. With a start, he realized she'd fight for him.

As he fought to protect her, she'd do the same for him.

It struck him anew. That realization rushed through him, a swift bolt of desire and acceptance. Love that warmed his heart and his body.

Kaya watched him steadily. Long strands of her hair had come loose from her braids and brushed her bare shoulders. He reached over and tucked the strands behind her back, his fingers caressing her soft skin. "We can leave," she said.

His head jerked back, his eyes widening. Blinking up at her as if she'd appeared from nowhere, he met her gaze. "What?"

"Leave. You don't want to stay here, and we only stopped in the village to buy food. We're still searching for the supplier of the opium." Kaya met his gaze, frowning. "It cannot be a coincidence that your friend—"

"He is not my friend!" Paul spat, venom burning his throat. His hand dropped from her shoulder and curled into a fist at his side.

"You are correct, I apologize." The crease between her brows stayed, and her face remained pinched with worry. She shifted until she lay half over him. "Harry Appleby is here, in a remote Calabrian village in the middle of the mountains. That cannot be a coincidence." She frowned, her head tilted. "I don't even know the name of this village. Did Marta say?"

"No." He blinked, caught off guard. "She didn't."

"We can leave now, purchase our food and never look back. There's enough daylight. We can walk far enough into the mountains where they won't find us in the dark."

"Then why did you insist we stay?" Mind whirling, Paul tried to follow Kaya's logic. It grounded him most days, but today he understood nothing.

"Marta." Kaya pressed her lips together. "I don't think she willingly...ah, what is the word? Befriends Appleby?"

Oh. Paul hadn't even noticed. His gut churned, and he closed his eyes against the anger choking him. "I wouldn't be surprised, knowing Appleby." Damn the slimy bastard, and damn him, too, for not noticing. Kaya had to be right.

"I thought he died in the opium dens." The words consumed every ounce of restraint he possessed. He held Kaya tighter.

"You never saw him after?"

"No." Eyes closed against the constant play of smoky darkness, Paul clung to Kaya like a drowning man. She deserved better than to be used like that, but he didn't know what else to do. "Oliver, when he found me and dragged me back to the barracks, he said he never saw Appleby."

"Do you believe that?"

"I—I never thought about it." Paul frowned and blinked away the past, even as it crawled up his spine, its tiny claws digging into him and dragging him backward. "By the time I had regained my wits, after the shaking and, well..."

After the desperation, the constant need to feel that floating bliss where nothing mattered. After the screaming and clawing and crying and begging. "Only weeks passed before the—before everything else."

"What happened to him in Bombay is a small matter now." Kaya pressed her lips to his, returning him to the present.

"Maybe." He shuddered and dropped his head to the pillow. "But you may be right about his reasons for being here."

Despite that, Paul still wanted to run. To take Kaya's hand and leave and never look back. He didn't want her to know the sort of man he'd been in Bombay. The sort of man who looked the other way when Appleby sold women or—

No. Not stopping Appleby here in this hamlet was the same as helping him. The same as looking the other way in Bombay. He wouldn't do that again. Never again.

"When I left Bombay, I thought that was the end." Paul's words surprised him. He tried to dam them, but they flew out. "Bombay was my past, Cairo my future. You."

He tightened his hold on Kaya, aware that his breath caught even as he tried to loosen his grip. He needed her close, a solid reminder of now. She shifted, her skirts rustling as she draped her leg over his and settled more comfortably atop him. She didn't move away. Kaya didn't ever stand or pull away. Or run.

No, she'd never. But what had he ever done to deserve her devotion? Her loyalty? Her love?

Her love.

It moved through him, the sheer vastness of it. He had no words to describe it, but it closed his throat and settled in him.

"We can't run from our pasts." She cupped his face and forced him to look at her. "Nor can we hide. I spent my life hiding because of my parents' choices. But it did not make their pasts disappear. It didn't put my life in any less danger."

Paul snorted and caught her hand, holding it over his heart. He liked the symbolism. "It only fueled your desire to see the world." He kissed her fingers, watching her. "And now I've placed you in more danger."

"Do you think I'm in danger?" Kaya asked so calmly that Paul knew she didn't believe herself to be.

"No. Maybe." He closed his eyes, then released her hand and

pressed the heel of his against his temple. "I don't know. I don't know why he's here or what he plans." He opened his eyes and met hers. "There's nothing in this place, unless he wants to smuggle those purple flowers you like to draw."

Kaya's lips curved, and Paul's shoulders relaxed just a little. "Is flower smuggling done? Is that someone's job, do you think?"

He felt laughter bubble in his chest, and when it broke free, so, too, did the remaining tension. "I'm not sure it's a job, or if smuggled flowers are in great demand, but I'm certain someone, somewhere has tried it."

She giggled, that light, carefree sound he adored. Paul tugged her closer and kissed her softly. Kaya hummed into the kiss and deepened it, rolling atop him, her legs bracketing his hips. Pushing herself up, she broke the kiss and looked down at him.

Paul bunched up her skirts and settled his hands on her hips, his fingers brushing up and down. He wanted to touch her skin, needed that connection. However, Kaya caught his hands and threaded her fingers with his.

"Do you think Appleby is still the same man? You're not."

"Of course—" He broke off and stopped to give her question the seriousness it deserved. But even after considering it, the answer remained the same: "He hasn't changed."

"How do you know? You only spoke with him a moment."

Jaw clenched, memories battering his mind and heart, Paul scowled. "I know." He consciously unclenched his jaw. "Even if you told me he built orphanages or paid alms to the poor or donated to churches or mosques, I'd still want to know what was in it for him. What angle he played. How much money he made from it."

"Oh." She offered a faint smile, but her eyes were serious. "I thought you were going to say you knew because he spoke in code."

Paul snorted, but whatever humor her comment elicited disappeared before it could take root. How did she know him so well after only months together? No wonder he loved her more than he thought possible.

"Do you think he's selling women here?"

Paul sat up impatiently, and brought Kaya to him.

Leaning against the wall, his gorgeous wife in his lap, he thought of several dozen far more pleasurable activities they could be enjoying. He ran his fingers under her skirts, felt the warm, bare skin of her thighs beneath his hands.

"This doesn't seem like the place for it, no."

"You do not sound certain."

Paul's fingers tightened on her legs, and he shook his head. He desperately tried to block out his time in Bombay. Eyes squeezed shut, teeth grinding together, he tried. God, did he try to push those memories away.

"Paul!"

Her voice broke through the roaring in his ears, through Appleby's harsh laughter, the crash of memories he wanted to wipe from his brain. He blinked Kaya into focus, concentrating only on her, and kissed her. He tangled his fingers in her braids. Her taste erased the self-loathing caught in his throat.

She wrapped her arms around his neck and rocked once against his cock. He growled, his own self-disgust at war with desperation for her.

Wanting Kaya won. Always.

She made that sound in the back of her throat, that breathless moan of need.

"I don't—Kaya."

"I know." Her fingers danced over his cock, her tongue teasing his. "Let go, Paul. Let go. I'm here. And I'll catch you."

Paul didn't answer. Instead, he cupped the back of her head and pressed his palm to the curve of her spine as she arched into him. Her fingers combed through his hair, her mouth hard against his. He deepened the kiss, the feel of her warm satin skin beneath his fingertips as arousing as her scent. As the feel of her mouth on his.

He easily lifted Kaya and laid her on the long, narrow bed. Slowly rolling up her skirts, Paul slid his fingers along her leg, felt the smoothness of her inner thigh.

"Kaya." Her name was the only sound that made sense.

It beat through him, pounding in time to his heartbeat.

His finger slid into her heat and she hissed, arching her hips so he could slide in deeper. She nipped at his throat, clawed at the buttons of his vest, bunched up his shirt. Desperate to expose his own skin for her touch. He cupped her face and kissed her softly but no less possessively. She was his as surely as he was hers.

He wanted to beg her not to leave him. Now that he'd found her, Paul didn't want to know what not having her might feel like. The words choked him, and again he deepened the kiss. Her legs widened to accommodate him, and her heat—her glorious heat —seared him.

He pulled back just enough to whisper against her lips, "If I had my way, we'd never speak to another human being again." The words were rough, guttural. Arousal caught him, hard and relentless, and pulled him inexorably toward the goddess in his arms.

His goddess.

"Difficult, that." She gasped and shivered, her breath catching, her fingers tightening on the nape of his neck. "We might have to speak to *someone*."

"You don't understand." He leaned his forehead against hers, his fingers trailing along her sides. She shuddered, her hips jerking against his, that low whimper shooting straight to his cock.

"Tell me." Kaya pulled him atop her, her hips arching into his touch. "Show me."

She kissed him again, harder, nipping his bottom lip with a hint of desperation. Her fingers jerked at his trousers and quickly pushed them down, her blunt nails grazing his skin. She stroked his cock, caressing him. She teased him, ran her fingers over the head of his shaft, then scraped her nails down to his balls.

He shuddered against her. Cupping her arse, her glorious

bum, he pushed her dress out of the way. He breathed deeply of the heady scent of her arousal and slid his fingers into the heat of her. Kaya gasped, moving against his touch.

"Paul," she moaned.

Paul pulled back just enough to see her. Kaya's dark eyes, heavy with arousal, met his. She deliberately raked her nails across the small of his back, and he hiked her legs higher on his waist. He slid into her and easily adjusted. They fit so perfectly, and the world burst into searing color.

Kaya tightened around him, and he slid deeper. Desperation beat through him, hard drumbeats echoing in his blood. Paul moved in short, hard thrusts and bent to kiss her. He'd never get enough of her taste.

She pulled back, her fingers between her legs, on her clit. Head thrown back, she tightened around him. Her lips parted, and a look of pure ecstasy crossed her face. She breathed his name, her hips meeting his with every thrust.

She shattered, clenching around his cock, her body shuddering.

In awe of her beauty, her passion, her driving need, Paul moved faster. Thrust harder into her welcoming body, tasted along her shoulder, nipped her throat. He wanted to cup her breasts, pinch her nipples, let the thundering of her heart echo around him. He wanted to see her come again.

Her nails dug into the skin at the small of his back, and he knew he'd have welts there later. Didn't care. Wanted them, Kaya's marks.

"Come for me, Kaya."

She whimpered, her fingers moving over her clit again, brushing his cock. He thrust harder as another orgasm crashed through her, nonsensical words falling from her lips. Whatever control he thought he possessed broke.

Paul kissed her, a sloppy, bruising kiss, and pounded into her, on edge. He fell. Shattered in her arms, her name a cry on his lips.

Only at the last second did he pull out, coming on Kaya's belly.

"I'll never let you fall."

Paul blinked, breathed in the arousal-tinted scent of her neck, her pulse still pounding against his lips. He rolled to the side and kissed that spot, breathing deeply as he tried to find the shreds of his control. The mantle he used to fool the rest of the world.

Not the man he was. Had been. Not the man Appleby thought he knew.

The man whose sins blackened his soul. The possessive, greedy, covetous man who tried to live in a world that didn't—couldn't—accept him for all he truly was. The one Kaya still wanted. Still understood.

Only her touch lightened that blackness, eased the selfish envy. Only she mattered.

"I'll never let you fall." Kaya's soft words wrapped around him more securely than his façade. She slowly blinked open her eyes and met his gaze. "I promise."

From the top stair, Kaya looked around the interior of the inn.

No matter what happened here, Kaya treasured the trust she and Paul had built. She refused to badger him for answers to satisfy her own curiosity.

She understood wanting to change. Not wanting to be defined by one's past. Kaya had loathed constantly living in the shadows of her parents' choices, her grandfather's constant fear. She refused to condemn Paul for his own shadows. He wanted to break from them, and she'd gladly walk beside him as he did so.

She meant it. She'd not let him fall. Her love for him beat sharply through her, and she promised herself she'd always catch him.

Paul stepped off the last stair and turned to wait for her. His eyes flickered around the room, constantly moving though he stood deceptively still. This Paul reminded her of the man who'd helped her escape Cairo in the middle of the night, not the one who'd held her in Mazzarelli while she recovered from seasickness, nor the man who eagerly, even joyfully, explored Sicily with her.

He held out his arm, a formal gesture he rarely made. Placing her hand atop it, Kaya stepped off the last stair and turned toward the room.

"Do you see any of your other former associates?" They'd agreed to speak in English until they gathered more information.

"No." His lips thinned, his muscles bunching beneath her hand. "Doesn't mean they're not here."

Kaya wrapped her fingers around his forearm and wondered if he even felt her touch. "Perhaps Marta might be able to tell us more about Appleby and his agenda."

"Agenda?" He slanted her an amused look, a little of his earlier humor returning.

"Plan?" She tilted her head. "What do you call such a thing?"

"Either works." Again his voice held humor—a good sign. She hoped. "I still don't like it."

That made two of them. "You didn't want to leave, either."

Paul held out a chair and rolled his shoulders, an impatient shift she recognized all too easily. Here she thought they'd moved beyond that point, the half lies, the withholding of information.

Her own fingers fisted into her skirts, but Kaya forcibly relaxed them. Their relationship, all four months of it, sparkled new and shiny around them. She couldn't blame Paul for keeping his past hidden, one he admitted to being ashamed of.

"Appleby's planning something."

"I'm in agreement; we should discover what."

"Then why do you keep bringing it up?" Paul snapped the words but immediately frowned. "Sorry. I'm sorry, sweetheart."

Kaya let it pass. Oh, yes, she knew him well enough to know he'd meet invasive questions with anger. It must've worked in the past to keep inquisitive people at bay. It had worked for her, once upon a trek through the desert.

"I don't want you to regret staying."

"I'd regret leaving, too." He scrubbed a hand down his face. "Christ. This is not where I pictured us when we woke this morning."

They settled into a small, round table nestled in the corner of the inn, and Kaya reached for his hand across it. She ignored the stares and the lowered voices around them.

"You continue to confuse me, Paul Hartley." Kaya smiled as Marta wandered to their semi-isolated table, which was pushed between rows and rows of longer tables with benches. "However, I don't want you tangled in something you'd regret."

Paul snorted, but Kaya ignored him and smiled brightly at Marta. The shorter, dark-haired woman smiled back—a forced, weak stretching of her lips—as she watched them carefully. Her brown eyes moved over them, their joined hands, and then to the rest of the busy inn.

"Do you search for someone?" Kaya asked. "Are we taking someone's table?"

"Oh." Marta laughed, a slight, nervous sound. "No. I looked for—" She lifted the bottle of wine she carried. "Wine?"

Kaya, far more used to this than she thought possible, shook her head. "Bergamot juice, if you have it. Or orange, please."

Surprised, Marta nodded. She looked to Paul, who shook his head to the offer of wine as well, and disappeared through the crowd. Kaya watched her set the wine bottle behind the counter and, just as silently, disappear through a side door.

"I had not realized the rest of the world drank only wine."

Paul snorted. "You've no idea."

Or she had. He'd told her a little about his past relationship with wine on their walk across Sicily. The perpetual drunken haze he'd preferred during those later years in Bombay, the lack of wine across the desert and in Cairo.

Kaya closed her mouth, uncertain how to ask and certain that this inn, surrounded by suspicious strangers and the thickness of Paul's past, was not the place to do so.

"Are you hungry?" Again his eyes tracked the same path over the inn's all-male population.

"Very." Kaya stopped when Paul stiffened.

She didn't need to look behind her to know Harry Appleby had entered the building. Paul's entire face changed—hard, flat, watching. Waiting. The rest of the inn changed, too, got slightly quieter, as if they collectively held their breath and waited.

"Paul, my friend!"

Appleby's voice echoed across the room, a booming sound that scraped along Kaya's nerves. She did not like it, the falseness of his tone, the way the rest of the inn watched him so carefully. She especially didn't like how Paul tensed.

It made her wary. She once more unclenched her fingers from her skirts and relaxed her jaw. How did one man's presence cause such unease?

Kaya's fingers brushed the hilt of her dagger. Just in case.

Eleven

"I insist." Appleby pulled a chair up to their table without asking. Quite rude, that, and Kaya scowled at him. He ignored her. "Join me for dinner."

"I believe *you* have just joined *us*." Paul scooted his chair closer to hers. With his back still to the wall, his gaze never left Appleby, but his hand rested on the back of her neck, warm and comforting.

Maybe Appleby's presence had caused his skin to crawl as well.

"Paul, my friend, your sharp tongue has not dulled." Appleby's gaze slithered over her. Kaya raised an eyebrow and waited.

In her experience, doing so often caused the other person to speak further and fill the silence. Well, in her experience with people who weren't Paul. Paul liked silence. He enjoyed conversation as well, but there was always a silent camaraderie between them.

Appleby's lips widened into what some might call a grin, but not Kaya. The sight of his lips pulling back at the corners—a more apt description—made her stomach tighten with tension.

He was missing a tooth, a lower molar, and his nose looked as if it'd been broken. Repeatedly. She had the sudden urge to break it again.

"Tell me, how did the two of you meet?" Appleby leaned across the table, his arms folded in front of him. Kaya wrinkled her nose at the heavy stench of wine. His body crowded the table, and his attention seemed to land solely on her. Kaya wanted to shove him to the next table. Or the next village. "How did my good friend find one such as you?"

"We met in Cairo." Kaya repeated the vaguely truthful answer she'd been giving for months.

People often asked such questions. According to Paul, they were considered small talk. Kaya wasn't sure how she felt about that. Those invasive, nonsense questions everyone wanted answered. Still, she forced herself to indulge. She met Appleby's gaze, determined not to feel intimidated by the man.

"Egypt?" Appleby laughed, though that seemed unnecessary. "That godforsaken place?" He shook his head. "Paul, what the hell were you doing there?"

Paul, as straight as the board they'd used for their tent and just as stiff, shrugged. To Kaya, it was an awkward movement, but Appleby didn't notice. Behind her, the tips of Paul's fingers pressed hard to the top of her spine.

"I wanted a change. Got tired of the humidity in Bombay."

Appleby laughed again, as if Paul had told the funniest joke. The sound scraped over her skin like a knife. Kaya pressed her lips into a thin line.

"It was stinking hot there." Appleby looked over his shoulder, his face darkening. "Stinking hot," he muttered, then shouted, "Marta!"

His voice echoed over the inn, hushing all conversation to the merest hint of a whisper. Kaya stilled, her hand on her dagger. Marta appeared from the back room, a dark bottle in one hand, her eyes wide. A flash of fear crossed her face and then disappeared so quickly Kaya thought she might've imagined it.

She had not. Anger made her hot, and only Paul's fingers on her shoulder stayed her.

"Is that bergamot juice?" Kaya nodded to the opened bottle Marta carried but seemed to have forgotten. "Thank you, Marta."

She took the bottle and smiled, but Marta didn't look at her. Instead, she turned to Appleby. "Sorry, Signore Harry," she whispered. "*Perdono*. I fetch the wine now."

Appleby's hand snapped out and grabbed her wrist, that slippery smile back on his face. "That's all right, Marta."

For a single long moment, Marta stilled. Appleby's fingers tightened around her wrist until Kaya knew it'd bruise. Then the other woman yanked her arm from Appleby's grip and whirled for the bar, her skirts flaring around her.

Kaya had never hated anyone before. Abstract anger and fear, yes. But not this hot, burning hatred she felt for Harry Appleby.

"She's pretty." Paul all of a sudden relaxed.

His fingers eased from her neck, and his shoulders lost some of their tension. Kaya whipped her head around, not sure if his words surprised her more than his sudden body language, or if the last few minutes had changed everything.

"Quite your type."

Appleby laughed, another loud, boisterous sound. Kaya wanted to shove the bergamot juice down his throat. The whole bottle. "Yes, yes. She's a handful." He winked at Kaya.

Paul raised his mug. Kaya wanted to stab the man. Marta returned and silently set the wine and a single cup on the table. Her eyes downcast, her lips pressed together so hard they all but disappeared, she didn't look at any of them before turning back for the kitchens.

Kaya glanced around the room, the juice sour in her mouth. Conversation picked back up, but it sounded more strained, as if to cover nervousness.

Kaya wanted nothing to do with this man. He made her nauseous. Paul's mood had changed in the last few minutes, and she did not understand how or why. She'd not learn anything from him when he was feeling like this. The problem was, she didn't know if she should leave her husband here with a man he clearly didn't trust. Would staying ease Paul's tension and get him to answer some of her questions?

Appleby watched her with that same look as earlier. The one that made her feel dirty and undressed. Exposed in the worst possible way.

"If you'll excuse me." No longer hungry, she stood and met Paul's gaze. "Good night."

"Leaving so soon, lovely?" Appleby leaned back in his chair and poured himself a generous helping of wine.

Tilting her head, unsure how a word as nice and complimentary as "lovely" could sound so greasy and rude, Kaya merely stared. Appleby blinked and looked down, draining his mug in one gulp.

Head held high, she turned and walked through the crowd. Though Paul rarely left her alone in strange places—which meant he rarely left her alone—Kaya knew he would not follow.

Based on their conversation earlier, Paul wanted answers about Appleby's presence in this little village in the mountains. Logically, Kaya knew Paul also wanted to stop whatever illegal operation Appleby employed here.

That wasn't the problem. The problem was, Kaya had a feeling she'd not like the methods he employed to discover the truth.

Kaya missed her husband as she climbed the stairs. Holding her skirts off the uneven wooden treads, she purposely didn't back, though she felt Paul's gaze on her. Once she was at the top of the steps, she couldn't help it and peered over the railing.

Paul met her gaze, barely nodding to Marta, who had returned with another bottle of wine. Appleby looked up at her and stared hard. Even with a flight of stairs and a mass of people between them, Kaya felt his interest. It disgusted her.

Unlocking their door, she slipped inside and undressed. The jewels they carried dug into her sides, but Kaya had long since grown used to that. She didn't like it, but they had no other method of safely transporting them. She carefully folded her dress over their single chair, placed her hijab atop it, and stretched her arms high over her head.

It felt wonderful to move so freely, without the confining bodice of the dress or the irregular angles of the stones cutting in.

The knock startled her.

Kaya grabbed her dagger from the table and whirled to face the sound. She carried their only key, so maybe it was Paul who knocked, but she did not believe so. He'd seemed entirely too intent on speaking with Appleby to follow her up so soon. Dressed only in her chemise, stockings, and boots, Kaya silently walked to the door and flattened against the wall by the knob.

She needed a crack, a spy hole of some sort, to look through and see whoever stood on the other side. But she couldn't move; the gap between the door and the floor would reveal her shadow.

A bad angle. She'd have to use her right hand to open the door, spring back, and keep the dagger in her left hand. Or she could open the door with her left hand, thereby reaching across her body. Kaya didn't like either option.

The knock sounded again.

"Signora Hartley?"

Marta.

Kaya lowered the dagger and opened the door, stepping back, well out of reach. A flood of noise entered the room.

"Oh." Marta eyed the dagger, and the tray of food she was carrying wobbled. "I bring dinner. Your husband, he said you were not well. Are you ill?"

Kaya waited a moment, then set her dagger on the table beside her before taking the tray from Marta, who hadn't set foot in the room.

"No." Kaya smiled and gestured for Marta to enter, though she did not. "I'm merely tired. Thank you for the tray, it's most kind of you."

Marta tore her gaze from the dagger, which was now resting

innocuously on the table, and glanced around the room. She spotted the dress draped over the chair. Only then did she step over the threshold and noticeably relax. "I clean your dress?"

"*Grazie*, but I can manage." Kaya rested her hand on Marta's arm—Marta flinched. Rage choked Kaya, a well of hot fury that stole her words. Dropping her hand, Kaya pressed her lips together. She wanted to hurt Appleby in every way he had hurt Marta.

"As you wish, Signora Hartley." Marta looked at the floor and stepped back, out of reach.

Kaya frowned. "Call me Kaya, please." After months of strangers calling her "Signora Conrad," she wasn't used to Hartley.

"A most unusual name." Marta's gaze flicked up but didn't make contact with Kaya's. Once again watching the floor, Marta stooped before the brazier by the table and set about lighting it. A long moment passed, then, over her shoulder, she met Kaya's gaze for a fleeting instant. "Is it English?"

"No." Feeling as if Marta was trying to pry information from her (and wondering if that feeling was a byproduct of traveling with Paul and his paranoia), Kaya dropped the subject. "Thank you for the meal. I hope it wasn't too much trouble."

"No trouble. You need more?" Marta looked around the room again.

"Not tonight, thank you." She wanted to ask about Appleby. What he was doing here, what he'd threatened Marta with, why no one had stopped him. Kaya also wanted to ask where Paul was, but she had a feeling neither he nor Appleby had moved from their table and bottle of wine.

"Good night, Marta."

Marta nodded and stepped into the hall, closing the door behind her. Once more in the relative silence of their room, the noises from below now faint, Kaya waited until she heard Marta start down the hallway.

She looked at the plate: noodles, chickpeas, garlic, all covered in olive oil. She saw no trace of meat. Paul must've told Marta not to serve her any pork products. Despite her worry for him, a rush of love enveloped her.

Kaya ate quickly, hungrier than she'd told Appleby she was. Several bites in, however, she set the fork aside and pushed the still-full plate away. Hungry though she was, food didn't agree with her. Not while she worried over Paul and Appleby.

Standing, Kaya paced to the small window and pushed the shutters open. The cold night air brushed along her exposed skin, and she shivered despite the fragrant brazier burning behind her. She didn't move away, however, and let the breeze revive her.

With the sudden change in their plans, she had a feeling she'd need to be alert to every possibility.

She leaned against the open window and closed her eyes. Some winter nights, the air in Cairo felt cool. Not like this, of course, but the temperature dropped noticeably. The crisp, clean scent of mountain air—that was new.

Open. Fresh. Crisp. Yes, she liked that word—*crisp*. It described much about this new land.

"Gidd would love this." Kaya closed her eyes against the grief that gripped her heart but felt her lips curve into a sad smile. "And Derya, she'd love these mountains."

Eventually, she took the blanket from the bed and wrapped it around her shoulders. The wool scratched her bare arms, but Kaya barely noticed. She tried calming her mind, to no avail. Paul consumed her thoughts.

She hadn't done enough to reassure him once they left Villa San Giovanni. The memory of Marco plagued him, and yet Kaya had no words to alleviate his pain. A failure at this partnership they'd forged, at this marriage, she curled her fingers over the window's ledge.

How could she help Paul if she left at the first sign of discomfort?

The moon, a bare sliver in the sky, rose higher, and Kaya tracked its progress. It glowed in the inky blackness, surrounded by twinkling starlight. She easily picked out *al-Jabbar*, the Giant, and *Ath-Thawr*, the Bull, and wondered what people gave them these names, what stories they associated with the stars.

Behind her, the doorknob rattled. Kaya dropped the blanket and noiselessly walked to the table where she'd left her dagger.

The din from below had stopped. If anyone remained in the inn, they spoke in low voices, careful not to let anyone overhear their conversation.

"Damn it."

Paul's cursing relieved and angered her in equal measure. Stalking across the room, her dagger gripped tightly in hand, Kaya unlocked the door and flung it open. The hinges squeaked, and it creaked unevenly but did not bang the opposite wall.

"You're awake." Paul blinked and stepped inside.

"You're drunk."

Disgusted, she closed and locked the door. Turning for the table, she set down her dagger—though she had half a mind to keep it nearby.

"Aye." Paul sat on the bed and scrubbed both hands down his face. The movement did not help his slurring. "I am. Damn good wine in this town."

Her lip curled, she watched him in the faint light. Several sentences ran through her mind, but she was in no mood to untangle them.

Tired, cold, aggravated, she crossed her arms over her chest. "What happened?"

"Appleby's keeping it close to the vest."

Annoyed at yet another idiom, Kaya made a noise in the back of her throat. Paul looked up. He looked tired. Drained. Kaya crossed the room and banged the shutters closed, latching them tight to give her another moment.

"He told you nothing?" She kept her voice low in case of eavesdroppers, though no shadow crossed beneath their door. Still, one never knew.

In the darkness, she vaguely saw Paul shake his head. His

shadow leaned over and removed his boots, only to stand unevenly and untie his trousers. They dropped to the floor, quickly followed by his coat and vest.

Half tempted to leave them there, Kaya sighed, and her fingers curled into fists. She hesitated for only a heartbeat before picking them up and laying them over her dress.

"Come to bed, Kaya." Paul sat on the bed again, and, despite the dark, she saw his hand reach out for hers.

"Will you tell me what you and Appleby spoke of?"

Paul faltered, his hand dropping. Her stomach churned with an emotion she couldn't place. Unease, perhaps. Worry. Disappointment.

"We didn't speak of his reasons for being here." Paul sighed, and she heard his hand fall against the bed. "He won't trust me with that. Not yet."

Kaya cautiously stepped forward, frustrated. Sitting next to him, she reached for his hand. Wrapping her cool fingers over his warmer ones, she rested them on his naked knee.

"I did not expect him to. I did not—" She cut herself off. Truthfully, Kaya didn't know what she'd expected.

"You didn't expect me drunk." Paul snorted and tugged her down, curling around her.

"Wait, I left the blanket." Kaya scrambled from beneath his arm and grabbed the blanket from where she'd dropped it. She shook it out and draped it over Paul before climbing back into bed with him.

"I'm sorry." His breath, heavy with the scent of wine and regret, wafted over her bare shoulder. "For everything."

A shiver ran up her spine. What, exactly, did *everything* encompass?

He didn't say more, but he didn't sleep, either. Kaya had spent so many nights with him, making love with him, being held by him, sleeping. She knew when Paul had finally succumbed to sleep and when he was pretending.

Problem was, she hadn't yet found a way to soothe him

during those moments. She'd tried talking, holding him. Sex until neither could move. Sometimes, her tactics worked. Other times, not so much.

Paul's breathing slowed, and he relaxed against her back, but Kaya knew he did not sleep. She closed her eyes but knew she wouldn't, either. Not tonight.

Twelve

P aul crept from their room feeling more like a thief than he had since leaving Bombay. He eased the door closed so as not to wake Kaya, who had finally drifted to sleep. His head pounded, and his mouth tasted like wet wool. He refused to even focus on his stomach lest he expel the wine he'd decided to drink last night.

He didn't deserve to sleep off the hangover. To lounge in bed like a layabout.

No matter how much the thought tempted him. Or how much Kaya, still asleep, enticed him back to bed, he'd made a promise last night. He'd discover what Appleby was doing in this village and stop him no matter what.

Before, Paul had always looked the other way. If it didn't affect him, he didn't worry about it.

He'd been wrong—of course it affected him. Was he any better for not stopping Appleby than Appleby was for doing the deed in the first place? No. It was time Paul admitted that.

These last months with Kaya had eased his guilt, but he hadn't yet atoned for his past.

Stepping into the tavern, he wasn't certain he could ever atone for all he'd done. But, for the man he wanted to be now, he'd try. No matter what he had to do.

A young girl was sweeping the floor, and she stopped to grin at him. "*Buongiorno.*" Her voice was cheery and her smile bright.

His head aching, his eyes squinting against the early morning sunlight streaming through the inn's open shutters, Paul raised a hand in greeting. "*Buongiorno.*"

His lips slurred the word, and suddenly his teeth ached, too. Wonderful.

Marta appeared from the kitchens then, her hair tied back in a long braid. She looked tired and troubled, and Paul had a feeling he knew the reason. Oh, yes—it burned through him, the knowledge that he had the power to stop Harry Appleby. He would. Appleby would never hurt anyone else ever again.

Appleby, who was nowhere to be seen.

Just as well. Paul wanted to pummel him to a pulp. Expel his anger and loathing and wind time back to yesterday morning, before they'd entered this hamlet.

Marta met his gaze, but it was there and gone before Paul could focus.

Winding time backward meant breaking his promise to Kaya. Paul vowed to see this through. Even at the cost of his soul.

Marta met his gaze again, a blink of inspection. He didn't catch what she said to the girl, but he didn't need to. The girl, confused, glanced up at him, nodded, and skipped happily out of the tavern and into the kitchens.

"Ah, happy morning, Signore Hartley." Marta forced a smile, another skittish glance, and looked up the stairs. "Your wife, she is not awake?"

"She's still asleep."

Kaya had finally fallen asleep not long before sunrise. She'd tried not to toss and turn in his arms, and eventually he rolled over and pretended to sleep. But he hadn't fooled her. One mad idea after another had raced through his mind in the quiet darkness of their room.

Only one stood out in the all-too-bright light of day.

Over the previous months, Paul had spent a lot of time shoving his past into a very small box and locking it. He hadn't yet managed to lose the key, but not for lack of trying. Oh, he brought out small pieces to share with Kaya because she wanted to know the man she married. At night, the memories forced their way out, pushing and prodding him. Reminding him of the past he couldn't escape.

He could leave this village, ignore Harry. He had that choice.

Paul resisted looking up to their room, as if he might see Kaya suddenly emerge. He was better off a selfish rat. He forced his gaze from the wine barrels to Marta. Those barrels called to him, a sweet melody of false promise.

So he smiled as charmingly as possible, ignored his throbbing head and dry mouth, threw caution to the wind, and hoped for the best. "I came to see if you had any mint, lemon juice, and fresh water." Paul cleared his throat, but it burned. "For my wife."

He used to be so good at this.

Marta nodded, that brittle smile frozen on her face. She called into the back, where he heard faint noises of cooking and talking, but she didn't leave him alone. Probably thought he'd steal the wine.

"Harry not awake yet?"

Paul looked around the empty room. Of course Appleby wasn't awake yet. The other man drank six bottles of wine himself, in addition to the two he and Paul had shared. Paul didn't even know how many more he'd drunk prior to sitting with them.

"Signore Harry still sleeps." Marta nervously cleared her throat but tossed her head back in defiance. "You wake him at your own danger."

Laughing, Paul shook his head—and regretted it instantly. Though the pounding drums refused to abate, Paul grinned. "Oh, I have no intention of waking him."

In the dark of night, with Kaya half asleep next to him and his thoughts tumbling over each other in rapid succession, a single thought stood out. If he killed Appleby now, he'd free the village from whatever hold the man had on it and ease his own conscience at the same time. It didn't matter if Paul ever discovered what Appleby was doing here, or why the town watched him with suspicious fear.

Or what hold he had over Marta.

He shoved that thought, and the dark pit that came with it, to the furthest corner of his mind.

"It's been a while since I've seen my friend." Paul forced his stiff shoulders to move in a careless shrug. He didn't want Kaya to see him now. "I've decided to stay a little longer. Catch up, as it were."

With her fingers bunching her skirts, Marta moved her head slightly in what might have been a nod.

Before she had the chance to reply, the girl returned with his items. "*Signore. Per tua moglie?*"

Paul took the tray from the girl. "*Sì, sì. Per Kaya. Grazie. Come ti chiami?*"

"Olivia, *signore.*"

"*Grazie,* Olivia." Paul winked at her and grinned. A little of the tar that coated his soul evaporated at the unaffected, wide smile from the innocent girl.

At least Appleby's blackness hadn't touched her. Yet.

Paul vowed it never would.

"I bring breakfast and water." Marta, though she still looked afraid and nervous, also seemed to relax.

Paul wanted to warn her not to. Relaxing around Appleby was exactly what the bastard wanted. He struck like a snake, waiting, quiet, sneaky. Just when you thought it safe, he attacked.

"*Grazie.*"

With movements slow and careful, Paul retraced his steps to the bedroom, Marta behind him. "Leave the bucket, Marta, please." He nodded and hoped his voice didn't wake Kaya. "Thank you."

Marta offered him an indecipherable look but left the bucket and breakfast tray by the open door. He waited until she'd walked halfway down the stairs before pushing the door fully open.

Paul wanted Kaya to sleep longer. She needed it after her restless night. Plus, he didn't want to tell her his plan, and he knew she'd ask.

The less she knew, the better.

"Paul?" The sleepy quality to her voice, low, sexy, intimate, cut him to the bone.

He closed his eyes, his fingers tight on the breakfast tray. "Go back to sleep, Kaya."

But the harsh words had the exact opposite effect, and she sat up. Her hair loose around her shoulders, her face pale in the dim room, her eyes too bright after a restless night, she stared at him as if he'd lost his mind. He probably had.

He set the bucket of water by the table, then he closed and locked the door.

"Why?" Her eyes narrowed. "What's on the tray?"

"Breakfast. Looks like fig preserves, *cornetto*." He sniffed the cup of juice. "Bergamot juice, and coffee."

He slid the tray next to the half-eaten bowl from last night. He hated waste and knew Kaya did as well—especially after surviving a famine. Stoking the fire, he set the bowl atop the small, round brazier.

"If you think not talking is going to work, you've obviously forgotten the last few months."

Paul snorted, his shoulders sagging. "You're a stubborn woman, Kaya."

She sniffed, and he heard her move across the room to the table. "Mint?" Her voice held a quality he refused to decipher. "And you." She sighed, a quiet huff of affection. "You're a strange man, Paul."

He let out a breath of laugh. "You should go back to sleep."

"According to you, I should do a lot of things." She ignored him, as he'd expected, and mixed several mint leaves into the cold mountain water.

After swishing the water around her mouth, she spat it into last night's empty cup. Then she crushed more leaves in the basin and washed her hands and face. The sharp scent of mint combined with the soothing routine of her morning.

He left her to her silence and her prayers and crouched before their pack as if he didn't know everything that lay within it. As if they were about to spend another morning traveling together, the two of them alone in the mountains.

Yesterday? Had it really only been a day?

"Thank you." Her prim voice caused Paul to look over his shoulder. Kaya stood straight, her posture as formal as her voice.

"The lemon juice is for your dress." The words sounded inane, and Paul leaned back on his haunches. Christ, what a mess. One of his own making. "Are you hungry?"

"What do you plan to do with Appleby?"

No, today was not a day for simple conversation. Paul stood, using the movement to buy time. He took the spoon from last night's tray and stirred the bowl, watching the tomato and pasta mix together. He left the bergamot juice and cappuccino for Kaya.

"I'm going to stop him."

He looked up and met her gaze. In the room's quiet gloom, with fingers of sunlight slipping beneath the shutters, Kaya did not look at all surprised.

He really should stop underestimating her.

"How?" She reached behind her for the blanket and stepped closer. Paul wondered if she only did so to be closer to the fire.

"Not sure yet." He casually dismissed it, then stopped himself. No matter how logical his plan to push her away, Paul found it almost impossible. "But I'm positive you won't like it."

"I am positive you are correct." Her eyebrow rose, and he sighed. "Will you tell me what you and he did in Bombay?" Her voice softened. "Trust me, Paul."

Paul opened his mouth—to dismiss her question or shrug off her concern or offer platitudes for her trust. But he snapped it closed without saying anything. Turning back to the brazier, he stirred the contents of the bowl again, his shoulders stiff, as if to ward off her questions.

"You don't want to know." The words didn't sound as dismissive as he'd hoped.

"I know. You said. You weren't a nice man." She didn't parrot his warning back to him but repeated its sentiment. It was a fine difference he never would've previously caught.

He loved her all the more for it.

"I don't want to dismiss the man you were," she said slowly. "I want to help the man I know."

Once more Paul opened his mouth, and once more he snapped it closed. At a loss for words, a rarity in his life but certainly not since he met Kaya, he stared at the pasta stew. It was the worst distraction he could think of. He used to be so good at distractions, too.

"I don't want you anywhere near Appleby." Paul dropped the spoon onto the tray. It clattered loudly in the quiet room.

He whirled toward Kaya and grabbed her by the arms. The blanket restricted his movements, but his fingers locked in place. Held there by fear and anger and remorse. He'd had his chance to stop Appleby long before he fled Bombay. Hadn't taken it out of respect for their friendship and their past, the shared memory of the two of them against the world.

Or maybe it was apathy. Or maybe both.

"He's dangerous. Mean. And he's after something here. Whatever this place has, it's profitable enough for him to stay."

Kaya's arms bent awkwardly at the elbow. Paul wanted to loosen his grip, but his fingers refused to obey. She clasped his arms, her fingers cool through the linen of his shirt.

"You think he smuggles opium through here?"

Unable to speak, barely able to move, Paul held her gaze.

"He holds Marta trapped—has something over her." Kaya

frowned but didn't look away. "She's terrified of him. I'm afraid he—forces her. And I think she spies for him, too, to keep in his good graces."

"Don't trust anyone." He shook her, a short automatic jerk of his hands.

"Not even you?" Her fingers tightened on his arms, her face set, her chin tilted in that stubborn angle he loved.

"Please stay out of it, Kaya."

She snorted, that unladylike sound he swore she learned from Tahir. "You're mad if you think I'll stay out of it. You are also delusional if you think telling me to do so will make it happen."

Somehow unsurprised, Paul heard the huff of his laugh before he realized he'd pulled her to him. Her hair smelled of the mountains, fresh and open, and her body curved into his embrace. Her hands flattened against his chest.

He pressed his lips to the top of her head. "You terrify me, Kaya."

"You have said as much before." She held him tighter, as if knowing he needed her embrace. Or maybe she needed it as much as he? "It does not change the fact that we agreed to live together, to carve out a life as husband and wife."

Before Villa San Giovanni, before Appleby, before the past reared its ugly head and bit him in the arse.

"I don't want you anywhere near him. Appleby is sneaky, dirty. He won't play fair."

Paul felt her frown before she pulled back and scowled up at him. He loosened his grip and touched his index finger between her eyes, smoothing the line there. She allowed him to, as always, and when he pulled away, she tilted her head.

"I don't understand what *playing* has to do with *fairness*."

"No, I guess you don't," he whispered.

Paul hated that she didn't have a normal childhood, but then he hadn't known "normal," either. He remembered Olivia's smiling innocence and vowed to stop Appleby before he took that little girl's "normal" childhood, too.

"Don't think breakfast means we're finished talking."

"Breakfast means the village is awake," he shot back. "It means Appleby will be shortly."

Kaya ignored him and picked up a mug of hot, milky *caffè*, breathing in the scent. "They don't make coffee like Egyptians, but it is good. Strong."

Paul watched her sip the drink and sigh. He deliberately squashed the impulse to make her sigh in pleasure using his hands, his mouth, his body. Even if his skin was crawling with the knowledge that time was slipping through his fingers.

"Kaya—" He scrubbed his fingers through his hair and tried not to whimper. His head ached. He'd forgotten the misery of too much drink.

"Don't." Her voice broke, and he dropped his hands, meeting her gaze. She watched him over the rim of the mug, serious. Sad. "You promised me three things—in Cairo, you promised we'd figure out our path together. In Damietta, you promised never to lie to me. In Mazzarelli, you promised you loved me."

Damn him and his promises. Paul sighed and sank to the single chair with his head in his hands. "I'm a damn fool for thinking I could promise you anything."

Kaya didn't call him on his cursing, a bold statement to just how dangerous this village had become in the space of a heartbeat.

"I don't—whatever you're thinking about Appleby, Paul, don't—" Kaya stopped again, and he looked up, curious. Hopeful. Terrified.

He held out his hand, and she instantly rounded the table. She set her mug down, then straddled his legs and wrapped her arms around his neck. Her lips were cool and dry on his temple, and Paul breathed in the scent of her.

Mint and *caffè*, sleep and Kaya.

Tightening his arms around her waist, he rested his head against her breasts. What a shithole of a mess. Paul's lips curved, and he almost repeated the phrase aloud, just to hear her scold him for his cursing since she hadn't before.

Instead, he closed his eyes and held her tight. He wanted to stay like that forever, in the quiet of their room, just the two of them. No village, no nosey innkeepers, no Appleby.

"I made you promises, too." Her words brushed over his hair, as light and gentle as her fingers caressing his scalp. He arched into her touch and closed his eyes, letting the soothing massage of her fingers ease his headache. "I promised I trusted you."

Kaya kissed his forehead. "I promised we'd work things through." She kissed his cheek. "I promised I love you."

She pressed her lips to his, a hard, desperate kiss. "And I do love you."

Paul held her gaze, his heart thundering in his ears, his own love for her wrapping around him. He was completely unwilling to break their connection. "You shouldn't."

"That is too bad. And too late. I promised. And I do."

Kaya leaned down and kissed him again, her lips rough on his, as if she tasted the same desperation he did every time he touched her. Looked at her. As if she knew as well as he that their time was slowly running out.

Thirteen

Kaya used a borrowed clothing brush to clean as much dirt off her skirts as possible. Last night, instead of standing in front of the open window and staring at the stars, she should've washed her dress.

Until last night, she'd been diligent about such things. But one day spent in the company of Paul's past, and all her old habits were gone. Now every too-rough stroke only rubbed the dirt deeper into the plain linen and reminded her of how little control she had in this life.

"I like this dress," she grumbled, but couldn't make herself stop her hard strokes.

"I'll ask Marta if she knows of a seamstress or has a spare one." Paul stood at the window with his back to her. Through the single open shutter, he observed the village square.

"No." Kaya hadn't meant to snap the word. Sleep fogged her mind and tugged her limbs, and fear settled like ice in her belly.

And anger, so much anger she didn't know what to do with it. It terrified her.

The cold breeze blew in from the window and curled around her legs. Kaya tucked her toes beneath her thighs and did her best to ignore it. Her fingers had bunched the fabric of her gown, and she forcibly smoothed her hands over the wrinkled material.

It wasn't about the dress. Not about the dirt on it or how she liked the light flow of the linen as opposed to the harder, more restrictive bone bodice of the blue gown she'd worn since Damietta.

Kaya flexed her fingers, dusty now and stiff with cold.

The trust she and Paul had built over the previous four months was now hanging on by a single thread—fragile, precarious. Or maybe it wasn't trust. Kaya couldn't name the disquiet scorching through her, choking her with uncertainty and insecurity. A vague apprehension that stiffened her fingers and tied her tongue in knots.

She licked her lips, staring hard at Paul's back.

He turned his head slightly, not enough to block his line of sight to the view below, not enough to truly see her, and sipped his coffee.

"You could leave."

She snorted and brushed the dress with vigorous strokes. She shook out the gown, movements far sharper than was necessary.

"You could."

"Without you, you mean." Kaya deliberately kept her voice light. Her stare, however, hardened. Had Paul turned to meet her gaze, he would've seen that. Maybe he instinctively knew. "I believe you wanted to discover Appleby's plans, if they had to do with the opium trade in Villa San Giovanni. Have you somehow discovered them between breakfast and now and not told me?"

Paul scowled over his shoulder. "No."

"Then I suppose we are not leaving."

"You're a stubborn woman, Kaya."

She dismissed that statement with a wave of her hand he didn't see. Then she stood up and dressed, watching Paul's back.

He stood a little straighter than when he'd first returned from downstairs. His head must not have been pounding as fiercely. His hair curled over the collar of his shirt, and she wanted to run her fingers through the soft strands. Instead, she pressed her traitorous fingers into the tops of her thighs. Paul lifted his coffee and sipped it.

Only then did she notice how tightly he held the cup. His fingers were gripping it so forcefully, his knuckles whitened.

"You've said." Kaya grabbed her dagger and strapped it to her waist. "Repeatedly."

"So I have." His voice sounded tired now. Defeated.

Kaya took a step toward him but stopped just out of reach. She couldn't say why and berated herself for her hesitation. "Why do you wish me to leave?"

His hand clenched around the cup before hastily setting it down. Slow, deliberately, he turned. "To keep you safe."

"You believe I'm not safe here."

Paul snorted and ran a hand down his face. "With Appleby here? And whatever his secret endgame is?" He shook his head. "No."

Kaya stepped closer, drawn to him as always. From the first, she'd been drawn to him, curious about the man who sneaked about Cairo so easily, so cleverly. "Or do you not believe I'm safe with you?"

Stricken, Paul stared at her. He opened his mouth, then closed it without sound.

She didn't know what to say, how to make him understand she would stay. Stay with him, help him in every way possible, and come out the other side.

Together.

What a terrifying word. She embraced it.

"I'm not leaving you." Closing the distance between them, she rested her hand on his arm, which was rigid beneath her touch. "Whatever you have planned, we'll see it through together." She squeezed, hoping her touch conveyed her intentions. "Together, Paul."

Paul met her gaze, and her breath caught. He looked so

broken, so lost. In all their months traveling, Kaya had never seen him so adrift.

"Paul—" Anything more caught in her throat.

His haunted, shattered gaze tore through her, and she physically ached. She took his hand and unclenched his fist. Her motions slow and careful, she wrapped her arms around him and guided his head to her shoulder.

He held himself stiffly at first, his arms at his side.

"Trust me, Paul."

With a whoosh of air, he wrapped his arms around her and held tight. His face buried in her shoulder, he shuddered in her embrace. Kaya pressed her fingers to the back of his head and held him there, hoping—hoping.

Half-formed thoughts fragmented as they raced round her mind. She hoped he'd see that they needed to be in this together, that she was here for him. That she loved him.

Both. All. Everything.

"I don't want you to see who I was before." Paul pulled back, his eyes sharp and focused and so fierce. "I never wanted you to know that man."

A number of replies rushed to her lips. When she spoke, however, the words came through the lump in her throat. "I can't return to the past and see who you were, Paul. Even if you pretend to be that man here and now with Appleby, it will make no difference to me. I know the man you are."

He snorted and stepped back, settling against the windowsill. He drew her between his legs, his hands on her hips. Kaya rested her hands on his upper arms, willing the tension in his muscles to ease.

"I'm not so sure they're very far removed."

"I disagree. I saw—" She stopped. "When we were in the desert, the Eastern Mountains, I saw how you fought the slavers. You didn't hesitate, didn't question, simply fought. Gidd never would've trusted you to smuggle me out of Cairo and see me safely through the desert if he wasn't confident in your fighting abilities."

"Tahir never knew all I did." Paul looked away but only for a moment. "He never knew the man I became. He saw the boy I was before, not that drunken layabout."

"He still trusted you." Kaya stopped and gathered her thoughts.

Knowing her grandfather, even those parts that were a mystery, he'd kept tabs on Paul. At the very least, he'd written someone in Bombay to discover what Paul had been up to during the intervening years. Otherwise, how would Gidd have contacted Paul? How would he have even known he was alive?

No, Gidd knew more about Paul's life in Bombay than Paul realized. Kaya would stake their jewels on that.

"In that desert ravine, you fought as if you had done it a hundred times before. You weren't afraid of two men against one and fought them without pause. You didn't ask what they planned with that woman, why they bound and gagged her. You knew."

"Aye." He shrugged, looked away again. "I've seen too much."

"Exactly." Hands gently on his cheek, she guided him to look at her. "You knew what they had planned, how they'd treated her already, and took action."

"So?" The word shot harshly between them.

"It was not the response of a man who does not care. Rather, of a man who knows what others are capable of and answers accordingly."

"Kaya."

Grappling with doubt, afloat on a sea of new experiences nothing could have prepared her for, Kaya pressed her fingers to the base of his skull. She didn't want him refuting her once more.

"What do you plan with Appleby?" She combed her fingers through his hair, hoping the motion eased the tension still tightening his jaw, his shoulders. Hoping it eased the tension tightening through her as well. "How do you plan to make him trust you?"

"I'll be the man he knows." Paul shrugged but drew her closer, tucked her head beneath his chin, and simply held her.

"The man he *thinks* he knows." She closed her eyes and held tight.

"Kaya," he sighed again.

She played with the hair curling at the base of his neck, lightly massaged his scalp. "Let's—"

Appleby's callous, loud laughter cut off whatever Kaya planned to say. She flinched, and Paul's arms tightened around her.

She'd wanted to say, *Let's get out of here,* or *Let's remember our promise.* Or even, *Let's go into the village.* Anything to keep him in the here and now.

It didn't matter. Paul instantly changed. His spine straightened, and his shoulders thrust back as if he stood in line for troop inspection. Or execution. He didn't look at her as he grabbed his coat and shrugged it on.

Kaya hurried to put her hijab on before joining him at the door. Paul reached to open it, but she slapped her hand against the wood.

"Don't do anything foolish."

Paul snorted and met her gaze, his blue-green eyes hard gems in the morning sunlight. "Too late."

He leaned down, kissed her hard and swift. For a heartbeat, Kaya thought she saw that desolate, broken look again, but then he straightened. Even though his fingers caressed her cheek, the mask he'd worn when they first met returned.

It made her want to vomit.

Paul dropped his fingers and left the room. Kaya watched him stride confidently through the door and down the stairs. She adjusted the bodice of her gown around the jewels cutting into her sides, checked for the dagger at her waist, secured her hijab, and followed.

She had no plan, no idea how to discover the information they needed to stop Appleby. Only her trust in Paul and the desire to help him kept her moving.

Kaya walked down the stairs, eyes on Paul as he crossed the inn to the open door. She ignored Appleby. Her love for Paul was a fiery awareness. The hot determination, the fierce resolve—not to right a wrong, though she felt that urgent need, too. No, the fire within her glowed solely for Paul.

It blazed alongside her blistering hatred for Harry Appleby.

"Paul, my friend!" Appleby's voice echoed over the village square, as drunk and rowdy as last night. Kaya wanted to stab him. "And his lovely lady-wife."

Appleby winked at her, but Kaya stopped a pace out of arm's reach. Lifting her chin, she watched him coolly as his broad smile faltered. Good. Whatever discomfort she made him feel, slight or otherwise, didn't disappoint her in the least.

Though petty, she felt a small stab of joy in that realization. She accepted that about herself.

"*Buongiorno.*" Kaya nodded to the man. "I'm afraid I have a bit of shopping to do in town." The words flowed from her before she knew what she'd planned to say. She wished her mouth would consult her brain before it spoke. "Will you"—*disappear into the mountains? Forever? Please?*—"keep Paul entertained while I'm otherwise occupied?"

Instinct told her not to say anything Appleby might use against them. She knew he was keeping every word tucked away in a neat corner of his drunken mind for future exploitation.

Appleby threw his arm around Paul's shoulders. It looked odd, given Appleby was more than a full head shorter than Paul. Paul looked at her strangely, standing stiffly beneath Appleby's too-friendly gesture.

"Of course, my lady. Of course." Appleby winked at her, and once more Kaya resisted curling her lip.

"Paul." She nodded, holding his gaze for a long moment.

He stepped forward and cupped her cheek. "What are you doing?" he asked in Egyptian.

Kaya had no idea a question could also sound like a demand. Most impressive. She reached up, covered his hand with hers, and grinned. His eyes narrowed further.

"Trust me."

He stared at her for a drawn-out moment. Then he shut his eyes and huffed a sound that one might call a laugh. If one was not Kaya.

"I do." He watched her seriously, the focused look that curled her toes and sped up her heart. His thumb ran over her lower lip. "You know I do. I trust you more—" He shook his head. "Be careful, sweetheart."

Her heart did a slow roll in her chest at the endearment. Dry-mouthed, Kaya nodded. Still so protective, her Paul. But they needed information. He wanted it from Appleby, and Kaya didn't want to spend any more time in that man's presence than was necessary.

"Be careful." His gaze flicked to the dagger at her side.

Kaya forced a smile but suspected it looked as false as it felt. "I will be. I promise." Then she stepped back and gestured to the soiled dress she wore. Raising her voice just slightly, she added in English, "I'm in need of a new gown."

Paul caught her gaze again and nodded, his lips pursed, his eyes flat. Kaya didn't look at Appleby as she returned to the inn. She needed a new dress, a warmer one, given the drop in temperature, and she wanted to speak with Marta.

A feat, Kaya suspected, that would be easier said than done.

She'd never investigated anything and had no idea how to go about it. But speaking with Marta sounded like a good place to begin. Kaya didn't know how to do so subtly, and she had the feeling this called for sensitivity.

At a loss, she walked past the empty courtyard and around the inn, letting the rising sun warm her. The day was colder than the last several, even those when they'd walked through the mountain forests. Still, the sun warmed her fingers and back and eased some of her tension.

It did little to wake her, however, but Kaya relied on the nervousness dancing along her skin to do that. The coffee helped. Her sleep last night had been anything but restful. What little she'd managed was troubled with dreams of Appleby's laugh and images of her standing helpless between him and Paul.

The cold wind blew harsher as she rounded the rear of the inn. Frowning at the empty stables, she examined the ground but saw no recent tracks. No sun penetrated here, between the inn and the mountain, and the temperature plunged.

She definitely needed a warmer gown. One thing at a time— find Marta. Discover whatever she could about Appleby, Marta's fear of him, and what that man wanted in the village.

Perhaps discover the name of the village as well.

Hmm, that came to more than one thing. Kaya sighed.

The back of the inn was a nondescript brown wood with a row of windows along the side, their shutters open to the cold morning air. A long table covered with various bowls and knives stretched between the building and where the mountain jutted against the inn. Two chairs leaned against it, both currently empty.

A bin stood at one end of the table, filled with rubbish Kaya preferred not to examine. Two heavy hooks held open the large double doors to the kitchens.

She stood at the open doors and called inside. "*Ciao?*"

A young girl, her hair tied in twin braids that hung down her back, popped in front of Kaya. Where had she come from? Kaya had seen no movement, yet suddenly the girl appeared.

"Oh!"

The girl curtseyed. "*Buongiorno*, signora."

Kaya nodded. "*Buongiorno. Come ti chiami?*" Proud of herself for remembering to stumble over her Calabrian, and for better understanding the necessity of greetings, she smiled—then suddenly realized she had no excuse for being in the back of the inn.

"Olivia, signora."

"*Buongiorno*, Olivia." She continued in English, "I'm looking for Marta." Kaya gestured to her dress, the only excuse she had, and wondered if little Olivia understood English as well as Marta. "I need to wash my dress, and I have nothing else to wear."

Olivia angled her head over her shoulder to call behind her but didn't take her gaze from Kaya. "Mama!" Olivia shouted in Calabrian. "The pretty English woman is looking for you."

It shouldn't have surprised Kaya that Olivia was Marta's daughter. Kaya tried not to show she understood the rapid Calabrian. She hated that. Hated pretending she was not who and what she was.

But Paul's fears were more than legitimate, and he had every right to fear for her safety.

Marta appeared at the doorway a moment later. She looked behind Kaya as if she expected another.

Paul? Or Appleby? Possibly both. Or Appleby's associates. Hadn't Paul stated that Appleby usually worked for others?

"*Buongiorno*, Marta." Kaya waited until Marta's gaze snapped to hers. "I'm sorry to sneak around the back like this." There was, no doubt, some sort of etiquette about showing up in kitchens uninvited. "I hoped I might borrow a dress until I wash my skirts?"

Oh. Hmm. This was a mess, and Kaya hated messes. Why couldn't life be more straightforward? Sneaking around to the inn's kitchens, pretending she didn't speak the local language. Looking for excuses to interrogate Marta about Appleby.

She didn't know if Appleby's hold on Marta was so great that the woman might run and tell him everything at the first opportunity. But the fear in Marta's gaze tempered that suspicion.

"I will wash, signora." Marta had already turned, as if expecting Kaya to follow.

Marta paused, her hand flying to clutch her side. Kaya

thought she heard a faint hiss of breath. Then, as quickly as she'd moved, Marta dropped her hand and straightened her spine.

"No, no. I don't want to trouble you." Kaya waved it off with a smile. She tried not to look too concerned, too curious. Appleby had hurt Marta. Rage colored Kaya's vision, and she needed a moment to steady her voice. "I'm perfectly capable of washing my own gown. And you were kind enough to bring me lemon water this morning. I simply need one to wear. I dislike being trapped inside all day while the skirts dry."

Marta looked at her oddly. Wonderful. Kaya didn't need her suspicious. However, Marta nodded, jerky movements of her head, and bent to Olivia. Again she paused, and again she slowly straightened, grimacing.

Olivia frowned. "Mama?"

"Olivia," Marta said slowly in Calabrian, her voice neutral despite her brief grimace of pain, "ask Nonna for one of her dresses. And be fast, darling. Don't let anyone see you."

Kaya plastered a smile on her face. Kaya, too, would've hidden her children from Appleby. Once the girl ran off, she turned back to Marta, who continued to watch her suspiciously.

"*Grazie.*" She breathed deeply and jumped into her next excuse. "What are you cooking?"

"Sausage stew."

"Ah. Might you have any lamb? Or beef?" Kaya knew better than to mention she didn't eat sausage. She'd as much to Letizia, in Mazzarelli, when she made tomato and sausage stew on their final night. Kaya still remembered the resulting, *blistering* lecture on what not to say in Sicily.

Marta eyed her hijab again but simply asked, "Goat? You prefer?"

"*Sì*, or more of the pasta stew from last night?" Kaya grinned and gestured to the kitchens, hoping Marta might be more comfortable there than outside. Well, it was worth a try.

Fourteen

Paul squinted at the sun rising high over the mountaintops. The constant breeze that had followed them from the coast chilled him now, but he suspected it had less to do with the dropping temperatures and more to do with his company.

His numb fingers clenched the waxy residue on the bottle, still full, though it tempted him. Called to him like the sirens of old, the seductive voice of rich red wine he could already feel sliding down his throat. Warming his belly.

Christ. One day. A *single day* with Appleby and months of sobriety disappeared like fairy dust.

Paul adjusted his hat so it blocked more of that disgustingly bright sunlight. Until last night, he hadn't a drink since leaving Bombay. He and John had run out of wine only a couple days into their less-than-distinguished flight, and Cairo hadn't a single drop of wine. Not that he'd found, anyway, and he spent considerable time searching.

With Kaya so ill, drinking on *The Cyprus Rose* hadn't even occurred to him. Once in Sicily, despite the abundant temptation, Paul had again resisted. It hadn't been easy—more than once, he'd spent their coin on a bottle of wine. But he hadn't taken a drink. Not one.

The couple times Kaya had caught him, she never censored him. Well, "caught" wasn't the right word—yes, it was. He'd always hid it from her. Hid how desperately he craved a drink. Just one.

They never spoke of his drinking, one of many topics they avoided, but Paul knew she wanted to ask. At meals, Paul always left the wine untouched. Each time, he'd taken Kaya's hand instead, and they continued on their way. Every single time.

Until last night.

Appleby had expected him to drink. Expected the drunken layabout he'd been in Bombay. The man who charmed his way into and out of trouble. Paul all too clearly remembered that man. He hated him with a loathing that choked him.

His entire being rebelled at the very thought of becoming him once again.

Maybe not his *entire* being. The clawing, clenching need for a drink had lured him into its clutches.

Christ, now he was overly dramatic.

Paul closed his mind's eye against Kaya's face, the trust and love that had shone in her eyes when they parted.

The Paul that Harry Appleby knew drank wine as quickly and as easily as the rivers flowed. No. Paul refused. He could do this; he needed to. If for no other reason than for Kaya. She believed in him.

The Paul who drank and stole and profited off others' expense died in the desert between Bombay and Cairo.

Unfortunately, Appleby had not died, physically or metaphysically, and was walking with him through town now.

"What are you doing here, Harry?" Paul swept his gaze over the landscape. A beautiful panorama stretched out before them, mountains and streams, distant villages nestled high in the mountains. An endless blue sky.

Kaya'd want to sketch this, and he half wished he'd brought her here first, before Appleby tainted the view.

"This is far too provincial for your tastes."

"Oh, Paul, if you had any idea."

He turned to face Appleby and was never as aware of the dagger at his hip as then. Appleby's pale blue eyes danced with wine and secrets and made Paul's stomach churn.

"I'm sure it's not the scenery." Paul kept his thoughts about the beauty of this land to himself. That wasn't the old Paul.

"Do you know what this land has, Paul?" Appleby turned to him. His own bottle of wine, seemingly forgotten, dangled precariously from his grasp.

Paul raised his eyebrows. "Trees?"

Appleby laughed, but it was muted now, and his eyes gleamed with the greedy craving for profit. Paul knew that look all too well. Had *he* looked that way, once upon a time? Had others only seen that greedy ravenousness of material conquest?

"Nothing."

Paul snorted. "I can see that."

"Its people are stupid and illiterate, with no ambition. They stay in these ridiculous, small hamlets with their cheese and their wine and don't do anything else."

The wine Appleby spoke of threatened Paul again. Instead, he lifted his own bottle in salute. "But they make excellent wine."

Wine smuggling? Increased production? That made no sense. Hard work for the sake of anything long-term equaled hard work for nothing. Appleby would work hard only if it promised an immediate and ample profit.

No, Paul would have bet their fortune—such as it was, stitched in Kaya's dress—that Appleby was smuggling opium. It made far too much sense.

I'm not that person.

Paul drank his wine. The once-rich red liquid tasted spoiled and sour, even as it flowed smoothly down his throat. He hated this. Maybe if he told himself that enough times, he'd think of another way to glean information from Appleby. Paul drank again, fingers twitching around the bottle, lips eager for another taste.

"Oh, it's true the Bourbons tax these people to within an inch of their profits." Appleby faked a shudder. "But that's not the wonder of this simple, nowhere place."

"I'm listening." Paul held his gaze and wondered if Appleby saw the changes Paul felt so keenly. The distaste for profitable exploitation, the annoyance in Appleby's mere presence. The burning desire to take Kaya and run. Paul swallowed another mouthful of wine before he realized he had.

Had Appleby paid for this wine? Probably not. Once, Paul would've congratulated him on such a feat.

"What if I told you, Paul, that these mountains contain the one thing Bombay does not?"

Paul snorted. "I'm sure they contain much Bombay does not." He gestured widely with his free hand. "We're in the middle of nowhere. People populated every inch of Bombay."

Appleby's enigmatic gaze grew mischievous. Paul narrowed his eyes, his mind racing. They were literally in the middle of nowhere. He and Kaya hadn't passed another village in days, at least not any that were close to the trail. There was nothing around this village for miles.

"Come." Paul turned from the view. "Let's return to the inn, I'm starved. On our way back, you can tell me all about the nothingness of this village."

Kaya wandered around the village—Casa Grigori, Marta had told her. Her gown was drying in her room, and she wore Marta's mother's much warmer one. She hadn't taken the time to transfer their jewels, and the freedom of movement made her giddy.

The village square, a small construct of only a hundred yards or so, housed Marta's inn, a small church, and several houses nestled into the mountainside. The stone structures reminded her of Villa San Giovanni: short, square, and sturdy.

The ground tremor that had leveled much of that town seemed to have missed this village. Either that, or Casa Grigori had rebuilt far more quickly than the larger city to the south.

Paul was nowhere to be found.

She'd told him she was looking for a new dress, but there were no shops to visit, no wares to purchase. Where did they buy their goods, or did they make everything they needed? Fascinated with that idea, Kaya walked the small square.

Several people avoided her gaze, but more stared back. Whether they were curious or suspicious or superstitious, she couldn't tell. Kaya adjusted her hijab, conscious of the fact that she moved unescorted through town.

An icy breeze ruffled her borrowed skirts and brought with it the scent of cooking. Not sausage, nor even the goat Marta had promised for dinner. This smelled like the noodles Kaya had learned were ubiquitous in the area.

Following her nose, and her growling stomach, Kaya retraced her steps along the dirt road toward the house attached to the inn. A woman with dark gray hair pulled back into a tight bun at the base of her neck stood on a small stool over a large, boiling pot.

"*Perdono*, what are you making?" Kaya asked.

The woman jerked upright, her free hand gripping the stool's back, and whipped around so fast her skirts brushed the heated pot. Kaya grimaced and muttered an apology. "*Spiacenti.*"

"You startled me." The woman pressed her hand to her heart but grinned. "You are the Englishwoman at the inn, *sì*?"

"*Sì*. Kaya."

"My daughter, she works the inn."

"Oh, you're Marta's mum!" Kaya stepped closer, gesturing to her skirts. "This is your dress, *grazie*."

"You are welcome."

"*Come ti chiami?*"

"Caroline. Kaya, a beautiful name."

Kaya nodded, pleased, and felt her smile loosen, become more natural. Caroline was the first person to ever compliment her name. "I'm afraid my husband wandered off with Private Appleby." Caroline's eyes widened then narrowed. Kaya noted but didn't comment on her reaction. "I had hoped to see more of this lovely village, perhaps sketch it."

Not a lie, though perhaps not the entire truth—but then again, Kaya had learned from the best when it came to mixing lies and truths. She'd feel better about that mixture if she knew where Paul *had* wandered off to.

"What is special about our village?" Caroline asked.

What indeed. Kaya wanted to know the answer to that very question.

"It's lovely. Very different from where—" She stopped herself just in time. *From where I grew up.* Kaya straightened her shoulders. "From Egypt, where my husband and I recently traveled from."

There. A complete truth.

"Egypt?" Caroline spat the word as if it had poisoned her noodles.

Kaya narrowed her eyes. "*Sì.* Egypt, a lovely country with friendly people. I much admired it."

Honestly, Kaya had seen so little of Egypt that she could not attest to its loveliness. She liked to think she could. Liked to think her country beautiful, rich with history and culture and the vibrant colors she'd seen in Damietta's souk. Even the vast desert she found beautiful, with the sun rising over *al-ṣaḥrā' al-kubrā* and glinting off the rocky *ḥammāda*.

What did Caroline have against Egypt?

"What are you making?" Kaya asked instead.

"Cooking noodles." Once again, Caroline glared as if it were obvious.

"Smells delicious. I look forward to supper." Kaya's stomach growled. Her worry over Paul had hampered her appetite. Despite the *cornetto* from breakfast, she'd barely eaten. "May I have a packed lunch? I wish to sketch the village."

"Olivia!" Caroline called her granddaughter, then muttered something too softly for Kaya to catch.

Olivia ran outside, her braids flying behind her. "*Sì*, Nonna?"

Caroline spoke rapidly, instructing Olivia to fetch food for the Englishwoman. Kaya pressed her lips together to prevent an angry retort. She hated being referred to as English. Oh, she had nothing against the English—she loved Paul, after all. But being referred to as such bothered her on a deep, visceral level.

"Wonderful!" Kaya grinned at Olivia when Caroline shooed her away. "I need to return to my room for my sketchbook and pencils. I shall only be a moment."

She nodded to Caroline, who continued to look at her suspiciously, and rounded the building to enter from the front. Kaya ran upstairs to their room and unlocked the door, grateful to Paul for having placed their normal precautions around the doorway.

No one had entered.

Kaya grabbed her satchel, checked her sketchbook and pencils, readjusted the dagger at her waist, and locked the door behind her. She slipped the key back into the deep pocket of her gown.

Olivia was standing at the base of the stairs, a wrapped bundle in her hands.

"*Grazie*." Kaya took the food and stepped around the girl, who didn't seem to want to leave.

"I'll be back before supper." Kaya waited, but Olivia only stared. "If my husband asks after me, tell him I'm sketching the mountains."

"*Sì*, signora," Olivia whispered.

Uncertain, Kaya looked around the deserted inn. "Would you like to join me? Show me around the mountains?"

Olivia's face lit up, and she grinned. "*Sì*! *Sì*!"

Kaya waited while Olivia raced to tell Marta. Even from the kitchens, she heard the girl's excited chattering.

"Signora Hartley." Marta exited the back room, looking equal parts suspicious and relieved. "You invited Olivia to walk?"

"*Sì.*" Kaya hoped to keep the child out of Appleby's path. "I was hoping Olivia might show me a nice place to sketch."

Marta looked hesitant, but she nodded. "Be careful, there are animals."

Kaya had a feeling she meant Appleby and his associates. She refrained from pointing out her khanjar and merely waited as Olivia left to gather more food.

"You need a cloak." Marta eyed her gown and shoes and followed Olivia.

Kaya didn't need to wait long before both Marta and Olivia returned, Olivia bouncing with excitement and Marta carrying a heavy wool cloak and gloves.

"Thank you." Kaya nodded as she tugged on the gloves and flexed her fingers. They'd take a little getting used to if she wanted to retain her complete range of motion with her dagger.

"Come, signora." Olivia, laden with a basket of food, led her from inn and around the backs of houses, through open courtyards. They squeezed between a house and the mountainside, and eventually found themselves on a path.

Lifting her face to the cold mountain breeze, Kaya kept up with Olivia's near-run from the village. Further from the village and Paul.

The sun was rapidly sinking behind the mountains, but she estimated she had at least two, maybe three hours of sunlight remaining. Olivia kept a brisk pace as they walked a well-worn path winding up the mountainside.

At a rock-wall ledge, Olivia stopped and gestured to the vista. "You wish to draw?" she asked in halting English.

The view stole Kaya's breath and made her pause. The surrounding vista, craggy mountains covered with greenery, the sea in the distance, several villages dotting the landscape, tempted her. Oh, it was beautiful from this height, which so few people ever saw.

Kaya's fingers brushed against her sketchbook. Sitting on the ledge, slightly concerned about its sturdiness, she pulled her pencils and pad from her satchel.

"Do you come here often?" Kaya asked as she sketched the vista. "It's peaceful."

"Sometimes." Olivia pulled their food from her basket. "I like water."

Accepting the cut fruit, Kaya turned to face the girl. "Have you seen the water before?"

"No." She sighed, looking wistful. "My papa, he promised one day we would travel. See water and fish."

Kaya wanted to ask after Olivia's father, Marta's husband. No one had mentioned him, and she very much doubted Appleby would force his way into a married woman's bed if her husband still lived.

Kaya nearly snorted. From the little she knew of Appleby, he would do just that. However, what husband would know such a thing and not stop it?

"What's the name of that village?" she asked instead, pointing to another small cluster of homes closer to the coast.

"I not know, signora." Olivia sighed and shook her head. "I never saw anywhere else."

Heart breaking for the child, Kaya packed up her sketchpad and pencils and stood. "It was many years before I left home." They walked further up the path, winding deeper into the mountains and away from the view. "Before I saw anything other than my house."

The words tripped over themselves. The loneliness of those years, the grief. The uncertainty and anticipation of leaving.

Kaya hated to ask the child for information, but she had little choice. "Did you learn English from Signore Appleby?"

"He speaks only English. Insist we learn."

Kaya hummed in annoyance, her lips pursing. "I see."

It didn't sit well with her. Appleby's presence, him having any contact with Olivia. Being away from Paul. This was the longest they'd been apart, and Kaya didn't like not knowing where he was. What he was doing with Appleby, what trouble the pair of them encountered. Or created.

Once more, that sickening worry tightened through her, squeezing her lungs until it hurt to breathe.

Desperate for a distraction, Kaya stopped at a large rock off the path.

"Let's sit and eat, shall we?"

Olivia seemed agreeable, or perhaps she was merely happy to be away from the village. Pulling out her sketchbook and the bundle of food, Kaya flipped to the purple flower she sketched—yesterday? The morning before? So much had happened since arriving in Casa Grigori.

The flower, whose name she still didn't know, grew everywhere, even here.

"Do you know the name of this flower?" She pointed to her drawing.

"No, signora." Olivia ate her bread and goat cheese in silence but seemed antsy.

"Do you wish to return to the village?" Kaya asked, chewing her own sliced fruit and cheese.

"No!" Olivia looked stricken and said more softly, "No, signora."

"Kaya," she corrected. "Please, call me Kaya."

It was a small thing, something she hadn't even told Paul. But, with so few people in her life, she liked being called by her name.

Olivia nodded. "Signora Kaya."

Grinning, she stood and gathered her things. "Kaya is fine, Olivia."

Having no idea what else to say to the child, she beckoned her to keep moving. Then again, Kaya enjoyed the silence. For as much as she craved new experiences, new places and people and things, she was used to the quiet.

"Why you wear mantilla not in church?" Olivia blurted out.

"Mantilla?" Hand flying to her hijab, she looked to Olivia. "Is that what you call this?"

Nodding, her face red with embarrassment, Olivia trudged ahead. They walked around another bend, away from the ledge and the view and deeper into the wooded mountains. Only the wind echoed here. She heard none of the animals Marta feared. No humans, either. Not a sound.

"I wear it whenever I leave the house. Your mother and Nonna wear similar coverings."

"They say—"

A noise stopped her. Perhaps she'd been mistaken. Kaya tugged off her gloves and drew her khanjar. Silently setting her satchel on the ground, she kept her eyes trained on the path ahead. Nothing. No one emerged through the trees, and no other sound reached her. Still, she sensed movement.

There. Careful steps through the brush.

A sharp growl stilled Kaya. Then, with her fingers tight around her khanjar, she cautiously turned toward the woods.

Fifteen

Unsteady, annoyed, hungry, Paul staggered across the town square toward the inn as the sun crossed its zenith. The wind whipped cold and fast along the streets, cutting through his coat and waistcoat a little too sharply. On one level, he felt it dig into his very bones. On another, the wine warmed him, and he felt very little.

Pushing open the inn's door, he let the heat smack him in the face. Between the cold outside and the heat in here, perhaps one or the other might clear his head.

All noise ceased. The long benches were already filled with men eating their noonday meal, and each and every one stopped their conversation and stared at him. Paul swept his gaze over their mistrustful ones and walked, as steadily as possible, to the small table along the far wall, the one he and Kaya had shared last night.

He sat with his back to the wall, and conversation started again, louder than before. It made his already pounding head pound that much harder. Unfortunately, he deserved it, and he damn well knew it.

An older woman, graying hair pulled into a tight bun, appeared at his table. Paul blearily peered up at her. Her dark brown eyes watched him angrily, though her face remained impassive. She tilted her nose up and looked down at him.

"You are Englishman."

His head felt like it might fall off, but Paul nodded, though it seemed unnecessary. She already knew who he was. He doubted the village had many visitors, though with Appleby here, who the hell knew.

"Your woman, she is not here."

His frown was a sharp tug on his face. Paul looked around the inn as if Kaya might magically appear. He didn't see her, and he hated that he hadn't looked the moment he entered.

Usually, he had a much better sense of her whereabouts. Not that they'd spent much time apart since leaving Cairo. Still. Damn drink—it fogged everything.

"Where is she?"

How long had he and Appleby talked? They'd walked a mile or more from town, eastward, toward more open mountains and empty land. Kaya said she was—what had Kaya said? Damn it, he couldn't remember. His hands shook as he ran them through his hair, and he forced his wine-soaked mind to focus. Had she said—

"You want food?"

"What?" He met the woman's hard gaze. Clearly, she trusted him about as much as he ought to be trusted. Paul snorted. Smart woman. "*Sì. Grazie.*"

He rested his head in his hands, the edge of the table digging into his elbows. The pain did little to clear his head. *Kaya.* What had she said this morning? Paul tried to think back, but the wine sloshed through his veins and continued to call to him.

It blocked all other sound, all other meaning.

The bottle snapped on the table in front of him. Startled, he jerked, cursing the painful move. The woman also placed a wooden bowl before him, though that noise lacked the sharp judgment of the wine.

Paul peered into the bowl: thick noodles and chickpeas.

"I add to your bill."

Paul snorted. Of course she would. Would probably add the bottles of wine Appleby had confiscated, too. Didn't matter. Money, for once, was the least of Paul's problems. Despite his shaking hands and sudden, deep, unquenchable thirst, he pushed the wine away. He ought to ask for bergamot juice, or some other unfermented drink. Anything but the wine beckoning him from across the table.

Licking his lips, he scooped up the noodles. It was hot and filling and helped to clear his mind.

He eyed the wine, tempted. So very tempted.

Chewing unnecessarily hard, he pushed the bottle further away, but its siren song only grew louder.

"No."

He needed to find Kaya. He needed to discover where Appleby had disappeared to once they returned to the village. He needed to shut down that evil man's operation and get the hell out of this place.

Hopefully with his soul still intact.

***

"Olivia. Stay behind me." Kaya spoke in Calabrian, low and quick. She no longer cared about propagating a lie. Olivia's life was in danger.

She didn't know what sort of creature lurked in the woods. In Sicily, they'd encountered wild boar. Huge things that roamed the mountains and charged angrily at any who dared disturb them. But this didn't sound like one of them. Whatever this was was stealthier. Lighter.

"No, signora. *Amico.*"

Kaya didn't look from the woods. "What?"

Olivia slipped around her, and, though she wanted to, Kaya didn't stop her. Reaching into her bag, Olivia took out a length of sausage and walked toward the shadowy woods, each step measured.

"She is Kaya." Olivia spoke in quiet Calabrian to the growling shadow. "She is nice, she won't hurt you. Come out, I want to show her to you."

The flowing words, soothing and peaceful, enticed the creature—or maybe it was the food Olivia offered.

Olivia continued to speak softly, lilting words of promises and encouragement. The girl waited patiently, but. Kaya moved steadily closer. Olivia didn't seem worried or scared, but unease slithered down Kaya's spine. Slowly, snout first, the creature exited the dark forest and limped into the sunlit path. Fingers tightening around the hilt of her dagger, Kaya watched the large, sleek animal step closer.

"*Che cosa?*" Kaya swallowed. "*Cane? Lupo?*"

"*Sì*, signora." Olivia held out a sausage, and the black-furred dog gently closed its teeth around the offering. Its piercing black eyes did not leave Kaya. "*Cane.*"

"I have never seen one before." Kaya lowered her dagger but didn't tear her gaze from the mesmerizing dog. "I have never seen one. She is beautiful."

Her short, black fur hung straight at her sides. Despite the heavy layer of fur covering her body, her face was visible, and she watched Kaya as steadily as Kaya watched her. Her pointed snout was aimed straight at her, as if waiting for a shift in her scent.

Forcing herself to relax, Kaya slowly sheathed her dagger and took a vigilant step closer. The large dog finished chewing her treat and waited. Kaya took another step as Olivia ran her hand down the dog's head. The dog's tail whipped about enthusiastically.

"She's alone," Olivia whispered, her hand running along the animal's neck. "I don't know where she came from, which flock she tended. It's just her and her *cucciolo.*"

"*Cucciolo?*" Unfamiliar with the word, Kaya eased another step closer.

A mixture of trepidation and excitement raced through her. She had never been so near a friendly animal, wild or otherwise.

She'd trapped them, yes. But befriended? If one could call this so... Kaya held out her hands to show she meant no harm, though she didn't know if this beautiful black dog would recognize such a gesture.

Over her shoulder, Olivia frowned. "Baby."

"She's protecting her young." Kaya wondered how one went about befriending a mother dog in the middle of the mountains. For that matter, how one befriended *any* animal.

She stepped another cautious foot forward, ready to grab Olivia and run if need be. The dog looked cuddly enough, loyal even. Kaya had absolutely no experience with this type of situation, but Olivia didn't seem in danger.

The dog's sharp eyes followed Kaya's every movement, and when she held out her hands, at a loss as to what to do, the dog snorted, and cold snot dripped onto her fingers. Mildly disgusted, Kaya nonetheless kept still. As if her stillness and acceptance of cold snot were an indicator of goodwill, the dog licked Kaya's hand.

Well, she *had* wanted to experience all possible firsts. Dog slobber was definitely a new one.

"How did you find her?" Kaya didn't bother with English; this was far too important to risk misunderstanding.

The dog nuzzled Olivia's belly, making the girl laugh. "Vita." Olivia met her gaze. "She is Vita. I found her close to the village months ago. Before Christmas. She was hungry."

Vita. Life. Kaya smiled and reached for the dog's side, lightly running her fingers through the dark, matted hair. Frowning, she looked at her hand and the flakes of dried blood that now rested there.

"Olivia, she's hurt."

"I know." The girl's wide, frightened eyes met hers. "I don't know what to do. I tried bringing her to the village again, but I always come here with food, so she refused. Mama helped, but she worries with Signore Appleby and Nonna—" She shook her head.

"Caroline does not know." Kaya frowned and gently prodded

Vita's side. The dog growled, and Kaya hushed her with soft, soothing sounds. "Where is her *cucciolo*?"

"There is a small cave in the mountainside." Olivia continued to run her hand down Vita's back. "I'm sorry, signora. The food —" Olivia looked on the verge of tears.

Utterly at a loss as to how to stop a child from crying, Kaya hastened to reassure her. "That's all right, Olivia. I don't eat sausage, anyway. Let's go feed the babe."

Though Olivia's eyes retained that glassy look, she ran back to the basket and picked it up. "I'm happy she likes you, signora. I knew she would. You shine so brightly, everyone likes you."

Kaya didn't know what that meant. Still, she smiled and followed Olivia and Vita deeper into the woods. Shaded by the thick cypress trees, the air chilled noticeably. Kaya shivered and rubbed her gloved hands together, wishing for the fire from the brazier in their room. And the blanket.

And Paul's warm body wrapped around her.

Shivering now, Kaya focused on the moment to keep from being eaten by a hungry, injured dog. As a precaution, she once more removed her dagger from its sheath, though the short walk to the small cave was free of any other animal. Or, for that matter, human.

Vita watched her warily, not that Kaya blamed her. After all, she watched strangers warily, too. The mother dog let out a short, low yip. Fascinated with the sound, which seemed very much like a language, Kaya wanted to ask her to do it again.

A small dog babe peeked its gray-black snout out of the den.

Kaya melted.

"Oh!" Olivia cried and knelt on the cold ground. "She rarely leaves the cave. See?" She beamed at Kaya. "They trust you."

Kaya didn't understand why.

Unable not to, she knelt beside Olivia and let the babe sniff her hand and lick her palm. Surreptitiously wiping her hand on her skirts, Kaya mentally apologized to Caroline for the soiled state of her dress.

Looking to where Vita lay, panting uncomfortably on her good side, she inched closer. Resting her hand on the dog's head, she looked to where the babe and Olivia were running around the small clearing, playing.

"You're beautiful," she told the injured dog. "I don't know how, but I will protect you and your babe."

Vita snorted, whether in acceptance or laughter, Kaya couldn't tell. Did dogs laugh? The little one looked a cross between her mother and something sleeker, grayer, and larger. Kaya had no idea who the father was, or where he was. Olivia had said Vita was alone.

Alone. Kaya's heart twisted at the thought. No one should be alone in the world. Despite the fact that she had no idea how to help, she vowed to do so. Somehow.

Sixteen

Exhausted, thrilled, hungry, cold, and bursting with excitement to tell Paul how she'd spent her afternoon, Kaya waved to Olivia as she raced up the stairs. Only a couple men sat in the inn below. Though they watched her intently, Kaya ignored them.

The sun had long set, and the night turned colder. A stiff wind blew through the village, but it could not dampen her sheer joy.

She unlocked their door and slipped inside. Their freezing room did not help her already chilled fingers. In the darkness, Kaya easily made her way toward the brazier. She crouched before it and instantly stilled.

Someone was hiding in the room.

Kaya clearly felt their presence. She had lived too long alone, always knowing exactly how many people moved around her house at any given time. She knew when people lurked outside her gates and stood just beyond her garden wall.

Unconcernedly turning toward the small bucket of wood and the grape vines beside the brazier, she caught sight of her dress and the hidden jewels still hanging over the chair.

Always hide things in plain sight, Paul insisted

She didn't know why she hadn't realized she wasn't alone the moment she entered the room. Even the darkness was no excuse. Kaya reached for her dagger just as the shadow moved.

It happened all at once—she grabbed her dagger, whirled on her heels, and the shadow spoke.

"Where have you been?"

Paul.

Breathing a sigh of relief, Kaya sank to her knees. The damp of her skirts bled through her stockings and into her skin. Jerking upright, she sheathed her dagger.

"You frightened me." She frowned. "Why are you standing in the dark?"

"Where have you been?" This time, the words were frantic, loud, harsh. They sent fear jangling along her nerves.

He'd been standing by the window. She clearly saw his silhouette now that her eyes had adjusted. His hands were clenched into fists at his sides, as if he physically stopped himself from reaching for her. Her heart lodged in her throat, Kaya wondered why he did not wish to touch her.

"I spent the afternoon with Olivia." Kaya took a guarded step toward him.

He made a frustrated, strangled sound and turned to the window. With an angry hiss, he pushed open the shutters and leaned on the sill. Shoulders tight, back rigid despite his bent position, he visibly shuddered.

"Paul?"

The sun had long disappeared over the mountains, and the starlight barely illuminated him, but she could see well enough to know he swayed on his feet—drunk and angry. Kaya stopped and fisted her own hands in her soiled skirts. Jaw clenched, lips pursed, she stared at him.

"Where have *you* been?"

Paul snorted. He straightened but continued to look out the window. "Prostrating before that bastard like a drunken fool in the hopes he'll just *tell* me what the hell he's after here."

Kaya blinked at his profanity. He rarely cursed since Damietta. He always seemed so uncomfortable with it, as if he didn't wish to speak that way in front of her. Taking another measured step closer, she rested her hand on his arm.

Beneath her touch, Paul's muscles bunched, hard as steel, hot to the touch.

"Paul? What happened?"

His hands shot out, his warm fingers grasping her arms. "Don't—Kaya don't—"

Paul didn't finish. He sucked in a breath, blew it out on a whiff of wine, and stepped back. Dropping his hands, he moved away from her.

She stood on one side of the window, he on the other, and they watched each other in silence for several painful beats of her heart.

"I'm sorry. I didn't—I don't..." His hands fisted at his sides again. "Kaya, I'm sorry. Did I hurt you?"

Kaya mutely shook her head, vaguely wondering if he could see her in the faint light. If he saw her at all. Tears burned her eyes, but she refused to let them fall. He hadn't hurt her; he'd frightened her.

His words, his actions, the heavy scent of wine on his breath.

"I'll light the lamp. I'm sorry."

She watched him move about the room, his steps silent despite the wine. Fear beat through her, painful heartbeats that physically hurt her chest. Kaya wanted to move, tried forcing her legs to turn and her hands to light the brazier. But her body did not listen.

"What happened?" She heard her voice before she realized she'd spoken. Loud in the dark silence, a shot in the fissure between them.

The flame sparked to life, illuminating him in flickering shadows. He lit the oil lamp and watched the wavering movement of the flame. Kaya watched him. Shadows danced over his face, more thoroughly obscuring his expression than the indifferent mask he wore in front of Appleby.

She wanted to touch him, hold him close, as if her mere presence might drag him from the intoxicated gorge.

"Appleby." He spat the name like a curse. "I told you I wasn't a good man, Kaya. I never lied to you, especially about that." Paul spun on his heel and banged the shutters closed, locking the latch with a ruthless scraping sound.

"Did he say anything?" She licked her lips, the pleasure of her day evaporating like rain in the desert.

"Oh, he talked about Bombay. Our time there." Paul ran a hand over his face, such a familiar movement, her heart stuttered.

Her Paul hadn't entirely disappeared.

"Paul." The word barely left her dry lips. He seemed not to have heard.

"Nothing about what he's planning here. Nothing about—" He shoved the chair hard against the wall. It crashed into the table, shaking the lamp and bowl and knocking over the empty cup. Her dress slipped to the seat, a lumpy pool of fabric. Kaya startled and closed her eyes, not against the violence, but against the helplessness in Paul's voice.

"Olivia said something today." The light shifted, and Kaya stepped forward. She didn't know if she wanted to comfort or confront him.

"What?" His voice sounded weary, tired.

"She said strange men come to Casa Grigori. Not just Englishmen like Appleby, all sorts."

Paul stilled. Awareness prickled along her skin. His fingers still gripped the table as he straightened, a slow movement of coiled power Kaya would normally find arousing. Now, a prickle of fear danced over her skin.

She didn't like it, fearing Paul. What he might do to stop Appleby.

He stood to his full height and released the table one finger at a time. Turning, he looked at her, and even in the faint lamplight, she saw the emotion caught in his face. The anger, the fear, the determination.

"What kind of men?" He spaced out each word, low and rigid, enunciated.

"She called them *semi di male*. Bad seeds." Kaya shook her head. "The village is afraid of them. The women shut up their houses, and the men disappear to work the vineyards and goat herds. Only Marta's inn stays open."

"He's using the inn as a transit point." Paul's hands opened and closed into fists. Open, close, squeeze. Open, close, squeeze. Kaya watched, mesmerized. "Why? Did she say?"

"No." Kaya stepped closer, bridging the gap, and took his hand. "She doesn't know. Marta sends her into the mountains when the strangers arrive. She—" Kaya stopped.

She wanted to share her discovery with Paul, of Vita and the baby dog. Licking her lips, she skipped over that. Now wasn't the time, though she longed to spark that excitement in herself again. To share her earlier joy with Paul.

"I don't blame her." He ran his hand down his face, his shoulders sagging.

"I'll ask Marta. She might know, might have overheard their conversations. Olivia didn't know what language they spoke, but she said Appleby speaks to them in the same language."

"Marathi." Paul snorted. "The only other language Appleby knows is Marathi. We learned it in Bombay." He barked out a laugh that was hard, brittle, painful to hear. "To better trade with the locals. Or cheat them."

Oh. Kaya's lips formed the word, but it never saw life. She pressed her lips together and tried to nod, but that didn't fully form, either. "Olivia doesn't know. She said sometimes they spoke English, but—"

"Neither Marta nor Olivia's English is good enough to eavesdrop."

Mind racing, Kaya tried to form a plan. The sooner they

solved this mystery and stopped Appleby, the sooner they could leave this place. The sooner she could have her Paul back.

"They come twice a month, at the first and last quarter moon."

"The full moon was days ago." He looked over his shoulder at the closed shutters, as if he could see the moon's phase. Looking back at her, he frowned. "That's not a lot of time between visits. Seven, eight days? Nine at most. Wherever they travel to, it's close by."

"The coast? We're not far. You can see it from the top of the mountain Olivia showed me today. Perhaps they walk over the mountains and stop here."

"They come from Bombay—have to. Appleby knows no other language and certainly has no other contacts. But why?" Paul paced around the room. He was normally still, alert, and watchful—always ready—and the fact that he once more paced concerned Kaya.

She could almost see his mind working, quickly leaping from one point to the next, a logical progression she much admired. In fact, she normally found it quite sexy, watching him think, learning how his mind worked.

Tonight, it clawed within her, churned her empty stomach with unease.

Paul strode around the room, down its center to the closed window, where he turned sharply, then paced to the door and back. Kaya stepped out of his way and allowed him space. She didn't know what else to do.

"It's a long trip from Bombay to Calabria. A lot of water." Kaya shuddered but resisted commenting. Yesterday morning, she would've joked about her hatred of the sea. Now, she doubted Paul would appreciate it.

The change she saw in Paul in so short a time hurt her.

"Smuggling, they have to be."

"People?" The word caught in her throat.

"Olivia would've noticed. They need to feed them, house

them, no matter how horribly they're treated." He made a noise she'd never heard before, a half growl, half snort. Kaya didn't like the sound. "Even slaves need food if they're to be sold later."

Yes. Yes, she supposed they did. Her voice dried up, and she worked hard to moisten her mouth. "They're the opium smugglers."

Paul stopped and faced her, his expression bleak in the flickering lamplight. "Yes."

He frowned and looked behind her, lost in thought. He looked worn and tired. So very tired. "What are the odds we find Appleby and the smugglers in the same place?"

Her fingers bunched in her skirts, numb and stiff. "We should've left."

She meant it, though she also knew she'd never have left Marta in such a position.

His head shot up, and he met her gaze. "Aye." He sounded defeated, beaten, but he didn't look away. "The Company, they sell the opium. I don't know." The words shot from him, frustrated and short. She knew they weren't in response to her unasked questions.

"Paul." Kaya reached out and grasped his hand.

She thought the feel of his fingers intertwined with hers would feel familiar, comforting. It did not. It felt like a stranger's hand, rough and hard and cold. Not at all like the warm fingers that caressed her skin and made her climax. Held her tight, kept her safe and warm.

"Appleby smuggles opium from Bombay through Calabria." Saying the words aloud made the realization settle heavy on her shoulders. "Or is there more to this smuggler's route than we know?"

"Operation." He said it absently, but it sparked hope deep within her. He often told her words she did not understand— things she missed or had never heard before, English terms or ideas neither Tahir nor Derya had taught her.

"We knew lots of people." Paul cleared his throat but looked at her sharply. "Some were short-term profiteers: steal it, sell it, be done with it. No sense keeping it around for the authorities to find or another thief to steal. Others were in it for the long term, the bigger profits. They had a network of people who moved it from one place to another, always after the largest buyer."

"All right." She squeezed his fingers, but he pulled away. Kaya stared at her empty hand for a moment, flexing her fingers around open air. "All right." She looked up at him, but Paul refused to meet her gaze, even in the uncertain light.

"He must've planned this." Her voice sounded stronger than she felt. "In Bombay. How else would he have contacted them? It's six, seven months since you left, yes?"

"About that." Paul was still staring at the wall behind her.

Kaya didn't turn around to see what he was looking at. She wanted to scream at him, grab him by the shoulders and shake him. Floundering, at a total loss, she remained still.

"He's not organized enough." Kaya didn't think he could see her any longer. Rather, he was drowning in the past he'd shared with Appleby. It angered her and made her irrationally jealous. "No, Appleby is the middleman, always has been. The idea man. But he drinks too much, can't keep up with the numbers, the product."

"Then he has people bringing the opium—how's it transported?" She couldn't picture it. All she had seen of it was in the dens when they searched for Marco. Kaya couldn't recall what any of it looked like, only the overwhelming stench that still rolled her stomach.

"Chests." Paul shook his head. "Large wooden chests."

"There are a lot of caves in these mountains. Easy hiding for chests, or carts full of chests."

"Haven't seen a customs agent here, either." He tried to lighten his voice, and Kaya tried to smile in return. "No one's going to question a caravan of men over these mountains. Not until the coast—if that. And I'm positive Appleby has men there waiting. He'd have to, to unload the chests quickly."

"And bribe the agents."

"Exactly." Paul sighed and sank to the chair. He lifted her dress from the seat and draped it over the table, as if he knew it was there but didn't *really* know. Elbows on the table, he dropped his head into his hands and stared at the floor.

Despite the brazier, the chill hadn't dissipated. Now it seeped into her bones, settling there as if it might never leave. Paul must've felt it also, because he shivered. Or maybe that was because of the impossibility of what they faced.

His hopelessness hurt her, and Kaya sank to her knees beside him. Once more, she took his hands, ignoring the strange emptiness holding them brought her. All she wanted was the laughter they'd nurtured these last months. The love and passion they'd shared.

"Paul." She waited until he looked at her. "Don't. We'll stop him and this opium smuggling. But please, *please*, don't give up."

"I'm not." His fingers tightened around hers. "I'm not, Kaya. But you aren't going to like the man I'll need to be to stop him. Hell, *I* don't like the man I'll need to be."

"I don't—" She licked her lips and tasted that desperation once more. "I don't understand."

But Kaya was afraid she understood all too well.

"Whatever I do or say, however I treat this village, remember, please remember…" He dropped her hands and cupped her cheeks, his fingers digging into her skull. Kaya didn't flinch or pull back. "I love you. I don't want to—hell, we should've run."

"Paul. Don't. Just—tell me. Whatever you need to do, tell me, and we'll do it."

"You'll remember?"

"Always."

He kissed her hard, his lips clumsy and brutal on hers.

Kaya rose to her knees, the cold damp of her skirts forgotten, and wound her arms around his neck. She held him tightly to her, as if her embrace alone would protect him from what he needed to do to stop Appleby.

"I'll remember," she vowed. "And I won't give up on you."

"You should." He breathed the words against her lips, his fingers slipping into her hair and angling her head to deepen the kiss. "You should. But I can't leave you now, Kaya. I don't know how."

Seventeen

P aul tugged her dress off her shoulders. He needed her, needed to taste her body, the softness of her skin, the warmth of her love. He kissed her, soft and gentle, and felt her shiver in his arms.

With a sharp rending sound, her skirts pooled at her feet.

"That's Caroline's dress," Kaya gasped. But she stepped out of its ruins without another word and returned to his arms.

He didn't know who Caroline was, and he didn't care. "I'll pay for a new one. I don't care. I need you, Kaya." She wound her arms around his shoulders, ran her fingers through his hair, and pressed her body to his. "Please, Kaya."

"Paul." Kaya's breath hitched, and she pressed her lips harder to his. She didn't want to let him go.

He groaned and kissed down her neck. Her pulse thudded against his lips, and Paul squeezed his eyes closed. He bunched up her chemise and slipped his fingers along her hips, over the lovely curve of her arse, and up her back. Kaya arched into his touch.

Pulling back only long enough to strip his boots and trousers, he let the cool air wash over him, but it did nothing to temper his arousal.

Paul swept her into his arms. Once, she might've laughed,

wound her legs around his hips and said something witty or seductive. Now, she only held tighter, kissed him harder.

Kneeling on the bed, he gently laid her down. He didn't break their kiss as he lay beside her, pulling her close. Paul tugged her chemise over her head and tossed it aside. He kissed down her body, tugging her nipples until she gasped wordless cries of pleasure.

He ran his fingers over her wool-clad legs to her boots. Quickly untying them, he tossed them in the general direction of her chemise. He untied her stockings and rolled them down, trailing kisses over her inner thigh, the back of her knee, along her calf.

"Paul." Kaya reached for him as he tossed her stockings onto the floor.

Then he slipped his fingers over her sex, teasing her wetness until she arched into him, her body humming for release.

Paul bent lower and kissed her, tasting her arousal, swirling his tongue over her clit, bringing her to the edge of orgasm, then backing off. He didn't purposely tease; he wanted tonight to last. Forever.

She stopped him, and in the faint lamplight he imagined her cheeks flushed from arousal. Her breath came fast, and he leaned over to take one nipple in his mouth, biting gently on the already hard peak.

"I'm never going to leave you." He clearly heard her promise.

"Kaya." Paul didn't know what to say. She should, of course. She should run back to Villa San Giovanni and Teresa's family and build a new life there. But his fingers clenched around her thigh, and he said, "I can't let you go."

He met her hungry kiss. Cupping her breast, he took his time. He stretched out their lovemaking, breathing her in, savoring her arousal. Her fingers combed through his hair, and he hummed around her nipple. The sound made her shiver, arch into his touch.

"I can't live without you." His mouth moved against her belly, his fingers tugging her nipples. "I don't know how to anymore." He kissed her hip, the sensitive skin of her inner thighs. "You're everything to me, Kaya. I love you."

Paul hiked her legs over his hips and guided his cock into her. Kaya rolled her hips, taking him deeper, and Paul clenched his jaw. He didn't want to come too soon, needed this to last. Needed *her*.

"Nothing can change that. Ever."

His slipped into her easily, a comfort, a promise. Kaya caught his hands and brought their joined fingers high over her head, stretching her body against his. She whimpered, cried out, embraced him.

"Paul." She whispered his name, her hips moving with his, her thighs sliding along his hips.

She needed more and he knew it, couldn't come from sex alone, but Paul didn't want to release her hands. As much as he wanted to watch her shatter, feel her tighten around him, he couldn't release her. Not yet. Not yet.

"Harder," she begged, and he obeyed.

Forcing himself to let go of her touch, the only thing anchoring him to this world, Paul found her clit. Arousal rushed through her, coiled tight around him as she came. Kaya shouted, her body stiffening as her climax crashed over her.

"I love you, Paul." Breathless words whispered in the space between them, and he felt their honesty clear to his soul. "Always."

"Kaya. Kaya." Paul thrust faster, pounding into her as he sought his own climax.

She shuddered as he did so. His fingers dug into the bedding, and he knew she slid a hand between them. Her fingers brushed over his cock as she sought her own pleasure, and Paul shuddered as his orgasm tightened through him.

Only at the last minute did he remember to withdraw, then he came with a cry. With his head thrown back, Kaya's body holding him close, he lost himself. She kissed his neck, shoulder, her calloused fingertips gliding up and down his spine.

Without a word, Paul rose and yanked his shirt over his head to clean her belly and thighs. Then he tossed the soiled garment back onto the floor.

"We should keep the handkerchief by the bed." Kaya, her voice sleepy, reached for him and curled around him the moment he lay beside her. "We'll have to wash your shirt now."

"I don't care." Paul tugged the scratchy blanket over them, angling his body to protect her from the harshness of the wool. "It doesn't matter."

He combed his fingers through her hair, loose now and tangled around them. Dropping a kiss to her forehead, Paul closed his eyes and willed this night to last forever.

"All that matters is you."

Paul held Kaya in the warming darkness of their room.

Neither slept. He thought Kaya might have dozed—she lay boneless in his arms for a little while—and he might've as well, though he certainly didn't feel rested. He'd risen to stoke the fire before immediately retuning to the comfort of holding Kaya, and now the room felt warm and cozy.

It was anything but.

The earlier tension choked him. Paul didn't know if he wanted to punch something or take another drink. He licked his lips, already imagining the slide of wine down his throat. His eyes snapped open, and he cleared his throat, swallowing hard.

"Are you hungry?"

Paul looked down. Kaya watched him in the shadows, her legs tangled with his.

"A little."

"I can ask Marta or Caroline to bring up a tray. I spoke with them about substituting goat for sausage."

He shook his head. "I don't want you to leave—" He stopped. "I don't want you downstairs if Appleby is there."

"I'm sure he's retired into a drunken stupor by now." Kaya shuddered. "No doubt in Marta's bed."

"No doubt." Paul held her closer. "When he doesn't get his way, Appleby flies into a rage. But I'll stop him. I'll stop him from returning to Marta's bed."

"You think he'll beat her?" She said the words far too practically, but Paul heard their underlying tremor.

"I know he will."

Damn it. He'd already raped her—Paul was under no illusions that Marta had gone to his bed willingly. Maybe she slept with the man to keep her family safe, but that didn't make her willing.

"I'm going to protect her." Once more, the fierce hardness in her words reminded Paul of all the reasons he loved her.

He kissed the top of her head and held her closer. "I know. I'd expect nothing less from you, sweetheart. Please be careful. Being my wife will protect you well enough, but Appleby... He doesn't like being denied. He's violent, unpredictable."

Kaya pulled back, and he didn't need the light to see the condescending look she gave him. "I'm perfectly capable of taking care of myself. And Marta, and her family." She softened and pecked a kiss on his lips. "But I shall be careful. I promise."

Paul wanted to argue. He wanted to beg her to stay in their room, to keep away from Appleby. But he knew better and swallowed the words. He wouldn't love Kaya so fiercely if she were any different, if she didn't fight for what she believed in.

They lay like that for a while, the room warm, her body pressed close to his. Neither slept again—not that Paul expected to, but he wished Kaya would. No, he had no desire to close his eyes and dream. He knew what his nightmares held for him, and he didn't want to revisit them anytime soon. Or at all.

"How are you going to convince Appleby to trust you?" Her words, a gentle whisper in the darkness, shot through him.

"I told you."

She pressed her fingers harder into his side and pulled back.

Paul didn't open his eyes; he didn't have to. He knew the frustrated look she gave him. Not angry—not yet—but challenging.

"Tell me again. In detail. So I know whether to smack you or not."

He huffed out a breath of laughter and met her gaze. "You'll probably smack me."

"Of that, I have no doubt."

Paul sighed and hedged, but, as always, Kaya didn't let him get away with it. She watched him, never wavering, and all his previous defenses fell. He framed her face and kissed her hard, hoping this wasn't their last.

"I have to prove to Appleby I'm the same man." He wanted to look away and dig up a lie or two but couldn't.

"You have to prove to him you—what? Still enjoy drinking and whoring?" She said it innocently enough, but the words held a hard disdain.

Paul choked and tried to find the lightness in this conversation, but darkness coated every word. His gut clenched, aching for another swallow of wine.

"Tell me." Kaya shifted and rested her head on her hand. She didn't remove her other hand from his body, and he appreciated the touch, the grounding.

"I'm going to lie to him." Paul didn't know what kind of reaction to expect—Kaya disliked lies—but she merely nodded. "I have to. I'm going to convince him I married you for your money."

Kaya jerked back. "You're going to tell him about our jewels?"

"No! No. I wasn't—no, not like that. Hell." He flopped onto his back and ran his hands over his face.

Kaya sat up, her hair falling over her breasts, and folded her legs beneath her. Paul reached out and played with the tips of her hair, purposely not looking at her. She caught his hand and stilled him, waiting. He sighed and met her gaze.

"All right." Her voice softened. "Tell me. What money if not our jewels?"

"I have to convince him there's a reason I married you other than the truth." Kaya snorted, and he grinned up at her. "So I married you for money and sex."

She laughed, a short, light sound that warmed his heart. "You did."

Paul grinned up at her then sobered. "I did. Originally, yes, I married you for money. But that all changed."

Sliding his hands along her thighs, over her knees, Paul watched her. He wanted to see her clearly, see her in the sparkling sunlight of Villa San Giovanni or Mazzarelli or in their tent in the desert. Wanted to know what she thought. How she judged him.

Maybe not that last bit.

"He already thinks you're English, and he knows we came from Egypt. It's a simple matter of telling him we're returning to England to collect your inheritance."

"He will believe this?"

"Kaya." Paul sighed. "He'll believe it because he will never believe I've changed. Appleby doesn't understand change, and I'm certain he's never thought of another person's welfare in his entire life."

"Not even yours?" she asked softly.

He snorted. "Never."

"Are you—were you not friends? And are friends not concerned with each other's well-being?"

"I suppose there are friends..." He stopped—yes. John and Oliver were those kind of friends. Who else would've dragged him from the dens?

"Damn it." He closed his eyes but saw only John's serious face —judging him. Oliver's disappointment. His eyes flew open, and he met Kaya's gaze, cool and calm and *not* judging him. Not yet. "It'll be easy to convince Appleby that I overheard you discussing your inheritance and persuaded you, with my charm and good looks"—Kaya snorted, and he grinned but didn't comment— "that I loved you and married you."

"And the sex?"

He frowned. "Our private life is none of his damn business."

"You are very confident he will believe you."

"I know Harry." Paul shifted his head on the pillow. "He'll believe me. It's not like he can check out our story. By the time any messenger sails for England or Egypt and back, this'll all be over."

"All right."

He stared at her, torn between hoping she'd agree with his plan, outrageous as it was, and hoping that she might possibly agree to keep out of it. But he knew better—she'd never stay behind when she could help.

"I don't see this ending well. However, I shall help. You know Appleby better than anyone, certainly better than me. If you say he will believe our story, then I believe *you*." She tossed her hair over her shoulder and lay beside him, one leg over his, her head on his chest.

"Just like that?" Paul lifted his head and looked down at her, but Kaya merely nodded. Her fingers curled into his chest, an anchor. She didn't move away.

"I don't like it, and I'm certain we haven't thought of everything. However, helping is never the wrong thing, and this village needs our help."

Paul tugged the blanket over them and wished they'd dressed. Even with the brazier burning, a distinct chill permeated the room. Kaya curled tighter into him and snuggled beneath the blanket.

"Any chance you'll stay away? That you'll keep your head down?"

"If I keep my head down, I won't be able to see anything but my feet." Kaya pulled back enough to look up at him. Paul grinned, and she sighed. "That is another one of your ridiculous English idioms, is it not?"

God, he loved this woman. Brushing her hair from her face, he kissed her softly. "I meant, is there any chance that you won't be involved, that you'll keep out of whatever is happening in this town?"

"Of course not. You speak with Appleby, become part of his plan. I'll befriend Marta and see what else I can gather from her. What else is going on here."

Below them, the noise from the breakfast crowd echoed faintly. Paul didn't need to hear him specifically to know Appleby was there. No doubt drunk—already or still, he couldn't say. His body jolted. He still craved the wine. His fingers tightened on Kaya's arm, her hip, and he tried to stop himself from giving into the clawing hunger. From running downstairs and grabbing a bottle for himself.

"You have to go downstairs." Her words barely carried to him over the noise from below and the pounding of his heart. It wasn't a question.

"Appleby is there. I have to make sure he—" Paul didn't finish. He didn't need to. "I'd rather stay here, with you."

"I know."

He hated that he needed to return. Hated leaving Kaya so unprotected. If he wasn't so afraid for her safety, he might've laughed. Kaya knew how to take care of herself and would take care of others. She'd stand against whomever she needed to in order to protect them.

"Any chance you'll stay here?" He had to ask.

"Of course not."

"I should've known."

"It was foolish of you to ask."

"Stubborn woman." He kissed her, deepened it until she wound her arms around his neck and tangled her fingers in his hair. Paul pulled back, breathing hard. Then he lifted her hand and kissed her inner wrist. For a long moment, he simply held her.

He wanted to stay like that forever. Holding his beloved wife in his arms. The sins of his past not yet caught up with him. But his soul screamed for atonement, and finally he stood.

They dressed in silence. Paul tugged his soiled shirt over his head and ignored the scent of their pleasure coating the fabric.

Kaya dressed in her own gown. She held up the ruined skirts to inspect the rend at the waist and nodded. "I can sew this. Fix it for Caroline."

"Good." The rest of his words stuck in his throat.

Paul held the door open for her and took her hand once more. He kissed it then straightened. "Whatever you hear, whatever Appleby says or I'm forced to say, don't believe it, Kaya."

She nodded, eyes dark and serious. "I know the truth."

They ventured downstairs, where Marta presented Kaya with goat meat and tomato stew. Ever gracious, Kaya thanked her with a sincere smile as she sat beside Paul, opposite Appleby.

Paul wanted to tear Appleby's eyes out for daring to even look at his wife, but merely accepted the bottle his former friend held out for him. He squeezed Kaya's thigh for support and took a drink.

The next morning, Paul slept late—rather, he was still passed out from last night, from all the wine he and Appleby drank. Kaya eased the door closed and slipped from their room. Sunlight flooded the hallway, streaming in from the open window at the far end. The temperature dropped even further overnight, and a sharp breeze bit her ankles despite her wool stockings.

Kaya breathed in deeply the scent of hot coffee drifting up the stairs and hummed in anticipation. No one stirred below, in the main part of the inn, despite the hour. Faint noises came from the kitchen, and she turned her attention there.

"*Ciao*? Marta?"

Marta exited the rear doors. She wore an expression Kaya couldn't place: gratitude, suspicion, wariness, even. However, she immediately cleared her features as she walked behind the long counter.

"*Caffè*, signora?"

"*Sì, grazie.*" Stomach jumping with nerves, Kaya felt the uncharacteristic need to fidget. To press her fingers into her skirts and bunch them or shift from foot to foot. Only the memory of her grandfather's stern voice admonishing her to keep still stopped her.

Instead, she smoothed her hands down her skirts and took a deep breath. Gidd may have prepared her to defend her very life, but he had never prepared her for marriage.

"Where's Olivia?"

"With Nonna." Marta eyed her guardedly, and only then did Kaya realize Oliva must have told her mother that the English lady spoke Calabrian.

Well.

"She told you about our afternoon in the mountains?"

Marta's lips pursed. "*Sì*."

Kaya tilted her head. No sense keeping the pretense. She switched to Calabrian. "Did Olivia also tell you I met her dog?"

Marta's eyes narrowed. Kaya met her gaze evenly. "I don't like that she goes up there alone." Marta turned for the coffee and poured a cup for Kaya. She set it on the counter with a sharp click. "A wolf!" Despite the strident tone, Marta's voice lowered. "Is this wolf friendly?"

Confused, Kaya sipped her coffee. "I don't understand what you mean by 'friendly.' She is not a wolf; Olivia said she is a dog. And she has not injured Olivia. She has even let her meet the babe."

It ached that she hadn't been able to share her experiences in the mountains, or her sketches, with Paul.

"I don't like it."

"But you have not tried to stop her." Kaya took another sip of the strong coffee and let the warmth do its best to seep into her bones. She hadn't been warm in days, and it had nothing to do with the temperature. "Why not?"

"She told me she told you." Marta scowled. Her hands pressed to the counter until her knuckles whitened. "About the men. Is your husband one of them?"

"Oh." She had not thought of that. Keeping her gaze firmly on Marta's, Kaya set the coffee down. She leaned over and made sure Marta understood every word she said. She wanted no misunderstanding.

"Paul knew Appleby in Bombay." She made sure not to say they were friends. Kaya had no experience with friendship. Based on what Paul had said about his relationship with Appleby, she had a feeling that form of friendship was not what she wanted. "That was a long time ago. He is *nothing* like that man. *Capire?*"

Marta didn't look entirely convinced, but she nodded. That had to count as understanding. Kaya picked up her coffee and sipped it, watching Marta carefully. They stared at each other in silence for several long moments, until the other woman straightened and pushed back from the counter.

"Breakfast, signora?"

"Kaya, *prego.*"

"Kaya." Marta nodded. "Breakfast, Kaya?"

Over bread and preserves and bergamot juice, Kaya listened to Marta explain what happened. How Appleby arrived in Casa Grigori one autumn's night with three other men, leading a donkey and cart.

"We welcomed him, of course." Marta kept looking behind Kaya, no doubt keeping an eye out for Appleby. Or perhaps Paul, though Kaya knew she'd hear the door open long before Paul heard their quiet conversation.

"It was bitterly windy. He paid for the room and food in gold, as well as the wine he drank, and I welcomed him back." She snorted and tapped her fingers on the counter. "My mistake."

"I doubt being less gracious would have stopped him." Kaya chewed a bite of bread, still warm from the oven. "These other people, they did not speak?"

"A little. Their English was like mine, poor, broken."

Kaya wanted to correct her. Considering it'd been mere months, she thought Marta spoke English very well. It was not an easy language to learn, and she'd spent years perfecting it. "What did they speak?" she asked instead.

Marta looked over her shoulder, then back toward Kaya. "Not

English, not Calabrian, not Spanish. I didn't understand any of it. Mama thinks it Egyptian or Turkish. Signore, he easily understood them."

At least that explained Caroline's anger when Kaya told her they'd traveled from Egypt. Kaya suspected Paul had been correct, that the men were speaking Marathi.

"What did they do?" Kaya shifted closer across the counter and dipped her last bite of bread in the fig preserves. It reminded her of Cairo, of Derya, of sitting in the courtyard and enjoying the early morning. "The other men, I mean. If Appleby was here, where were they?"

"They ate. Then they left." Marta shrugged, as if to show her confusion. Kaya kept silent. "They returned three, four days later, stayed the night, paid. Then they left again. Appleby waited here, stayed two weeks until they returned. Different men from the east, but with two carts. They ate, paid for Appleby. Then the four of them traveled west." Toward the coast. But they were on a peninsula, so perhaps they were crossing from coast to coast with donkeys and carts.

"Different men?"

Marta nodded.

"They traveled from east to west, stayed here, then returned west to east?"

"*Sì*, through the mountains."

"What do you mean they paid for Appleby?"

"Appleby, he did not pay." Marta spat on the floor beside her. Kaya wrinkled her nose but didn't comment. She'd seen many people do that, and she had no idea why. It disgusted her. Marta corrected herself: "He *does not* pay."

"I don't understand. Why do you not force him?" Kaya looked the other woman up and down and frowned. "You have not threatened him?"

Marta met her gaze, the anger in it hot enough to burn through Kaya. "He has people."

"I thought those men came and went. No? Appleby has others here?"

"No." Marta shook her head. "I mean he has people—he's taken people. One person from every family. Twenty-seven in all."

It took her only a moment, but when she realized what Marta meant, her anger flared. Her face flushed; her hands curled into fists. The dagger at her side felt heavy, and her fingers begged to take it to Appleby's throat.

"He kidnapped people from this village?" Kaya barely recognized her own voice.

"*Sì*. My papa is one. You saw him when you came into town, you and your husband. Signore, he allowed my papa to remain here so long as I—" Marta paled, but Kaya understood. So long as Marta shared Appleby's bed, he'd ensure her family remained free. "That night, they took Papa, forced him from his bed. We don't know where they take them."

"Who does he take?" All the men? No. Yesterday afternoon there were men eating in the inn. Kaya saw them.

"Men, women, children." She shrugged, an expressive movement of her shoulders that turned into a shiver. "He does not care."

"Where?" Kaya swallowed her anger. It burned through her, hot and sharp. "You don't know where?"

"No. No one does. We don't know if they are alive."

"No one followed him when he took your father?"

Again Marta shook her head. "No one knew until morning. Mama—" Marta closed her eyes and swallowed hard. "Olivia slept through it." Marta quickly crossed herself in thanks. "But in the morning, she found herself tied to the bed."

Kaya felt sick. Her nausea nearly choked her. No longer hungry, she pushed away her plate of bread and fig preserves.

"Olivia was not injured?"

"No. Scared. Angry. But unharmed."

"He took the villagers to ensure you do nothing to stop him." Kaya closed her eyes, tried to wipe the vision of Appleby's grinning face from her mind. She wanted to hurt him. Badly. Instead, she glanced up to the landing, where their door remained closed.

Paul didn't know. She was certain of it. She remembered the way he'd fought in the desert against the two slavers who dragged the nameless woman between them. How he'd fought to protect her in Damietta's souk, knocking out four others, though Kaya fought off the man who'd tried to kidnap her.

She remembered that village in Sicily, the one whose villagers wanted to burn her. Kaya had never seen Paul so angry. Though they'd managed to run, she knew he'd have fought each and every one with his bare hands before they had the chance to harm her.

No. If he knew, he would've told her. If he knew, he never would've come up with the plan he had.

"What was in the cart?" Her heart thudded painfully. Kaya wondered if Marta knew what Appleby was smuggling through her village.

Even a description of the contents might help, though it hardly mattered in the end. Kaya needed to stop Appleby before he destroyed Paul, and this village, more than he already had.

Hands still fisted, shoulders stiff, Marta shrugged. "Wooden chests."

Though it was the answer Kaya had expected, her bread and fig threatened to come up. She hastily drank the last of her juice and hoped it might settle her stomach.

She doubted it very much.

"Signora?" Marta rushed around the counter. "Signora!"

"I'm fine." She waved off Marta's concern.

"You do not look fine." Marta huffed and poured a cup of wine.

Kaya wrinkled her nose and refused it. "No, *grazie*. I do not drink." Marta gave her yet another odd look but set the cup beneath the counter. "What does Appleby do here?"

"*Perdono?*"

"Appleby." Kaya sat straighter and hoped her concerns did not show on her face. "When he is here without his friends, how does he spend his time?"

"Drinking." Marta grimaced. "Sleeping." She started to say more but looked to the landing where their room was. "Now that your husband is here, he does not spend as much time in...the village."

As much as she hated that Paul spent all night drinking with Appleby, she was grateful it meant that the hateful man spent less time with Marta.

Kaya had spent her life hating and fearing the Ottomans, the sultan who'd rather see her mother—and her—dead than accept Esme's choices.

She'd been so jealous of the outside world she never saw. Hated the restrictions Tahir and Derya had placed on her.

But never had Kaya felt such pervasive loathing as she did for Appleby. She thought her love for Paul the strongest emotion she'd ever felt. She was wrong. Appleby was repellent. Hateful. Evil.

Kaya tilted her head from side to side and tried to release her anger at Appleby. It would bring her only distractions, and she needed all her intelligence to stop him, to help Paul do so. "Where does he sleep?"

Marta busied herself with clearing away the empty plate and cups. Kaya reached across the counter and rested her hand on Marta's arm, stilling her. "Marta." She waited until the other woman looked up. "Where does Appleby sleep?"

She straightened, defiant. "In my bed."

Kaya was not surprised. No, she understood what measures people went to simply to survive. Some hid, like Gidd had hidden her away. Others fought—died. Others fought in different ways.

"Does Olivia know?"

Eyes closed, face pale, nose pinched, lips pursed, Marta didn't say anything for a long moment. "She sleeps in my mother's house now. She does not like it, but I can't have her in that house with—"

"No," Kaya agreed. "No, you can't." She paused and tried to connect everything. She knew she was missing something, a gaping hole in the center of this mystery. It eluded her no matter how she tried to grasp it.

"I'll take breakfast up to Paul." Kaya looked at their door, though she had a feeling he was already awake. Even with the amount of wine he consumed, he didn't sleep long. "I'll make a tray, if you don't mind?"

Several minutes later, with fresh *caffè* and a plate of bread and preserves on a tray, Kaya climbed the steps. She hadn't locked the door behind her and now balanced the tray on her hip, jiggling the handle with her free hand. She pushed the door open into the bright morning light, chillier than she expected. The shutters opened to the day, letting in the cold breeze and streaming sunlight.

Paul sat on the bed and stared at her sketchbook, turning the pages slowly, as if reluctant to leave one drawing for another.

Her heart flipped at the sight—it was so quintessentially Paul. Sitting on their bed, his hair mussed from sleep, focused on the task before him but eminently aware of his surroundings. He angled his head to acknowledge her but didn't look up from the sketchbook.

Kaya vaguely wondered if their window faced east, if they could see the carts Marta spoke of coming into the village.

"These are beautiful." He met her gaze.

His eyes were bloodshot, his curls more disheveled than mussed, his face wan. Her heart clenched, and she closed the space between them. Kaya set the tray on the floor and knelt before him. She cupped Paul's chin, raising his face to the sunlight.

He winced and closed his eyes, but he dutifully allowed her to study his face.

"Paul." She swallowed the admonishments and stood, kissing his forehead. "What are you doing to yourself?"

"Everything I can to stop Appleby. It's the only way."

"Don't," she pleaded. "Don't do this."

"I have to." He wrapped his arms around her waist and leaned his head against her belly. His body warmed hers, and she held him closer, running her fingers through his hair. "I don't know any other way."

"Paul—"

He pulled back and kissed her belly, just above where the jewels rested, though Kaya doubted he realized it. "Why didn't you tell me you met a wolf?"

"I—last night—" She shook her head and released him. "It didn't feel right last night."

"I wish you had, Kaya." He picked up the sketchbook again and showed her one of her hurried drawings of Vita and her baby. "These are beautiful. I don't know if I told you that." He didn't meet her gaze but traced the lines of Vita's fur with his finger. "You have real talent."

"Thank you." She swallowed the lump in her throat. "That—thank you. It means much that you think so."

He put the book beside him on the bed and stared at the closed cover. "A wolf, eh?" He deliberately lightened his tone. "Where did you find one? They're extinct in England, and I've not seen one in Bombay."

Paul lifted the tray and walked to the table. He merely glanced at her. She hated that, hated the distance already between them. How did she close it? How did she fix this problem she couldn't accurately name?

Last night, Kaya thought they'd work through this. That they'd survive what was happening. Then Paul stumbled into their room near dawn, startling her from what fitful sleep she managed.

"Olivia." Kaya swallowed against the dryness in her mouth and sniffed, straightening her shoulders. "She brought me up to one of the mountain peaks yesterday. The mother, Vita, is injured. She's not a wolf, but one of the herding dogs. Olivia believes the baby—what does one call a baby half wolf? The Italian word is *cucciolo*, but I don't know what that translates to."

"Cub." Paul frowned at her as he sipped his *caffè*. "Wolf cub."

She nodded. "Vita's cub. Olivia believes it is part wolf."

"You—" He set his cup down. "You did not spot the wolf from a distance?"

"No." She tilted her head. "Olivia made friends with her. She gives her food. Vita is injured and can't hunt for herself and the cub."

He choked out a laugh and turned back to his breakfast. "Kaya, you're the only woman I know who would befriend a she-wolf."

Kaya frowned again. "Are they dangerous?"

He nodded. Of course they were.

"Egypt has no wolves. Jackals, yes. I wonder if they are the same?"

"Are jackals dangerous?" She nodded, and he grimaced. "Then they're close enough."

"Vita is a dog," she reminded him. "Olivia befriended her, plays with the cub. How can they be dangerous if a child plays with them?"

Paul opened his mouth, closed it, frowned, and tried again. "No, I have no answer to that."

Kaya tried to smile in triumph but worry knotted her stomach. She shivered and closed one of the shutters, which was still allowing the weak morning sunlight to penetrate the room. It was positively freezing outside. She was unused to such change in temperature.

"Now." She met Paul's gaze and braced for the fight ahead. "I also discovered that Appleby usually waits here for a caravan to arrive from the east. He spends the night at the inn, then continues west."

Paul slammed down his cup and stepped forward. "How did you—who told you that?"

"Marta." Kaya frowned. "Appleby has been here since autumn."

Paul was as still as a mountain. It would've warmed her—at

least he stood immobile and didn't pace—but she saw the crazed look in his eye and hated it. Hated the way he planned something she knew she would not like. Something she knew would end up hurting him. Them.

"He said as much. Said he arrived one cold night and decided to stay."

"He's kidnapped people from the village." Her words shot between them, hard, angry. Paul closed his eyes and nodded, as if he'd expected as much. That simple acceptance twisted through her like a dagger. "Marta doesn't know where he's hidden them." She managed to keep her voice even, though she would never understand how. "They're kept away from the village, so no one says anything to the authorities."

"Aye." Paul sank back in the chair and ran a hand down his face. "He doesn't want them to try to stop him, either. It's simple enough to terrify a large group by threatening a smaller one—no one rises up. Not usually."

Kaya snapped her mouth shut on an angry retort about standing for what was right. She knew that look, the haunted, devastated look on Paul's face. He was remembering Bombay and the massacre that had happened when the people did stand up.

Angry at Appleby, worried for Marta and Olivia, furious at Paul—and absolutely terrified for him—she was unable to keep *all* her thoughts to herself. "Marta, she is forced to entertain Appleby," Kaya spat.

Paul dropped his head into his hands and looked at the floor. Kaya knew he didn't see uneven wooden boards, but his past. She licked her lips, though they felt numb, as unfeeling as her fingers. Her heart.

Mouth dry, heart thundering in her ears, Kaya stared at the man she thought she knew. "And you?"

His bleak eyes met hers. "I never forced a woman." He snorted, bitter and tired, and looked out the window. "Never had to. Wasn't my way."

"Forcing women—this is Appleby's 'way'?" Paul met her gaze, and Kaya felt sick. "What sort of man were you in Bombay?"

"The sort you didn't want to know. The sort I never wanted you to know." Paul closed his eyes and shook his head.

"And now you're becoming that sort again." Additional words crowded her tongue, but they didn't leave her mouth.

Kaya didn't see him move. One minute he sat, looking away from her, and the next he stood before her, his eyes blazing, his face set.

"To stop him. Only to stop him. He's smuggling opium, putting these people in danger. Teresa and Marco, too. He's kidnapping people so no one tells the customs agents or any authority." His voice lowered, pleaded, and he gently gripped her arms. "It's the only way."

"I know. I just—I know."

He held her gaze for another moment, as if to discern her honesty or her belief in him or—Kaya didn't know. Slowly he released her, as if afraid to do so. Sighing, he once more sat and turned to his breakfast. Paul poked at the bread, uninterested, but he broke off a piece.

"If they travel east to west, they could be using the coast." He dipped his bread in the coffee and chewed silently. "But if they're coming from Bombay, I don't understand why they don't continue overland. They need to cross through the Ottoman Empire anyway, once they're on the coast, they could easily take a ship to wherever."

"If they use a ship, they don't have to declare their cargo, yes?" Kaya heard her words, but they sounded very far away, as if someone else were speaking them.

Paul's eyes sharpened on her, alert and understanding. "He knows a captain who either collects part of the profit or orchestrates the entire shipment. But why cross through Calabria? Why not sail about the peninsula?"

"I don't know."

"Pirates? Spanish navy? English navy? Ottoman navy? It makes little sense."

Kaya walked to the window and let the cold breeze slap her in the face. In the distance, she heard the howls of animals and wondered if one was Vita. Her fingers curling around the window frame, she leaned out and closed her eyes against the knowledge standing right behind her.

Paul was only doing this to stop Appleby and the smuggling. The drinking, the late nights, the reverting to the man he once was, all of it was only to reunite these people with their families and end the horror gripping the village.

So why did it feel as if Paul was walking away from her?

Nineteen

Paul grabbed two bottles of freshly dispensed wine from a reserved and skittish Marta. He eyed the barrels behind the counter, but turned from them. He did his best to ignore Kaya's worried, watchful gaze from beside him. Failing, he tried to smile. Failing that, he stood before her.

His beautiful wife. The only one who believed in him. Who would support him so unconditionally. He never thought he'd have this. The peace that came with such intimate companionship. He hadn't really understood it before, what that meant.

Now it lay fragile between them, held steady by a single thread.

Kaya held his gaze, her dark eyes steady and understanding. She laid her hand atop his. "*Ya rouhi*," she whispered.

He didn't understand, and she offered no explanation. But the passion in her voice wrapped around him. Perhaps their intimacy wasn't as fragile as he believed.

Despite the small crowd, the way Marta watched them, and the very real danger Kaya was in by simply being his wife, Paul set the bottles on the counter. Taking her hands, he kissed the back of each one.

He wanted to tell her again how he loved her. That she was his life, his light, his purpose. He'd crawl across broken glass to protect her. Paul met her gaze for a long moment and could only nod.

Picking up the bottles, he turned for the inn's door and headed toward what was apparently Marta's home. It was, more importantly for his purposes, where Appleby slept.

He wanted to drag that bastard from bed and beat him as mercilessly as Appleby had treated these people.

Instead, he carefully planned what to say and hoped it'd be enough. Paul snorted. Of course it would be—Appleby rarely looked past the obvious. He saw profit and took it, uncaring who it hurt or what problems it caused.

Paul was no better.

Was, past tense. He tried to remember that. Atonement. He'd stop Appleby and, hopefully, redeem part of his soul.

At the top of the small hill that separated the inn from Marta's cottage, he stopped. He didn't need to look behind him, but he did anyway. One more glimpse.

Kaya stood in the inn's doorway. The wind whipped around her skirts. Though he knew she was cold, she stood perfectly still and watched him. Her hands folded at her waist, her chin held high, she didn't move. From this distance, her expression was unreadable, but he knew.

He wanted to tell her he loved her again, but with every step away from her, every drink of wine and every moment he spent in Appleby's company, he felt less and less worthy of her love.

He'd never been worthy. Doubted he ever would be, could be. But somehow, for some reason, Kaya loved him anyway.

Spinning on his boot, Paul kicked the door open and banged into the house. "Harry! Wake up!"

It sounded as if the noise had startled Appleby literally out of bed and onto the floor. Good. Paul hoped it hurt.

"What the bloody hell, Paul!" Appleby's voice, barely audible, slurred from the rear room.

The small stone structure, short and square, resembled many

other homes he and Kaya had visited since hastily disembarking from *The Cyprus Rose* in Sicily and making their way overland. Paul waited for Appleby to emerge and noticed the small decorative touches around the house. Wood carvings, abandoned needlework, miniature religious statues in an alcove. An empty hearth sat along one wall, cold to the touch.

Where was Olivia's father? Kaya hadn't said if Marta told her, but based on what he saw here, the black lace over one of the statues and the fact that Appleby had easily moved into the bedroom, Paul suspected that the man was dead.

Another one of Appleby's casualties?

Hands shaking, Paul let the bottles clang onto the stone table. He pressed the heels of his hands to his eyes. Did Appleby kill him? As a warning? Paul had seen it happen—kill someone close to the person you need to ensure their cooperation.

It sickened him in Bombay, and it sickened him now.

He hadn't stopped it then. He'd damn well stop it now.

But first he had to stand here, complete with wine offerings and a plan to spend the day drinking with Appleby. Paul needed Appleby to lead him to the kidnapped villagers, but how complicit was he in these dealings? In Bombay, he hadn't stood up until it was too late. Then he ran. Now, in this nothing little town in the middle of the Aspromonte Mountains, Paul vowed to do more.

Take a stand, fight any way possible. Kaya was right to stay away.

He missed her. The way her body curled around his, the softness of her breathing. Her laugh as they walked the land, her sheer joy in life. Last night, the wine helped him sleep more soundly than he had since leaving Bombay. The tradeoff, keeping the nightmares at bay versus losing Kaya, churned unpleasantly in his stomach.

"You better have brought wine, Paul." Appleby stumbled out of the bedroom, rumpled and dirty, his trousers hanging off his waist by a single suspender and his stockings loose about his ankles. One toe peeked through a growing hole in the stockings.

He looked a mess. Worse than Paul had ever seen him.

"Course I did." Paul smoothly handed a bottle to Appleby. The fingers of his other hand curled into tight fists. Despite their shaking, he didn't reach for his own bottle.

It called to him, lured him in with its pungent scent, the rich red of the local vintage. Paul swallowed hard and licked his lips. He could taste the flavor already. Kaya's disappointed look, the worry in her dark eyes, stopped him.

"You look refreshed." Appleby smirked. Paul jerked his gaze from the wine. "Your wife make you feel better?"

Paul grabbed Appleby by the throat and slammed him back against the table. Snarling, fingers digging into the soft tissue of his neck, Paul leaned over Appleby's flailing body. One leg kicked out, but it was weak, and Paul easily ignored it.

"Don't." He squeezed tighter. Appleby's hands clawed at Paul's wrist, but he didn't let up. "Don't *ever*. Not one word about Kaya. Ever." He squeezed harder, enjoying Appleby's wheezing gasps. Appleby's eyes bulged. "Not one word about her. Am I clear?"

Appleby tried to gasp out a word, tried to nod. Paul waited another moment, as tempted to finish Appleby here and now as he was by the bottle of wine by the man's head. Slowly, he released Appleby's throat and stepped back.

"Damn." He tsked, though it was a struggle to control his breathing. "Look what you made me do, Harry." Paul reached over and lifted the second wine bottle before it crashed to the floor. "You made me spill my wine."

Most of the liquid puddled on the floor by the table. Paul wasn't so far gone as to want to lick it up. Not yet. Instead, he took a casual sip. Paul kept his gaze on Appleby, who was kneeling on the floor, gasping, wheezing, his shaking fingers probing his throat. His other hand strangled the neck of his bottle, as if afraid to release it.

"What the hell, Paul?" Appleby reflexively swallowed. "What happened to you?"

Paul shrugged as casually as he finished the wine. "Kaya is mine."

Appleby snorted and coughed. "Well, look at you." His voice chafed in the small room, and he grimaced from the effort. "Not the Paul I remember."

"Oh, I'm still that man." It sickened him to say. Not because it wasn't true—because it was.

"The Paul I knew had a dozen women at a time. Didn't matter who they were, so long as they were willing." Appleby stood on shaking legs and guzzled the wine. It dripped down his chin, onto his shirt, staining the already soiled garment. He coughed up wine-flecked spittle. "Never kept one woman longer than was useful."

"One more word." Paul stepped forward, his body coiled for a fight. He could easily take Appleby, drunk or not. Always had been able to since they were kids.

Appleby snorted. "I figured you married her for money."

"She's mine. You'd do well to remember that, Harry." He stepped forward, purposely intimidating Appleby, who wisely backed down.

Paul waited, wanted him to attack. Restless anger throbbed through him, and he was ready to release it any way possible. He wanted to pound on Appleby until the other man confessed everything. Wanted to expend this dark, burning energy with violence and viciousness.

His jaw clenched, but he remained still. For Kaya. The only reason he had anymore.

"Bitch has you—"

Paul wrapped his hand around Appleby's throat again. Appleby snorted, his eyes widening again, and he stopped. Stilled. Understood.

"Now then." Paul pulled up a chair and sat, feet propped on the table, gaze hard and direct. "Why don't you tell me why you're sleeping in Marta's bed?" He swallowed the dregs of wine sloshing around the bottom of the bottle. Had he finished it already?

Appleby scrubbed his free hand through his hair and shrugged. He did not, however, rise from his kneeling position on the floor. "Wench had no one else to warm her bed."

His hand clenched around the thick glass, but Paul kept silent.

So Marta's husband was dead, then.

The closed-in smell of the house made him sick; the wine churned dangerously in his stomach. Marta definitely hadn't aired out the place since Appleby's arrival.

"Why are you here, Harry? It's a nothing town with barely any entertainment. Sure, the wine's good." Paul held up his empty bottle and craved more. Wanted to snatch Appleby's from his hand and down it himself. Instead, he dug his heels into the table and pressed his free hand into the top of his thigh.

"Oh, I have plans." The cagey look returned to Appleby's face. "I know people, Paul. And if you play your cards right, and keep from strangling me, maybe I'll let you in on the payday."

"Unless it's enough to set me up in the south of France with all the wine I can drink, forget it." Affecting boredom, Paul sighed. "I'm tired of petty payouts." He upended the wine bottle, but it was still empty. "Besides, I have Kaya's money."

"Oh, it's enough. Can anyone have too much coin?" Appleby moved with surprising stealth from the floor and across the room. Hands flat on its surface, he leaned over the table, blue eyes gleaming in the weak sunlight coming from the still-open door. "You want in?"

Paul forced an uninterested, lazy look and shrugged. "Sure. Why the hell not?"

"End of the week." Appleby nodded sagely, as if he'd said the most profound sentence in the history of sentences. "The quarter moon; that's when they arrive. It'll be big. Bigger than we've ever had before, I promise you that."

"All right." Paul abruptly stood, his gut clawing at him for wine. Or urging him to run. Or both. "Let's get more wine and take a walk. You can tell me all about it."

Appleby licked his lips and nodded. "Trust me, Paul. It's big. Bigger than anything we've done before. All those petty schemes in Bombay are nothing compared to this."

"Bigger than stealing the princess's ruby and selling it to the English merchants?"

The memory made him itchy, but Paul grinned anyway. That had been a payday all right, and one that still made him sick. Enough coin for all the opium he'd wanted.

Oliver, after dragging him from the dens, after ensuring he'd sweated out all that opium from his system, had told him what happened. Told him that the princess had been killed. They were all complicit in the girl's death. Appleby may have arranged it, but none of the rest of them had asked questions.

They stole her ruby and sold it and didn't look back. Then they pocketed the money and forgot about her.

Until Oliver told him about the rumors swirling around the city. That the girl's husband beat her to death for its loss.

Slinging his arm around Appleby's shorter—and smellier—body, Paul shoved those memories aside. Not this time. "Oh, I'm sure it is."

They walked out of the house, Appleby stumbling in the cold sunlight, and Paul hauling him up. Kaya no longer stood in the inn's doorway, and Paul prayed she'd disappeared into the mountains once more with Olivia. He didn't want her to see him like this.

"All right. Tell me about it. Tell me what you have your hands in."

"You remember Major Rogerson?"

His blood like ice in his veins, Paul slowly turned to Appleby. "Yes."

Oh, he remembered the major all right. Remembered him sitting high atop his horse, his sword drawn, red-faced. Remembered him shouting orders to murder the hungry people begging for food in front of the Company's buildings. To slaughter the women and children, the old and the young, because he didn't care if they starved or not.

Yes. He remembered the man who ordered that massacre all too well.

"It's opium. They bring it across the peninsula for distribution north. Throughout the Empire, into Prussia, Russia, France...everywhere."

"Who is 'they,' Harry?"

"Major Rogerson's men." Appleby met his gaze. "He's made a deal with me. I see that the opium makes it safely across Calabria, north into the Papal States and beyond. We split the profit."

"You trust that bastard?" Paul stalked forward, not sure if he wanted to strangle Appleby again or shake sense into him. "He'd as soon sell you out as he would slit your throat."

"Opium is a profitable operation, Paul." Appleby shrugged and dismissed everything they both knew about Rogerson. "The whole world wants it. And Rogerson will ensure I see part of that profit."

"Why?" Body suddenly hot from anger, Paul shook his head. "Why, Harry? The money might be good, but it's not worth it. Trusting Rogerson isn't worth it."

"Why? The money and the wine." Appleby looked back toward the path before turning for the village again. "As long as I have both, that's all that matters."

"And the Company? I assume you're stealing the opium right out from under them."

"Raw." Appleby nodded, clearly warming to this subject. "Transport it right here, where the locals pack it into chests."

Paul stopped. Ah, now they were getting somewhere. "Locals?"

Looking cagey, ready to close up and stop talking, Appleby looked around the clearing as if Rogerson might leap from behind a tree and scream at him.

"Come, now, Harry. You need more to drink. Let's head to the inn and see about that."

Wrapping a slightly friendlier arm around his shoulders, Paul led him through the cold mountain air and back to the inn. "Now then, old boy. Tell me about the locals."

Twenty

Kaya had gone into the mountains with Olivia, but they stayed only long enough to tend to Vita, who looked weaker and thinner than even yesterday. Olivia offered the dog and her wolf cub food before Kaya urged her to return to the inn.

Olivia had wanted to play with the cub, but being out in the open made Kaya's back itch and the hairs on her neck stand up. She didn't like it, no matter how much she told herself no one could have possibly followed them. While she suspected the girl had walked these mountains many times, with Appleby and his smugglers in the area, Kaya worried about her alone.

She needed to return to Paul. She hadn't liked leaving him.

"The cub needs a name." Olivia slipped her hand into Kaya's with this announcement and looked up at her with dark, all-too-serious eyes. They were nothing like little Teresa's, in Villa San Giovanni, who laughed and walked with her head high in fiery determination. Even with the worry about her missing brother, Teresa let nothing stop her.

Little Olivia had seen too much already, and it broke Kaya's heart.

"Oh. Yes, if her mother has a name, I suppose the little one must as well." Kaya frowned. She did not understand naming animals, but her experience with them was nonexistent.

"I have never named an animal," Kaya confessed. "What do you suggest?"

Olivia thought on it as they walked down the mountain at a slower pace than their exuberant race up. "I don't know. She does not answer to anything I call her. Vita, she comes when I call. The cub, she does not."

Kaya frowned as they walked into the village. She didn't understand that, either, but let it go in favor of returning to the inn. Did animals come when you called them by name? As if you'd asked a human to "come here"? If that was the case, did they have names of their own in their animal language?

She shook her questions off as they reentered the village. Today was not the day to think on animal names. Not with the cold descending like a veil and her constant worry about Paul. The village was quiet when they entered, though dozens of people wandered throughout the square. Women carried jugs of water, and men returned from wherever they worked during the day.

Quickly scanning the eerily quiet crowd, she did not see Paul. She hadn't expected to. The tingle that raced across her skin whenever she felt his eyes on her was noticeably absent. Saddened, but not yet disheartened, Kaya walked to Caroline's house and returned Olivia to her nonna. Caroline scowled at Kaya but said nothing as Olivia raced inside, already telling her grandmother about their afternoon.

Kaya nodded to the older woman and left. She honestly had nothing to say and was so very tired of judgmental looks. As if she wasn't aware what was happening in this village. *To* this village.

Shivering in the cold wind, the sun barely peeking over the mountaintops, Kaya rubbed her gloved hands together. She needed to find Paul. His absence had scraped along her nerves all day, making her jittery and nervous.

Scared.

Marta wove between tables at the inn, her hands wrapped

around bottles of wine, looking about as calm as expected. Her gaze skittered over the long benches, to the door, and back over the waiting crowd again—a noticeably subdued crowd. Kaya hurt for her.

Paul was nowhere in the room.

Stomach twisting, Kaya caught Marta's gaze and jerked her head toward the room she shared with Paul. The other woman shook her head. Throat tight, struggling for breath, Kaya stalked back outside.

She looked up and down the square. The wind howled through the village, coming down from the mountains, constant gusts that slammed into her. Shuddering with the cold, she glanced to the west.

In the rapidly spreading darkness, she could barely make out any individual walking through Casa Grigori. Heart pounding, she stepped toward Marta's house but stopped.

No, they weren't there. Marta would've said. Where, then? Paul had walked Appleby out of town hours ago, well before luncheon.

At a loss, Kaya whirled, hurried back inside the inn, and ran up the stairs. Their room was empty, of course. Kaya fumbled with the lamp, her hands shaking around the flint.

Struggling for breath, her hands no steadier now that lamp-light pooled across the floor, Kaya turned in a small circle. Her gaze bounced from table to bed, from bed to chair, from chair to table, again and again.

"Paul."

Lungs threatening to burst, she exhaled, finally calm enough to *see* the room. All their items lay where they'd left them. His pack, their bedroll, the tent and post, her bow and quiver and satchel. Her sketchbook on the bed where Paul had left it this morning.

Everything as it was when they'd parted ways.

He hadn't left. He hadn't. Unless he walked out of the village with nothing but the clothes on his back—which was possible, but she doubted it. Kaya's heart only now slowed, and she managed to take in another deep breath.

The thought of him leaving—

She hadn't realized that fear until now. The trembling worry that had followed her all day.

Shaking, she took off the cloak and gloves and lit the brazier. Standing beside it, she hoped for some semblance of warmth. She shouldn't have left him this morning. He said he planned to spend the day with Appleby as part of his scheme to learn information. Kaya didn't know how she could've stopped him; Paul was far too determined.

Looking back, she realized that perhaps disappearing into the mountains to visit Vita and her cub may have been a bad idea.

Now she had no idea where Paul had vanished to and no idea how to find him. Her knees gave out, and she fell to the floor with a thud. Kaya barely noticed.

"Paul, where are you?"

The empty room offered no answer.

Below, noises ebbed and flowed. The crowd sounded different now than they had when she and Paul first arrived—was it only two days ago? Seemed like a lifetime. Now, closer to the quarter moon, they sounded far more subdued.

Suddenly, the chatter silenced altogether.

Kaya scrambled to her feet, tripping over her skirts.

At the top of the steps, she paused and looked to the people below. They stared at the door. Paul and Appleby had walked in.

Paul looked up then, met her gaze. She felt that look straight through her, as if he drew her to him, and Kaya was halfway down the steps before she realized it.

She didn't run to him, though she dearly wished to. No, she calmly crossed the inn—or thought she crossed it calmly—and stood before Paul. The lines around his eyes softened, though those eyes remained bleary with the wine he'd obviously consumed.

"Ah, the missus." Appleby's voice cut in, slurred and stark.

Kaya didn't spare him a glance. Paul did—an unforgiving glare, a warning growl. Part of her wondered what had happened between them, but only a small part. Her attention was solely focused on Paul. He was all that mattered. The only thing she cared about.

Words tumbled through her brain but stopped up in her mouth—*I missed you, where were you, come to bed.*

"Later, Kaya." Paul leaned down and pressed cold lips to her forehead. "I'll meet you upstairs."

She narrowed her eyes at the obvious dismissal. "I promised Marta I'd help her here."

She'd promised no such thing. Marta might not even want her help. But Kaya refused to be dismissed, told to wait upstairs like... like she was no more important than the bottle Paul carried.

Kaya ignored his clear displeasure, the annoyed huff, the snarl in the back of his throat. As steadily as her legs allowed, she turned and walked to the counter, where Marta was pouring wine. The other woman had no help and stood alone in the inn, serving all these people.

"Let me help." She couldn't serve the wine, but she could serve the food.

"Kaya." Marta shook her head but instantly stopped. She grimaced, and a whimper of pain escaped her lips.

"Marta." Kaya lowered her voice though she was positive no one could hear them. "Did Appleby hurt you?"

Marta's gaze swung from the wine to the man in question then wildly back to Kaya. She shook her head but stopped again, sucking in a quick breath through her teeth. "He—no. He—"

Kaya tried again. "Marta." She didn't know what to say. What to promise. Instead, she gently took the bottle from the other woman's hand and placed it on the counter.

"You don't want to see what men are like when they drink." Marta's anguished whisper lanced through Kaya, painful and damaging.

Kaya kept her gaze steady. She was quite proud of herself for not looking at the small table in the back of the room where Paul and Appleby sat. "Let me help you."

She did not beg, though *please* formed on her tongue. Going back upstairs was out of the question. She'd either pace the room until Paul returned, or she'd grab her bow and shoot Appleby where he sat. Neither option truly appealed.

Well, maybe shooting Appleby did.

"*Grazie*," Marta murmured.

Kaya moved steadily from the kitchens to the long tables, setting bowl after bowl of pasta in front of men who ignored her. All the while, she kept an eye on Paul. They spoke in quiet tones, their words indistinguishable in the hum of the crowd. Finally, *finally*, the crowd trickled out like a rain-starved brook, until only Paul and Appleby remained.

Hours passed. Kaya stayed with Marta until the kitchens were ready for the morning. She scrubbed the counter, gathered all the mugs, and swept the floor.

Paul never looked at her.

Kaya worked until she wanted to collapse. It was very late, the sliver of moonlight barely enough to penetrate the mountain darkness. Raw energy continued to spark through her. She didn't want to leave until Paul left with her.

Unreasonable though it might have been, Kaya was afraid if she left without Paul now she'd lose him forever.

"Your wife, she watches you." Appleby finished another bottle of wine and banged it on the table, as if signaling for another.

Marta disappeared into the kitchens, no doubt preparing herself for another night with Harry. Hatred curled in Paul's stomach, but he kept his gaze level on Appleby. He'd seen Marta's limp, the way she held her side, the quick shake of her head, as if her neck pained her.

No more.

"I am aware." Paul knew Kaya's every move. Her every glance, the frown between her brows, the downturn of her lips. The way she watched him, a closed off, aloof look that might've fooled everyone else in this place, tugged at his heart.

The wine churned in his gut, and he pushed his half-finished bottle toward Appleby. He didn't want any more—well, no. He did. No use lying to himself. His stomach tossed unpleasantly with the knowledge that Kaya was disappointed in him. And frightened for him. For was going to happen after he left Appleby.

He couldn't let that happen.

In fact, as far as Paul knew, he was the only one able to stop it. The only one with even the slimmest chance of seeing Appleby passed out and unable to force Marta.

Over the night, with Kaya eyeing him steadily, he listened to Appleby rant about the unfairness of their time in Bombay. About each and every past slight—or perceived slight.

It was worse than listening to the plans Appleby had told him about in the freezing wind as they stood in the shadow of the mountains.

The money he was promised, the upcoming meeting with Rogerson.

Paul forgot how Appleby blathered on. "Drink up, Harry." Paul nodded to his bottle of wine, one of at least a dozen littering the table. It sickened him. It called to him. "It's the only way to keep warm in these godforsaken mountains."

Appleby watched him with eyes unfocused. "What are you doing here, Paul?"

Paul raised a patronizing eyebrow. "Drinking with you. I thought you knew that."

"No." He shook his head, a slow, soppy movement. "I mean in Casa Gri-ri. Griggggi..." He stumbled over the village name again, slurring the letters together, then gave up with a shrug. "What are you doing here?"

He had no bloody idea, that was for certain.

"Fate." Paul leaned back and tipped his chair, folding his

hands behind his head. "I never expected to see you again, Harry. Thought we'd parted ways for good in that opium den. Thought you'd died." He grinned, a forced twist to his lips. "How'd you get out?"

Appleby flashed him a sly smile. "The major. He found me."

Paul desperately wanted to look at the bar, where Kaya continued to stand. He remained deeply aware of her every move. Of the distance between them.

"Did you travel to the peninsula from Bombay?" Paul watched Appleby, who looked a little too in his cups to be cognizant of anything.

"Yes." Appleby cleared his throat, as if that might steady his words, but it didn't help. "Sailed through the Red Sea and crossed Egypt to the Mediterranean."

Paul leisurely lowered all four legs of his chair and fought through the fog of wine in his brain. "Interesting place to end up." He leaned across the table. In the freezing mountain wind, Appleby had talked at length about the plan he and Rogerson had concocted while they warmed themselves with Marta's wine.

Paul didn't need to hear it again, but he grasped at anything that would keep Appleby talking. He would not spend another night forcing Marta. "Why here? Not exactly your usual haunt."

Appleby snorted. "Yours, either. What were you doing, walking through these mountains?" He gave Paul a cagey look. "All that coin, you could have hired a carriage to take you anywhere."

"In these mountains? Not likely." Paul waved the question away. "Kaya wanted to see the countryside. We're staying with friends of hers in Genoa, at their villa."

Huh, maybe his ability to lie hadn't completely deserted him. Good to know, he supposed. Appleby bought it, of course.

"Yes, your wealthy lady." Appleby leaned across the table as well. "Tell me, how'd you convince her to marry you?"

Paul shrugged, a careless move that belied the tension in his shoulders. Appleby wasn't the wiser. "I told you, Harry." He flashed a grin. "Charm. She wanted to believe in love, and I provided her with that belief."

Appleby snorted again and drained the bottle. "I'm impressed, Paul. I'm impressed. Good on you, finding a beautiful heiress."

"Marta is a beautiful woman." Paul waited, watching Appleby carefully.

He merely grinned. "She's a screamer."

Paul half rose, ready to leap across the table and punch Harry for his cruel, crude comment. Instead, he pressed his fingers into the rough tabletop and clenched his jaw.

It made him sick, doing nothing, and Paul felt the wine threaten to come up. He'd deserve that. He deserved far more for using Marta to further his own plans to stop Harry.

Paul glanced at Kaya, who was disappearing into the kitchens. "What happened to her husband?"

"Died in the earthquake. Half the village did."

Paul leaned back in his chair and crossed his arms over his chest, his gaze firmly on Appleby. The *terremoto*. They were still rebuilding in Villa San Giovanni, but he hadn't seen any sign of construction here.

Typical Appleby. Using a weakened village to establish himself in a position of power.

Kaya exited the back and moved around the room, gathering mugs and plates as she helped Marta tidy the inn. Though he forced himself not to look at her, he knew she purposely didn't drift any closer to this table. Paul didn't blame her.

"I saw no signs of rebuilding."

"Eh." Appleby waved it away. "Provincial people. Look at these houses. They're made of nothing but wood and rough stone. Easy to bring down, easy to rebuild. Worse than after the monsoons in Bombay." He drank again, draining the final bottle.

"Nothing is worse than the monsoons." Paul shuddered.

Paul hadn't thought they would live through their first year stationed in Bombay. The entire monsoon season had terrified him—the massive flooding was shocking, and the rains wiped out everything. Houses, people, livestock, temples.

It'd taken months to rebuild.

"Is that why you took me around the mountains today? Lovely as that tour was, all it did was make me cold." Paul waited, coiled, ready to strike. "You wanted to check their progress in rebuilding?"

Appleby laughed, banging his hand on the table. The bottles shook precariously, but none fell. "Wanted to check on my investment."

"So you keep saying, but all I saw were cold mountains. I'm tired of your vague references."

Appleby once more looked cagey, his eyes bouncing around the empty inn. "Rogerson. Told you, told you. He'll arrive with the opium, then we take it across the Tyrrhenian and up to Rome and Venice."

Paul licked his lips. The missing people were the key piece. Not Rogerson or the ultimate destination of the opium train. It nagged at him, pushed him on, that feeling that something was missing.

Why take the villagers? This was a small, nowhere place. Why kidnap people to ensure the rest of them cooperated? And cooperated with what, exactly?

Paul pushed his chair back from the table and stood. He ignored Appleby and stalked to the bar, where Marta hid the wine.

The fire burned low, a faint source of heat in the large room, and the wind beat against the doors and shutters. Paul swore the temperature dropped even further with every minute that passed. Or maybe that was the glare Kaya leveled in his direction.

"We're going to owe Marta a lot of money." Kaya appeared before him, blocking his access to the bar. She guarded the wine like a warrior princess.

His gaze found hers as easily as always. Paul tried to smile and find a lighter tone, but the words died on his tongue.

He stepped cautiously forward but, naturally, she didn't back away. Wrapping his hand around her upper arms, he shifted so he blocked Kaya from Appleby's line of sight. "Kiss me."

Kaya frowned but didn't look behind him. "I will not. You reek of drink."

That wasn't the only reason, and he knew it. Nonetheless, Paul leaned in just enough to make it look as if they were sharing an intimate moment.

"I miss you, Kaya."

Damn it. Those were not the words he wanted to say. But the truth had ripped out of him, honest and desperate.

Kaya's eyes widened, as if she hadn't expected that, either, and her fingers wrapped around his arms. Paul pressed his lips together and tried again.

"I know who his contact is. Our former major."

Jerking back to look at him, eyes wide, she looked as surprised as he had been when Appleby told him. "The man who ordered the massacre?"

"Aye." Paul rested his forehead against hers. For a precious moment, the room stopped spinning.

Kaya sighed and wrapped her arms around him. "I don't like it. This has a bad feeling to it."

"I agree." Paul slipped his fingers up her arm and cupped the back of her head. Just to feel her. "He trusted me with the plan. That's something. Don't wait up for me. The quarter moon is too close."

He hugged her tightly, felt her sigh and lean her head on his chest. Paul took what comfort he could from the embrace. Kaya pulled back and pressed her lips to his cheek. Without a word, she retreated upstairs.

Paul grabbed two more wine bottles and grimaced. Kaya was right. They'd need to pay Marta for not only what he and Appleby drank, but also what Appleby had taken from her before they arrived.

No coin would ever be enough for what Appleby did to her.

No amount of money could ever erase the nights he'd forced her into his bed.

Returning to the table, Paul set down the bottles with a hard click. The noise startled Appleby, who looked bleary-eyed up at him. Damn, he should've kept quiet—maybe Harry would've passed out and slept at the table. No, best not take the chance. He owed it to Marta to free her from at least one night with this man.

"Your wife, she's very open about her affections."

Paul snapped. His arm moved before he fully realized his intent, and his fist connected with Appleby's face. The satisfying crunch eased the burning hatred, the self-loathing, the angry, clawing tension within him.

"I told you never to speak of Kaya again." Paul spoke to an unconscious man. He hoped he'd broken Harry's nose.

Returning the bottles to their rightful place, he paused and— no. He wouldn't take one for himself. Not even to keep him company during the long night ahead. Resolutely turning his back on the temptation, he walked through the kitchens and out the back.

He needed to tell Marta that Appleby wouldn't bother her tonight. At least one of them should have a decent night's sleep.

Twenty-One

Paul hadn't come to bed.

Kaya lay awake in the stifling room, the brazier working hard to heat the small space. She'd tossed and turned all night, rising far too many times to add more wood to the fire, to check that the door remained unlocked, to pace the room. Unaccustomed to sleeping alone, she tried to doze in the chair, but that only proved uncomfortable.

She'd spent only four months sleeping with Paul, but it amazed her how quickly she'd grown used to him. His large, warm body beside hers, sometimes touching, holding her close. Other times, just there, within arm's reach.

Giving up on any sort of sleep, Kaya rose before the sun.

The cold seeped through the shutters, fighting against the brazier's heat. Not bothering to open the window, she washed and dressed in the dimness. She quickly braided her hair, then wound it tight at the base of her neck and secured it with the pins she bought in Damietta. She smoothed her hijab and finished her morning preparations.

Today, she'd ask Marta to tally what they owed. What Appleby owed. They'd been very careful not to flaunt their wealth. They bought only what they needed, traded where they could, and hunted for food as they walked Sicily. Yes, they'd enjoyed the Spanòs' hospitality in Villa San Giovanni, but they had also left a small pile of coins by the bed to pay for whatever inconveniences they'd caused the family.

The Spanòs would need the help, especially with Marco recovering from the opium.

She'd pay Marta all she was owed, and she'd do so looking the other woman in the eye. No hiding, no backing away.

Kaya stepped from the room into the dim hallway. The far window was not open today, nor were the windows below. The wind continued to beat against the front door, which also remained closed to the weather.

She needed to find Paul. Find Paul and—what came next didn't matter. She needed to find him. It burned through her, a despondent echoing deep within her blood.

Paul wasn't in the main room.

Kaya's mind blanked. She'd expected him passed out at the table, bottles of wine littering the tabletop and floor. Snoring in the sleep he'd so craved and she desperately wanted for him. The main room was completely empty; only the faint noises from the kitchens dented the heavy silence. It caved in on her, crushing her lungs and her hope.

Her hands curled into her skirts. "Where is he?" she asked the empty room.

"He and signore, they left very early this morning."

Marta appeared from nowhere, and Kaya's head wrenched around as if the other woman had yanked it. "What? Where? Where did they go?"

"I don't know." Marta shook her head. "Signore, he did not —" Her lips pursed. "He did not come to the house last night. Your husband, he saw to that. I am most grateful."

Glad Marta hadn't had to face Appleby, but no less worried for Paul, Kaya managed a faint nod. "Good. He'll never bother you again," she promised.

Where had Paul and Appleby headed? They needed to stop

Appleby, but not at the cost of themselves. Not at the cost of the man she loved. It hit her then, right in the heart, sending the little air she had in her lungs rushing out in realization and fear. The love she felt for him.

Standing in an empty room, her love for Paul consumed her. It overwhelmed her, beat through her with every thud of her heart. However it was the...the *vastness* of what she felt that frightened her. How deeply she'd come to care for him in so short a time.

How easily she'd accepted him in her life. In her heart.

Very much alone in this foreign village, far from home, Kaya couldn't imagine Paul not being there. A part of her life. Couldn't imagine walking through strange lands without him there. His warmth beside her when he rose to stoke the fire. She couldn't fathom not being able to share any new experience with him.

Kaya blinked, bringing the dim room into focus. "He's gone to meet the smugglers." She knew it as surely as she knew the feel of his body moving against hers. "Where do they come from? From the east, *sì*? What path do they take?"

Marta nodded. "Sì, but not until tomorrow or the next day, with the quarter moon."

"He's gone to meet them," she repeated, strong in her conviction.

Paul had figured it out.

Where did one hide twenty-seven or so people who knew this area, knew the mountains, had worked them, lived in them? Her thoughts whirled like a haboob, so fast she couldn't catch one, let alone hold onto it.

"Divert them. Paul plans to divert them around Casa Grigori. Or—or discover where they're keeping the villagers." There. That. He had either finally convinced Appleby to tell him where the villagers were hidden, or Appleby was going to show him this morning.

"They could be anywhere," Marta snapped. "Don't you think we've looked?"

"I'm sure you have," Kaya agreed softly. She tore her gaze from the empty table and met Marta's. "But there are hundreds of places to hide them. It needn't be in mountains you're familiar with."

Once more, Kaya remembered the woman they met in the desert. She closed her eyes and thought of the intense brightness of the desert sun in the valley of the Eastern Mountains. They hadn't even realized another had set foot in their path until it was too late.

"It's possible," she whispered, "to stay an entire day in one cave and not realize there are others one cave over."

"We've looked," Marta snapped again.

Kaya only nodded. She didn't wish to argue with Marta over such a thing. Of course they'd searched. Assuming the villagers Appleby had taken were still alive—the alternative was a possibility she did not mention—they could be scattered across a dozen caves.

"Food." She whirled toward Marta, who stepped back, startled. "The people Appleby kidnapped, they'll need to be fed."

Marta's eyes brightened. "Of course."

"Does Appleby take food anywhere? How long since they were last seen? Months you said, yes?" Kaya didn't wait for Marta's agreement. "They'd need to be fed, and in winter they'd also need clothing, though I very much doubt Appleby cares for their well-being."

"I've noticed nothing. Other than here at the inn, where would he find so much food?" Marta followed Kaya to the open door, where the cold morning wind whipped violently.

Kaya couldn't believe she hadn't realized it sooner. Those people needed food if Appleby cared about keeping them alive. But assuming he did was a big assumption.

"They're dead, aren't they." Marta's words hit her as sharply as the cold breeze from the open door. A statement, not a question, filled with too much acceptance. "Appleby does not care if they live or die," she spat.

Kaya didn't answer—she couldn't. It'd been months since they were taken. Even a storage of food would've disappeared by now. She stilled and stared toward the east. Unless Appleby was feeding them when he met the carts. Marta hadn't said Appleby took her father, only "they." *They* had come that night and taken him.

"Does he care?" she heard herself say. "Those people, does Appleby care about them? At all? Why keep them alive? If the village discovered they were dead, would you continue to lend your cooperation?"

"No," Marta scoffed. "Of course not. We keep silent because he has our families. If he killed them—" She stopped, swallowed. "If they're dead, we have no reason."

"Have you followed him?"

Again, Marta shook her head. "He threatens us. The women, they search the caves while the men work the goats and lower vineyards. Once the frost came, many searched the mountains, but only a few at a time. We couldn't alert signore."

"No," Kaya agreed. "No. Plus, there might be others guarding the caves. The men who travel overland with the carts might leave others behind, with Appleby here to ensure the village cooperates. No." Kaya shook her head, an odd energy propelling her forward. "There have to be others guarding the caves."

Every word Gidd ever taught her about military tactics, campaigns, and overcoming one's enemy suddenly made sense. She'd studied each book and manual he brought her, memorizing all of them. Never had she needed that knowledge as she did now.

"Twenty-seven hostages and how many guards? Paul figured it out." Kaya breathed deeply of the mountain air, refreshing now rather than bitter. "He did it. He found them."

Relief eased a bit of the tension in her shoulders, and Kaya relaxed her neck, let it fall backward. The rising sun shone brightly behind the clouds, its weak light bouncing off the mountaintops. The wind cut through her gown, battering her. She shivered, unaccustomed to such cold.

"It's going to rain," Kaya murmured.

Pioggia, the word for rain, was one of the first she learned from Letizia. It often rained in Sicily, far more than Kaya had expected. Though Gidd had told her stories of the lush valleys in Bombay, the annual rainfall in Cairo barely mattered, and she never realized how much it rained elsewhere.

"*Neve*." Marta looked at her oddly, wrapping her hands around her arms and rubbing briskly to ward off the chill.

"*Neve*?" Kaya shook her head and shivered again. The cold seeped into her bones. "I don't understand the word."

Marta frowned harder and dragged her inside, slamming the door behind them. The sudden warmth tingled through her fingers, heated the tip of her nose.

"*Neve*. It is—*neve*. I don't know the English word." Marta trickled her fingers through the air, but Kaya didn't understand the gesture. "Frozen rain, white frozen rain."

Kaya brightened. "Snow." She laughed and ran to the door, wrenching it open again. "It's going to *snow*? I've never seen snow."

It was a sight she wanted to share with Paul. A joy she wanted to experience with him. But she had to find him first. Kaya nodded and turned back to Marta, who continued to look at her as if she were mad.

Well, she might be.

"How many trails to the east? Does Appleby always take the same ones? The men leading the carts, do they always enter the same way? Or is it a different path every month?"

"I don't—I don't know." Marta looked helpless.

"Marta." Kaya took the other woman's hand and rubbed it between hers. "We will find them, and we will stop Appleby. I promise you. Now. Answer my questions or find me someone who can. This will be their last trip through these mountains."

Paul didn't notice the cold, the falling snow, or the ice crunching beneath his feet. Part of that had to do with the vast amount of wine he'd consumed. The other part was his burning drive to discover Appleby's hiding place.

Drink always loosened Appleby's tongue. Frankly, Paul didn't know why people went into business with him. The man had never kept a secret while in his cups.

Paul had let Appleby sleep off some of the drink. And the broken nose. Then, in the predawn light barely denting the village, he'd roused him. Sure enough, in the early hours, with the inn silent and the wind howling outside, Appleby had cracked. Paul feigned disbelief that Appleby and Rogerson had built such a vast smuggling operation in the space of less than half a year, and he forced Appleby to show him.

Hence their forced march through the bitter cold, deeper into the mountains.

At least he'd successfully kept Appleby from Marta's bed. That had to count for something against all his sins. A tick in the good column, so to speak. What had Kaya said about weighing good deeds versus bad?

He missed Kaya. God, he missed her. Missed her body wrapped around his, seeking warmth. Her smile and her pure delight in life. Holding her hand as they walked, strolling peacefully through the land.

Maybe this was his punishment. Or atonement.

He looked over his shoulder in the general direction of the village. The wind threatened to take his hat, and he clamped a hand to keep it steady. From here, he couldn't see Casa Grigori but imagined he saw Kaya anyway, imagined she stood framed in the inn's doorway, watching him with dark, concerned eyes. Waiting for him.

He hoped she'd forgive him. Eventually.

"I missed this." Appleby snorted then groaned. Good. Paul hoped his broken nose pained him greatly. Appleby stumbled over the freezing, uneven ground, cursing around the wine bottle.

"What?" Paul shook his head and refocused on the moment. "Walking in the cold?" He huffed. "I sure as hell don't. Damn cold in England." He sighed, his voice quieter than he'd have liked given the swindle he currently played on Appleby. "Fucking hot in Bombay."

"Aye." Appleby cleared his throat. "I don't miss it, England or Bombay. Sure as hell don't. Don't miss the damn Company, either." He sniffed and met Paul's gaze over his shoulder. "I miss the way we were, you, me, John, Oliver."

Something in Paul twisted. His heart or soul or conscience. "Aye," he lied, forcing a smile. "Me too, Harry."

Until that moment, Paul hadn't realized how truly dead his past was. He'd dreamt about it nightly, tried to atone for it with every sunrise. Here, with Appleby, he'd drowned in it, suffocating and clawing inch by inch.

It meant nothing. Oh, not his deeds and actions—those, he'd make amends for, probably for the rest of his life. But now there was no feeling there. When he talked about his past with Kaya, he didn't feel any connection to his former comrades. All he felt was Kaya's hand in his. Her soft kiss of understanding.

Perhaps he truly had left his past behind.

"Why did you leave Bombay?" Paul finally asked. "I really thought you had died in the dens."

"I didn't tell any of you I was coming here." Appleby sent him a sly grin. The swelling around his nose distorted his expression, turned it grotesque. "Still don't know how you found me."

"I don't know either, Harry." Paul shivered in a blast of wind and snow. "Just luck, I guess."

The poorest of luck, as it happened.

"Seriously, Paul, what are the chances you stumbled into my little village while I happened to be in the square? You could've gone any number of ways; why were you even in Calabria?"

"We started in Egypt," he reminded Appleby.

"Yes, but why not sail straight to England?"

"Harry, I told you." Paul shoved his hands under his armpits and flexed half-frozen fingers. They hadn't needed gloves in the south. He was woefully ill-prepared for this walk. "Kaya wanted to see the countryside. We're on our way to Genoa, to visit her friends."

"But to walk? A woman like that—" Appleby shook his head. "Rich women, English women, they sail for their destination."

Paul growled. "You know nothing of Kaya. If you don't want me to punch you again or leave your body here for the wolves to find, shut your damn mouth."

Appleby shook his head. He seemed bemused and oddly sober, considering he hadn't had the chance to sober up at all today.

"Oliver's woman, Rose, she's English, and she preferred to walk the countryside." What happened to Rose once they left? Maybe that's where Oliver went—maybe he returned to Bombay, to Rose. Or at least sneaked her out of that city and the Company's hold on her.

Appleby rounded the corner and stopped. "We're here."

In the rocky, narrow mountain pass, high trees bracketed each side. It looked about as inviting as the immense emptiness of the desert. The cold wind tunneled through the pass and hit Paul square in the face.

It did much to clear his head.

In the distance, he heard the lone howl of an animal and wondered if it was Kaya's dog and her wolf cub. The sound startled Appleby, who flinched and jerked around. Eyes wild, he gripped the neck of his empty bottle like a club, ready to swing.

Paul eased his hands from beneath his arms and looked around cautiously. Oh, what he wouldn't give for a greatcoat. He scanned the area for any sense of danger, but the wind cleverly hid any hint of sound, digging through the pass. Trees swayed and groaned in the gusts. Other than the howl, no sound penetrated the corridor.

He didn't see any footprints other than theirs, though the snow continued to fall heavily. Anyone, or any animal, who'd recently passed through here did so at a convenient time; the snow covered their footsteps.

This was it, then. Time to play the dutiful friend, the fellow schemer, the partner in crime. Paul stepped up and clasped a hand on Appleby's shoulder.

"Little jittery there, Harry." Paul grinned, though the obligatory lightness crushed his shoulders with tension. "Here, have a drink. It'll help calm your nerves."

Appleby nodded, grateful. "Thanks, Paul." He guzzled the wine even as his eyes, wild and frightened, darted around the area. "There are wolves in these mountains."

"So I've heard. I've never met one." Paul casually shrugged it off and rubbed his hands together in a vain attempt to warm them.

"I have." Appleby shuddered again. "Vicious black beast. Tried to tear me apart."

Paul stilled. What were the chances? It was almost unfathomable that he'd found Appleby in a little village in the middle of Calabria, that he and Kaya had walked through said village just as Appleby stood in the square.

Was it possible that Appleby had met Kaya's wolf?

"When was this?" The words sounded slow and uneven to his ears, but Paul kept his gaze on Appleby's.

"Oh, weeks ago." Appleby waved it off and grinned viciously. "Cut a hole into the thing, that's for sure."

Paul raised his head in a half nod. "Where?" He cleared his throat and blew into his hands. It was viciously windy here, and bitterly cold.

"Oh, north of the village somewhere."

"Didn't realize these mountains were so dangerous." Paul eyed Appleby warily. "We walked through them for days and didn't meet anything larger than a rabbit."

"Ah, yes, you and your wife." He eyed Paul, but the broken nose had evidently delivered its lesson. "Good thing you found me here, then." Appleby grinned around the swelling. "Now you can be a part of my new venture."

"Yes." Paul stepped back, giving the other man room. He looked around the woods, into the darkness of the tree-lined path and up the mountainsides. "Does this venture involve killing *me* and leaving *my* body for the wolves?"

Appleby snorted. "No. But don't think I haven't thought about it! Choosing a woman over me, your oldest friend." He shook his head as he held up his hands and backed away from Paul. "Not another word. Promise."

"So you've said before," Paul warned him.

"I want us to be partners again. Like we were in Bombay." His voice lowered. "Like in England."

"We've known each other a long time, Harry." Paul once more shoved his fingers beneath his armpits, but the biting wind didn't ease, and the cold seeped further into his bones. "Christ, I need a greatcoat. It's freezing here!"

"Bloody mountains." Appleby sighed and finished the wine.

Paul wanted to fight him for those last drops. He imagined the rich, sweet taste sliding down his throat. He wanted to lick the bottom of the bottle. He curled his hands into fists and stayed where he stood, even as he ached for more wine, a physical ache that made him want to crawl out of his skin.

"They should arrive shortly. Tonight or tomorrow."

Paul was not staying out in the open, with nothing more than his shirt, vest, and jacket, in the beginning of what seemed to be a ferocious snowstorm. "I'm afraid I didn't dress the part," he said dryly.

Appleby laughed, a louder sound than Paul expected with these contacts of his slipping through the mountain pass. He tossed the bottle against the rocks and slung an arm around Paul, steering him deeper into the woods.

"Come, I know where we can keep warm."

Finally. The caves where they kept the villagers. Of course they kept the prisoners and the merchandise in one place. That way, Appleby would only need the one set of guards to watch both.

Anxious to find this cave, Paul followed Appleby on the quickly darkening path. They'd walked perhaps an hour northeast of the village. Far enough from the grazing grounds to go unnoticed by search parties.

Paul had meant it when he said they hadn't seen anything on the road he and Kaya walked. Not even a field of grazing sheep. The waterfall they'd camped near had been so off the trail, Paul wondered if another soul even knew about it.

The villagers could search for a year and never find every cave.

Paul nodded to Appleby's lamp. "That's not enough heat for the night. Are you planning to stay until sunrise?"

"They usually arrive an hour after sunset. If they're not here shortly, we'll return to the inn, and I'll let you buy me another drink."

"You've never bought a damn thing in your life." The words came out clipped, but Appleby didn't seem to notice.

Appleby hesitated near an outcropping of large boulders, then slipped between them. In the darkness, snow swirling around them, Paul nearly missed the opening. No light shone from the entrance, no sound.

Appleby shouted for someone, Paul didn't hear who.

The entrance wasn't where Paul thought. It was on the other side of the cave he'd been looking into. From around the corner of yet another outcropping, the guard stood, holding a lamp.

"You're early, Harry," the man said in English.

Another Company man, then. Paul didn't recognize him, but that didn't mean anything. Appleby motioned him forward, and Paul silently took a step.

"Who's that?" the guard demanded.

The hard snarl told Paul all he needed to know about what sorts of men Appleby surrounded himself with. These weren't the kind to look back in sorrow or regret. These were the kind to live hard and die in a gutter.

"Paul Hartley. A friend."

"The major won't like that," the man warned.

Paul agreed, but merely snorted. "*The major* won't mind. Especially if it doubles his profits and expands his network."

Appleby waved it off, his eyes darting around the area. Searching for the wolf? Rogerson? Another bottle of wine? "Paul is trustworthy. And we need another man if we're to continue into the rest of the peninsula."

Ah, so despite his assertations to the contrary, they hadn't managed to move north. A small operation still. Paul filed that away, promising little Teresa he'd stop these people. If she had the fire and determination to enter the dens in search of her brother, he could face his past and stop the opium from reaching Villa San Giovanni.

For the time being, at least.

"It's freezing out here." Paul ignored the still snarling guard and stepped around him and Appleby. "Let's have a bottle inside, eh?"

He'd thought he'd prepared himself for this. The missing villagers. The chests of opium. He had heard what the opium factories looked like but had never seen one in person.

The sight hit him doubly hard.

Old men, young children, and women continued to work despite the darkness. Several oil lamps sat on tables, illuminating just enough to be able to see the heavy chests. They worked methodically, taking the raw opium from the chest to another table with smaller chests. The children carried the balls to a row of bags lining the table.

Easier to sell that way.

They wore no gloves, and Paul honestly did not know if the opium seeped into their skin. Did merely touching it affect them? Were they all as addicted to the opium as he had been?

Sickened, he turned away from the scene. He wanted to vomit. He wanted to push them all aside and take all he could carry.

Hands fisted at his side, all thoughts of cold and snow now banished in the face of such barbarism, he met Appleby's gaze. The other man's eyes, swollen from the broken nose, looked dispassionately on the scene.

Paul wanted to punch him again. He wanted to gut Appleby, the guard that had greeted them, and the two nameless guards standing watch over the villagers.

"Efficient," was all he managed.

"Best way to keep the village in check." Appleby eyed the opium balls greedily but made no move to snatch one. He'd no doubt been threatened. Plus, stealing would only cut into his profits.

"Impressive."

Paul was going to stop this. All of it. That silent vow burned through him.

Twenty-Two

That night, restless to stop Rogerson, to show Kaya where the villagers were being held, to end all of this, Paul stood before the hearth. The inn's fire barely dented the cold seeping in from the outside.

It certainly did nothing to ease the fist from around his heart.

Behind the counter, Kaya helped Marta serve large bowls of pasta and hot bread. She moved effortlessly, as if she had always been doing this, keeping a sharp eye on Marta whenever the other woman exited the kitchens.

He knew these men had families, knew their wives and children waited for them at home. Did they come to the inn to watch Appleby? Or simply to share a bottle or two? Maybe it was more than that—maybe it was the friendship, the camaraderie the tavern offered.

Paul missed that, missed gathering with John and Oliver around a bottle of wine and dice or cards.

Unable to help himself, his eyes drifted to Kaya. She watched him as steadily as he did her. As if she expected him to disappear. Paul didn't blame her. He'd left all too often these last days.

One more night. Maybe two, depending on if the snow hampered the carts traveling over the mountains.

"Are you hungry?" Marta asked, then she looked guilty and scared. "Um, signore?" she asked again, louder and in English. "Are you hungry?"

"*Sì*, Marta." His eyes flicked to Appleby, too fast for either Marta or Appleby to tell. Appleby hadn't noticed anything. "I am, *grazie*."

As casually as possible, Paul walked to the counter, where Kaya continued to guard the wine. It tempted him, lured him in, each open bottle an enticement all its own.

"Where have you been?" Her dark eyes deepened, and he reached across the counter to take her hand. The instinctive gesture soothed him, and he grasped her fingers and held tight. His only lifeline.

"Waiting for his suppliers." He shook his head, the faintest movement. He'd tell her more in their room, far from eavesdroppers. "Why are you here?"

Kaya tilted her head, the movement so familiar it clenched his heart. "Here serving food?" She wrinkled her nose. Paul stared; he'd never seen her do that. How endearing. He wanted to lean over the bar and kiss her. "Or here in the inn?"

"Serving food."

At the inn—why are you still here? You should've run when you had the chance.

"I'm helping Marta. She has no one but Caroline to help." Kaya squeezed his fingers and leaned forward. "Paul—"

"Later." He promised her with a wordless squeeze of his now-warm fingers around hers and hoped he could keep that promise.

Kaya sniffed. "You're coming to bed, then?"

There was nothing he wanted more than to wrap around her and hold her as if the last week hadn't happened. "Yes."

"And Appleby?"

"I'll see he passes out before Marta closes the inn tonight." He didn't look away from her. Couldn't.

Kaya pursed her lips. "All right." She sighed and lifted an open bottle to the counter. "Then you're going to need this. He'd better be worth the coin he drinks."

Paul snorted and lifted her hand, kissing the inside of her wrist. He knew what it cost her to offer him that bottle. Not money—her beliefs. She shivered, eyes darkening further, and he smiled against her skin. "He's not, I promise you that." Paul stood and grabbed the bottle. "I'm not sure I am, either."

"You are." Kaya tightened her fingers around his before letting him go. "You are to me."

Kaya watched Paul drag Appleby's unconscious body from the inn.

She helped Marta close up. "Where will you sleep tonight?"

"By the fire with Olivia." Marta sighed, but there was no relief in it. "Perhaps I shall sleep well tonight."

"Try," Kaya urged, though she doubted Marta would be able to. How did one sleep well when forced into such an untenable situation? "I'll latch the front door and double-check the window shutters."

"Thank you, Kaya." Marta squeezed her hand. "For everything."

Kaya tried to smile in return but could only nod. She watched Marta disappear through the kitchens, into the attached house where Caroline and Olivia now slept. The winter winds cut through the small village, and even standing in the doorway was too much for her to bear. Despite her wanting to watch Paul deliver Appleby to the floor of Marta's house, Kaya closed the inn door and stood next to the dying fire.

It felt like ages before Paul returned, but the embers had barely warmed her hands before the door opened. Kaya turned and watched him latch it before leaning his head against the thick wood.

"Appleby won't wake before noon tomorrow."

"And you?" She stepped across the floor. "What of you?"

His laugh was harsh and acidic, and he banged his forehead against the door. Paul pushed off with flat palms. He stood there, arms straight before him, hands on the door, staring at it as if it held the answers he sought.

Kaya wished it did, if for no other reason than to keep him from blaming himself.

"I haven't had nearly enough wine tonight."

"Good." She hated when he drank, even if he hadn't had any nightmares these last few nights. Kaya reached out and took his hand, one then the other, and forced him to look at her. His normally bright eyes were bleak, bleary, his face wan and pale.

"Where did you sleep last night?"

"Here." Paul closed his eyes. "Appleby passed out. Well." He stopped and grinned. "I knocked him out. Then I slept in the chair."

"You punched him?" Kaya grinned. "This is why his nose is swollen?" Paul nodded. "Good." She added viciously, "He deserved it."

"Yes." Paul quieted, that intense look back in his eyes as they focused on her. He brushed his fingers along her cheek. "Yes, he did."

"Were you—did you find out anything?" Kaya threaded her fingers through his and tugged him toward the stairs. They were alone here, but she wanted a closer comfort. "Did he say anything?"

"Oh, yes." Paul snorted and leaned his head against her shoulder, his hands wrapping around her waist.

Kaya stopped at the first step, leaning into him. She covered his hands with hers and simply held tight. Paul's lips grazed her cheek, soft and light, as if afraid to do more. It broke her heart. It also gave her hope.

"We were right. It's opium. They're smuggling it out of Bombay, right under the Company's nose. I also found the villagers."

Kaya stilled. Voice barely audible, she asked, "You did?"

"They are in the mountain caves. But it's easy to miss. I didn't see it at first." He sighed against her shoulder, tightening his hold on her. "About two hours' walk northwest, down a well-trodden road. I didn't see any animals, but then, with the snow, I doubt they'd be out anyway."

She remained silent and simply held him. Paul mattered. Retracing his steps into that cave mattered.

"And the cave?"

"Up the mountain, a pretty steep climb. The opening is hidden by an outcropping. From the other side, you can't even see it." He shuddered and held her tighter. "They're using the villagers to package the raw opium into smaller, more easily transported chests. Easier to sell."

"How easy is it to find? That cave?"

"Damn near impossible. But I left a trail. Tore my stocking and tied pieces of it round the branches. My right foot is damn near frozen."

"You brilliant man." Kaya kissed him, hard, holding him tighter. "I'll find you another stocking. And Appleby?" Kaya cupped the back of his neck. Despite the persistent chill that had permeated her these last few days, his body warmed her. "What's his role in all this?"

"Middleman. As always. He oversees it through Calabria, then they ship it down the coast. They're small yet. Haven't expanded north. They want to."

"And yours?" The comfort of his arms around her settled her. His warm breath on her cheek reassured her despite their next step. "What's your role?"

"I'm his new partner." The bitterness in his tone stung her. "Just like old times."

His arms tightened around her then loosened. He shuddered but didn't release her. Kaya wanted to hold him tighter, afraid if she didn't, he'd drift away.

"He thinks we're heading to Genoa, that your friends own a villa there."

"We know no one in Genoa." Kaya wasn't even certain where the city was, though she'd heard of it.

She felt his grin against her cheek and lifted her head. "Appleby doesn't know that. With us traveling north, we can expand not only into the Papal States and Piedmont, but Austria and Prussia, too."

"You're going to stop him." She turned her face into his neck and breathed him in. He still smelled like Paul, felt like him. Her Paul. *Hers.*

Her fingers played with the curls at the nape of his neck. His hands settled on her waist, and he pulled her tightly to him. She leaned her cheek on his shoulder and kissed the side of his neck. For this one moment, this one perfect moment, her world righted, and she knew peace.

Kaya corrected herself: "*We* are going to stop him."

Paul slid his hands up her back, over the curve of her spine to her shoulders. His lips brushed her temple, down her cheek. The faint scent of wine hit her nose, but Kaya ignored it.

"Paul." Kaya raised her face and met his lips. She didn't deepen the kiss; she let him lead, soft, languid brushes of his mouth on hers, his tongue teasing her lips, tasting her. This wasn't the rushed desperation of three nights ago. This was care and love and trust.

This was everything she'd come to expect from Paul, and more.

"Let's go upstairs." She didn't pull away. Didn't want to.

"I need you." His breath brushed over her cheek, as gentle as his lips. "I need you so much. My Kaya."

She tangled her fingers in his hair, the curls soft beneath her fingers. He groaned deep in his throat, and she deepened the kiss. Fire licked through her veins, sparking within her. Kaya refused to pull back, refused to let him go.

"Come with me." She kissed him again, held him close. "Paul, come with me."

"Anywhere." His hands hooked beneath her arse, and he easily lifted her, pushed her against the wall and kissed her. "Everywhere. I'll follow you everywhere."

Kaya's gown tangled in her legs, and she scrambled for purchase. She wrapped her arms around his neck and dug her fingers into his shoulders and back. She trusted him with everything in her, and she knew he'd not let her fall.

"Make love to me." Kaya nipped his lower lip. "Now. I need to feel you inside me."

"Your wish is my command."

Paul didn't carry her up the stairs. He took her hand, and despite the darkness, never looked from her. Together they walked up the stairs, and he led her to their room, where he closed and locked the door.

"It's cold in here." He drew her close again, unwrapping her hijab, his fingers combing through her hair to loosen the braids. Her pins fell to the floor, faint dings in the quiet darkness. "Do you want me to light the fire?"

"No." Even in her head it sounded overly poetic, but the truth was, she already burned for him. "I don't want to let you go, Paul."

His hands were quick on the ties of her gown, spreading it open to his touch, his mouth. Paul kissed along her shoulders and the tops of her breasts, lifting their weight in his hands and teasing her already hard nipples.

Kaya arched into his touch, shrugging out of the dress and cursing the many layers of material in her way. She gasped when his teeth tugged one nipple and then the other, and she shuddered beneath his touch when his thumbs brushed over the moist, hard peaks.

"Untie your trousers." Kaya pushed off his jacket and vest. "I want to feel you. I need to touch you."

He did as she commanded, silent as she ran her hands down

his back and over his hips. His hips jerked at her touch, but Paul only watched her.

The room was too dark to see clearly. Light didn't matter—she felt his gaze. It wrapped around her heart and settled in her soul.

"Come back to me, Paul." Kaya pushed him onto the bed and straddled his hips. Her fingers wrapped around his cock, and she stroked him gently, grazing her fingers along the sensitive underside, around the tip of him. "Please come back to me."

"Kaya." He twitched in her hand, hips arching up in short jerks. "You're the only thing worth fighting for." He held her hips as she guided his cock into her.

Kaya rolled her hips as he slid in, rocking gently against him until he was deep inside her. Nails digging into his chest, she leaned over him and kissed him hard. His words seared through her, sharp and so very real.

"We." She sat up and lifted her hips off him, then slowly slid back down. "*We* are worth fighting for. *Ya rouhi.*"

He didn't answer. It'd been four short months—was that enough time to believe in something? Kaya thought so. Believed it with everything in her.

"Come for me, Kaya." His thumb pressed against her clit, moving in short, hard circles. "Scream for me, my Kaya."

She moved faster, straining for her orgasm. Pleasure shot through her in short bursts, and she reached for more, that glorious ending. The gratification Paul made her feel, the tingling sensation of pleasure.

"That's it, sweetheart. Let go. Come for me."

Kaya did. Her orgasm shot through her, curling her fingers and toes and enveloping her in a cocoon of sensuality and desire. Paul rolled them, hovered over her for a long minute as she gathered her wits. He pushed her legs up higher on his waist and moved, pounding into her in long, uneven strokes.

He was close, she knew from the uneven thrusts, the change in his breathing. Kaya pressed her hand to the small of his back.

Closer, she wanted him closer. She slipped a hand between them and stroked her clit, another orgasm already tightening her belly.

"I'm here, Paul." She wrapped her other hand around the nape of his neck, scraped her nails down his back. Another orgasm burst through her, and she cried out, a wordless sound of contentment.

She tightened her thighs around his waist, her heels digging into his thighs, and held tight. Afraid to let him go. Afraid he'd never return to her if she did. Head thrown back, muscles straining, he pulled out as he came.

"Kaya." Breathing heavily, he rolled to the side.

She tried to speak, but love, fear, and worry closed her throat. Kaya blinked back tears and pressed her lips hard to his chest, his shoulder.

Paul stood, reaching for his handkerchief to clean them both.

"I'm not letting you go," Kaya vowed. "Do you hear me? Not in any way. Never."

He didn't meet her gaze as he gently cleaned her. He worked in silence, and she watched his shadow move above her, his fingers warm on her skin.

"You should. You deserve better. You should've left me in Sicily when you planned to." His voice broke, and when Kaya reached for him he flinched. She ignored it and rested her hand on his shoulder. "What Appleby is doing—it's nothing I wouldn't have been a part of before."

"Maybe," Kaya allowed, her voice thick. Her fingers curled into his skin, as if to anchor him to her. "Maybe not. That was before. You're not that person anymore."

"No?" Paul shook his head and sat on the edge of the bed. Her hand slipped from his shoulder and fell, useless, to her lap. Even in the darkness, she saw his shoulders sag. "Feels like it. It was so easy to slip back into that man. The drinking, the gambling, the scheming."

Kaya wanted to ask. Badly. The words waited to burst free, to demand to know if he thought of whoring around, too. But she didn't. Part of her knew that wasn't the case. Not when he still looked at her so intensely, as if he clung to her as fiercely as she to him.

As if he'd read her mind, Paul said out loud, "I didn't." He shifted on the bed, laid a hand on her calf. "I never would. Not when I have you."

"Does that mean you'll never leave me?"

"I can't." Paul snorted, his fingers tensing on her leg. "I'm not strong enough."

Twenty-Three

Paul didn't sleep that night. He didn't think Kaya did, either. Wrapped around each other beneath their blankets, the brazier finally warming the room, he held her throughout the night. He didn't know what else to do. What to say.

Toward dawn, he rose to add more wood to the fire. The sun hadn't yet penetrated the mountains, but Paul heard the faint stirrings of the village below. Kaya moved, and he felt her gaze land on him, but neither spoke.

The fire sparked to life, and Paul stared at it, thoughts circling from Appleby to Kaya, from the smugglers to last night.

"Don't leave."

Paul returned to bed. He gathered Kaya in his arms, nuzzling her neck with his cold nose. Her hand cupped the back of his head and pressed him close. He thought he felt her smile—normally they'd laugh, and she'd push him away only for him to grab her again. They'd have fun, enjoying themselves with silly games.

Maybe her smile was more wishful thinking than anything. Paul hoped not.

"Not yet."

Paul kissed the underside of her jaw, shifting them until they lay back in bed, the scratchy wool blankets covering them. He rested his head on her belly before drawing back and propping his head on his hand. Unable to *not* touch her, however, Paul traced random patterns on her skin, over her ribs, under her breasts, circling her nipples, hard beneath her thin chemise.

"We're meeting the smugglers today. Unless the snow delayed them, they should arrive just after sunset." Kaya's hands tightened around him, one pressing into his wrist, the other catching his roaming fingers. "I'll draw a map to the mountain cave before I leave. Maybe Marta knows how to get there. Or one of the shepherds."

"I'll find it," she promised. "I'll follow your very clever stocking trail."

He almost smiled at that, but it refused to form. "Don't go alone." He held her tighter. "Don't argue with me, Kaya. I know you can handle yourself, but I'd rather you take someone else with you."

She wanted to protest, he could see it. Pride over practicality. Her fighting skills versus the very real threat lurking in those mountains. Eventually, practicality won out, and she nodded. It did nothing to loosen the chains tightening around his chest. His fear for her a pulsing, suffocating thing.

"I should be with you." She cleared her throat and exhaled slowly. "I don't trust Appleby."

Paul snorted. "No."

"No to trusting Appleby? Or no to meeting the smugglers with you?"

"Either." Paul stretched up, trapping her between his arms. He easily settled between her hips as Kaya opened to him. "Both. I don't want you anywhere near those men. Major Rogerson, he was a madman. Whoever these men are he hired, they're just as dangerous."

"I can take care of myself, Paul." Her reminder was gentle,

serious. Kaya's hands slid down his spine, over his arse. "You don't have to worry about me."

"Kaya." Even in the darkness, he couldn't meet her gaze. Kissing down her neck, he bared his soul, every word true. "I always worry about you." Paul pressed his lips over her heart. "You're the only thing I care about, the only thing worth worrying over. You are worth everything. Even dying for."

Her fingers combed through his hair. "And living? Am I worth living for?" Her voice caught, but she hastily cleared it. "Are we?"

Paul kissed her. She was, of course she was—were they? He deepened the kiss. Her hips rose to meet his, and Paul rocked gently against her. When he pulled back, Kaya whimpered, her short nails digging into his arse.

He eased into her, her body welcoming him, and Paul shuddered in her embrace. That same desperation that had beat through him from the first moment they set foot in Casa Grigori still gripped him. He forced it away, to the black pit of his soul that once more threatened to overwhelm him.

Instead, he kissed her softly, moved slowly within her, kissed her breasts, teased her nipples, circled her clit until she sobbed in his embrace.

"Paul." She gasped, panted, her body wound tight around him, eager for release. "Paul."

He couldn't speak, had no words to tell her how he felt for her, the sheer scope of love and affection and adoration. Paul pressed hard to her clit and watched her shatter beneath him, coming hard against his hand. He continued to move, thrusting faster, harder, even as he built her back up.

Kaya arched into him with a wordless cry.

Thrusting harder, Paul watched his wife, his beautiful Kaya. Seated deep within her, he felt a peace he hadn't ever felt before. "I love you, Kaya."

"I feel like we should have a strategy." Kaya tried to keep her voice low, but the words crackled in the quiet morning.

"We have one." Paul rubbed his hand over his face and stretched.

Though tiredness tugged at her, a strange buzzing pushed her forward. As exhausted as worry and sleepless nights made her, the thought of finishing this energized her.

"What we have is no strategy."

He ran his fingers down her arm, up again. A constant touch, a steady connection. Kaya hadn't realized how desperately she needed his touch until the last few nights without.

"Perhaps not the sort Tahir taught you, no. We do, however, have a...plan."

She snorted. "Is that what you call this? A plan?"

"What sort of strategy are you thinking?" he eventually asked. "Other than me going with Appleby to meet the smugglers while you and Marta free the missing villagers."

She sighed. "Yes, that's *a* plan. But I was hoping for a little more. Marta is in no position to fight, and I do not believe we can trust the rest of the villagers." She paused and corrected herself. "I do not believe they trust us enough to be trusted."

Paul let out a laugh but didn't move. His chest rose and fell evenly, his breathing steady. Kaya turned her head just enough to press her lips to his throat. His heart beat beneath her lips, a tangible reminder of all she'd gained these last months.

All she stood to lose if today didn't go as they hoped.

"I don't know what you want me to say." His hand tightened on her arm, and his chest heaved with his sharp exhale. "Appleby trusts me enough to have told me everything in the few days since we've been reunited."

Kaya grimaced at his use of "reunited" no matter how his own voice twisted it. She refrained from commenting, however—she didn't know what it felt like to have the very past you were running from suddenly rear up and snap at you like a crocodile lying in wait. But then, she supposed no one could run from their past forever.

"Did I tell you I think he met your wolf?"

Kaya leaned up. Though she couldn't see him, she leaned onto one elbow and shook her hair over her shoulder. "What makes you say that?"

"He said he met a wolf, a large black thing. Also said he hurt it, and you said the dog was injured, yes?"

She slowly nodded. "Yes. Her side. She won't let me see it, but it's crusted with blood."

In the darkness, Paul made a face she couldn't adequately see and shook his head. "I don't know how; we're not in the same area you said the wolf was. But I think it's the same one."

"How extraordinary." Kaya breathed out in wonder. "I can't believe how connected things are in this village. First we meet Appleby"—Paul growled—"then you learn he was the one who injured Vita."

"I hate coincidences."

"You think that's all this is? That all these occurrences are mere coincidences?" Kaya snorted. "The hand of God or fate or something else at work?"

"What else could they be?" Paul sounded tired, drained.

"I don't know," she admitted. Kaya rested her head on Paul's chest and closed her eyes. "But I think we're here for a purpose. A reason."

Perhaps to stop running, though she understood his reasons for that all too well. Perhaps to challenge them. They'd shared a beautiful four months together, but how much of that was based on a story Paul had told himself? How much of it was Kaya wanting to start fresh and not look back?

"To stop Appleby." His voice, though quiet, rang thick in the room. Final. "To prove—"

He didn't finish, but Kaya didn't need him to. Yes, he wished to prove to both himself and to her that he was a changed man.

"You think you've changed," she whispered into the darkness.

"That you had to. But I think you forget the man you used to be, the one who drink and opium clouded. I think that man has always been beneath everything you dislike about yourself."

She stopped, positive she'd muddled her words. She had no experience with this sort of thing. With placating or encouragement, or—Kaya sighed. She had no idea. But she knew Paul.

"You tell me you aren't a good man, but I've yet to see that side you insist lies in wait, lurking in the shadows." She took his hand and kissed his fingers, then held them over her heart. "Everyone has done things they wish they hadn't, I'm sure. Actions they wish to change. However, the man in bed with me now, the one who promised to show me everything in this world, has only shown me what a good man he is."

"You're wrong," he whispered.

Kaya let those words sit between them for a moment then shook her head. "No, I don't believe I am. If you weren't a good man, you wouldn't have instantly defended that woman in the desert. You didn't bother to ask those men what they were doing. You attacked them."

"I—" He broke off, and she felt a stir of triumph. "I'm selfish and greedy, Kaya. I always took things for myself. Never cared about anyone else."

"If that were true, you wouldn't have left the East India Army after the massacre. If you didn't care, you wouldn't mourn Basu. Wouldn't regret your actions. And even here." She turned to look at him, though she felt time ticking down inexorably. It wouldn't be long before they needed to leave. Before she let him go, before they did what she knew they both must, she had to tell him.

"You're doing what needs to be done. You knew what you had to do, who you had to become."

"It was all too easy to fall back into that life," he whispered.

"Was it?" She shook her head. "I don't believe that. Because you regret it. You regret having to be that man. You do not revel in it; you fight it. But you do what needs to be done because you care."

He tightened his arms around her, burying his face in her shoulder. He didn't speak, but Kaya took that as a positive sign. If he wasn't fighting her words, he was listening to them. Right now, that was all she asked.

They'd make it through this. They would. She refused to give up on him, no matter how he tried to give up on himself. But that was talk for after—after rescuing the villagers, after stopping Appleby and Rogerson.

After, they could pick up the pieces and move on from this place and rediscover who they each truly were.

They lay in the darkness until the faint sounds of the awakening village stirred below. In silence they dressed, a touch of the hand here, the slightest caress there. Enough to remind each other, she hoped, of their connection. Of all they'd experienced these last months and all they promised for the future.

The skies were a heavy gray. Snow was swirling in the whipping wind, and the rich aroma of coffee was thick in the air. Kaya watched Paul leave with Appleby. She didn't hold him, didn't even kiss him goodbye in front of the small crowd, not because she was worried what these people thought of her obvious affection for Paul, but because she was afraid she might not let him leave without her.

Paul needed her to watch his back; they made a good pair in a fight.

Still, there were many unknowns. What did one call a walk to meet known smugglers? Kaya doubted there was a strong enough word to encompass the sheer scope of absurdity in this quasi plan.

What was done was done. Paul and Appleby walked out of the inn, Appleby ignoring her as always, Paul sending her one final glance before closing the door behind him. She didn't want him to leave, but of course none of them had any choice. There were smugglers to stop, villagers to find, Appleby to—what?

What were they to do with Appleby once all this ended?

Kaya sat down hard in one of the chairs. The spindles of its back dug into her spine, but she hardly noticed. Honestly, she hadn't thought about what to do with Appleby until now. Did one turn such a man over to the authorities? As far as she could see, no authoritative figure existed in Casa Grigori.

Even if they did, Appleby knew Paul's real name, and their papers clearly said Conrad instead of Hartley. Plus, there was no guarantee he wouldn't try and implicate Paul in his scheme. Marta knew the truth, but did her word—a woman's word, a woman who might also look complicit to an outside view—matter in a Calabrian court?

Kaya pressed her fingers to her eyes, but it didn't settle her thoughts. Dropping her head into her hands, she let the quiet of the inn wash over her.

Paul needed enough time to get Appleby to the eastern trailhead to meet Rogerson before she left to follow his stocking trail to the caves. Which meant she had precious little time to decide whether to trust Marta with this information.

"Breakfast?" Marta asked softly from the long counter.

Kaya looked up and smiled, standing as she did so. "Thank you, please."

The mere thought of food unsettled her stomach, but she accepted the fruit and croissant anyway. Chewing slowly, her mind raced. There had to be a subtler way to say this, but time was running out.

"The smugglers arrive tonight."

Marta closed her eyes and nodded. "Yes, I know."

"I need your help. Are there any in the village who you trust?" Kaya stumbled awkwardly over the conversation, hoping for help, positive it would not be offered.

"What do you mean?" Marta, pale and defeated, shook her head. "You want to attack the smugglers?" She laughed, a bitter, harsh sound. "No, we cannot. They have our families."

"Yes." Kaya swallowed a sip of coffee, but the rich brew tasted like ash. She pushed her meal aside. "Do you trust anyone to help?"

"To fight?" Marta shrugged, looking smaller than she was, as if she caved in on herself at the very idea of fighting. "No, the men they—it's hard to explain to an outsider. There is very little law here. In all of Calabria. The men will attack in groups, there and gone to steal from the rich landowners or wealthy travelers. No one says anything, nothing is done about it. These smugglers?" Again Marta shrugged. "There is no law to see justice done."

Kaya understood, but she had a feeling there was more to it than Marta said. She wondered how long Paul had been gone. Whether it was long enough or not, she needed to move.

She was careful about her next words. "If no one will take Appleby to the authorities," she said slowly, moving to catch Marta's eyes, "then I may have a solution."

"A solution?" Marta frowned but her voice sounded stronger.

"You are certain you cannot trust anyone in the village?" Kaya didn't necessarily want to forge up the pass alone to fight three to five armed guards in a cave, but if she needed to, then she needed to.

"I think they want to take over the operation," Marta admitted. She shifted and grimaced. "They see how much money Signore Appleby has and want it for themselves."

"All right." Kaya nodded. A burn of anger swept through her, but she had no time for the petty village politics of opium smuggling. "We're going to stop him today. Paul is with Appleby now, meeting Rogerson."

Marta only nodded, but she looked around as if someone might overhear. Though Kaya saw no one in the inn, and they spoke softly across the counter, she lowered her voice.

"I'm going to free the villagers Appleby has taken." Kaya paused at Marta's wide eyes. "I'd like help, but if you have none you trust, I shall go myself."

"I'll go with you." Marta stood straighter, her chin tilted in defiance. "They have taken too much from me already."

"What of any others?"

Hesitating, Marta nodded. "I'll let Mama know. Perhaps she can convince them to come after us."

"Here." Kaya took out a hastily drawn map Paul had made this morning and handed it to Marta. "Give Caroline this. It shows the rough area where he found them." Kaya stepped from the counter. "We must move quickly. Have you a weapon?"

Marta's gaze flicked to the khanjar Kaya wore, then back to the kitchens. "I'll take one of the knives."

She didn't ask if Marta knew how to use it. She clearly wielded it with great precision when cooking. That had to be good enough for what Kaya planned. She almost smiled. "Plan" was still too strong word, but it was all she had.

If Marta, whose family had lived in this village for who knew how many generations, trusted no one here, then Kaya certainly could not. Within moments, Marta returned, bundled against the snow, a large butcher knife held securely in hand.

In the deserted courtyard, they turned east, and Kaya offered a quick prayer that they all survived this day.

Twenty-Four

In a greatcoat borrowed from Marta's dead husband, one that had ripped beneath the arms when he'd shrugged it on, Paul once more found himself standing at the smuggler's pass. He wondered if that was its name, or if decades from now local legends would call it that.

He hoped not. He hoped that what happened here today would be forgotten. That no one would remember all that these villagers experienced these last months.

He drank another mouthful of wine and let the liquid burst through his veins.

"Are you sure you don't want to stay in the caves now?" Paul looked to where Appleby walked ahead of him, a bottle of wine in each hand. He wanted to stop, wanted to shove his own bottle into Appleby's hands and not taste another drop.

His fingers curled tightly around the neck, fighting to keep the wine even as he fought himself to let it go.

Paul rubbed his gloved fingers over his face and grimaced at the scent of wet wool. At least the gloves kept his fingers warm against the gusting winds and swirling snow. He rolled his shoulders and heard a faint rip; stilling, Paul sighed.

This was not at all how he'd envisioned their walk through the Aspromonte Mountains.

In the desert they battled the sun and heat, slavers and each other. In Damietta, they fought off potential slavers, and they stopped their own fighting. Well, they didn't argue as much. Now, away from all that and finally happy, was it too much to ask that they had an easy walk through beautiful mountains?

No smugglers, no old friends looking to turn a quick coin and drag him back into that pit he hated in Bombay.

Apparently, it was too much. His good luck with Kaya had run out, and now he stood exposed and vulnerable. All his secrets, the deceitful things he'd done in the past, lay spread out before him like the snow they trudged through. He wanted to tell her—eventually. Later. In his own time, at his own pace, with no specter looming over him. When it didn't matter, when his past wasn't staring him in the face.

When who he had been wasn't a threat to Kaya.

"No, no, not yet. We can't visit the caves yet." Appleby looked evasive, his head twisting this way and that, his eyes darting over the land as if he expected the windy snow to conjure up a ghost. "We'll wait for Rogerson here. He knows where I normally meet them."

"Harry." Paul forced Appleby to look directly at him. "What's wrong?"

"Nothing." Appleby vehemently shook his head. His gaze slid from Paul's, once more roaming the area. "It's bloody cold here, and I told you about meeting a wolf." He drank his wine but didn't stop looking around. "Don't want to meet another one."

Paul didn't believe he would, given what Kaya had told him: that the she-wolf was actually a dog, and she stayed in the caves to the north of the village. What had Appleby been doing there? Wandering? Hallucinating? The drink could do that to a man.

Christ, this was a mess.

"I don't see any tracks." Paul swallowed a mouthful of wine. "We should be safe."

"Safe. Aye. Safe." Appleby shuddered, and Paul didn't think it was from the cold.

Appleby couldn't be that scared of Vita, could he? Paul hadn't met a wolf before, or even a wild dog, so he couldn't say, but this seemed extreme. He lifted the bottle to his lips and paused.

Angling his head, he listened over the howl of the wind.

Voices.

Paul lowered the bottle and turned to face the path. Appleby stumbled beside him, but Paul doubted he had heard anything. Appleby continued to mutter beneath his breath and look around, as if he expected a wolf attack.

Rogerson and his men, then. They were early. Paul looked to the sky, but the heavy clouds hid the sun. The snow obscured everything. How long since they'd left the village? Long enough for Kaya to have followed his trail and found the caves?

He hoped so. This whole plan—and yes, all right, "plan" *was* too strong a word, he'd give her that—hinged on strict timing. The only luck Paul could see was the snow. It would make slow going for the carts, thereby delaying Rogerson.

"Harry," Paul hissed.

Over the wailing wind, Appleby didn't hear him. Paul stalked the few steps between them and grabbed the other man's arm. Jerking him around to face the path, he ignored Appleby's yelp and the fallen wine.

It stained the snow red, spreading on the ground as vividly as it had on the dirt road in Bombay.

"Damn snow." Paul heard the words carried on the wind. "This might be our last shipment until spring."

Appleby straightened, choking and spluttering. Paul ignored him. Alert, fingers tingling despite the cold, he shifted his stance. He carried two knives: one strapped to his thigh beneath the greatcoat, and one at his hip. Though he wanted to, he reached for neither.

The cart, pulled by a single donkey, breached the hill and came into view.

Three men walked beside the cart as it made its slow way up the snow-covered path. The donkey looked less than impressed with the men, the weather, and its payload. However, the men, despite their heavy coats, looked armed and ready for a fight.

The moment they realized Paul and Appleby were standing there, two of them pulled their knives, and the third aimed a musket. The back of Paul's neck itched, and his entire body tensed, but he did not move. It took everything in him, but he kept perfectly still.

They were too close to the mountain wall to dive for cover should the third man fire. There wasn't enough room for a knife fight. He could use the mountain walls, he supposed, but he didn't want to chance it with an unpredictable Appleby.

Four against one. In short, Paul did not like his odds.

"Harry."

Bloody hell.

Major Richard Rogerson stepped from behind the cart.

So it was five against one.

His greatcoat billowing in the wind, Rogerson pushed his hat back just enough to look them both over. Paul dropped his hand to his thigh. One second to move the coat, another one to unsheathe the knife. Two seconds to grab it. The wind was too strong to chance throwing it at Rogerson—Appleby first? Or one of the guards?

He was too far away; a dozen or more steps separated them.

No, he still didn't like his odds.

"And Paul Hartley." The way Rogerson said his name made Paul want to attack, odds be damned. "Well, Sergeant, I didn't expect you here. I thought you died on that street in Bombay."

"Sorry I survived." His voice sounded far smoother, far easier than he'd expected. His heart pounded, and the wind roared in his ears, but he remained perfectly still. Waiting. Watching.

Rogerson merely grinned, a slow, snakelike movement of his lips.

"Moved on, you know."

"Married some chit in Egypt," Harry said in the groveling voice Paul had expected.

"Did you now?" Rogerson asked, all joviality and kindness.

Paul's stomach turned. Forcing a shrug, he lifted the bottle of wine to his lips and pretended to drink. The few drops that touched his tongue seduced him, but, despite the clenching in his gut, Paul did not swallow.

"Had to," Paul said easily. "She's just inherited a fortune in England."

"Good on you." Rogerson's shoulders relaxed, and Paul knew he'd accepted the lie as the reason for his presence here in the Calabrian mountains. "Stand down," he told the guards in Marathi. The third man raised his musket back over his shoulder, and, while the other two didn't sheathe their knives, they did lower their arms.

"It's been a rough journey over these damnable mountains," Rogerson said, as if Paul had been part of the plan all along. "We need all the help with can get with this damn stubborn donkey."

"We should shoot the thing," one of the guards muttered and scowled at the animal.

The donkey bared his teeth and brayed back, causing the man to stumble out of the way. Paul suppressed a grin. He liked that donkey.

"Let's move." Rogerson ignored the donkey and the man and took up position behind the cart once more. "I want to get over these mountains while we still can. We have product to deliver and money to collect."

He was going to kill Harry Appleby for putting Kaya in danger. But first, Rogerson.

"Your husband, he left this trail?" Marta asked as she and Kaya trudged up the mountainside in the winter storm.

"You sound as if you don't believe it." Kaya kept her voice low so it wouldn't carry on the wind.

She didn't know who else might be in these mountains during a snowstorm, who else was foolish enough to venture outdoors. However, considering they were looking for a cave full of villagers and a caravan of who knew how many guards was heading their way, the mountains seemed busier than the port at Damietta.

"I am—I don't know," Marta admitted. "I had thought he and Signore Harry were friends. The same sort of man."

Breathing heavy, Kaya only shook her head. "I told you, Marta. They are nothing alike. But Paul needed to discover what Appleby was up to here."

"You said." Marta huffed.

Kaya wanted to stop and let Marta rest, but they couldn't chance losing time. Still, she paused on a slight level and leaned against the tree. Mountain climbing in snow was far more exhausting than walking the desert at night.

"We can rest," she offered. "But only for a few moments."

"I am usually more accustomed to climbing," Marta said. She grimaced but straightened and looked straight at Kaya. "The babe makes me uncomfortable."

Babe? Kaya blinked and ran through the words again. "You're with child?"

Marta flushed, more than the exertion allowed for, and looked down. "Aye."

Certainty settled over Kaya. It was Appleby's. She met Marta's gaze, as uncertain how to feel about that as Marta seemed.

"Does he know?"

She snorted and stalked forward. "No. No one does, but I can't hide it for long."

That much was true. Kaya followed after her. "What do you plan to do?"

Marta looked slyly over her shoulder but shrugged. She didn't seem the devious sort, and the uncomfortable movement of her shoulders and faltering words only confirmed that. "Perhaps I leave with you. I can't stay here." She sighed and stopped again, tears in her eyes. "I can't even find the words to tell Olivia."

"We'll figure something out," Kaya promised.

She had absolutely no idea what that might mean, or even how she could make promises, given what they were attempting to do. But leaving Marta here? In a village that would most definitely shun her? No. She refused to even think about leaving a woman she considered a friend in such a dilemma.

Searching for a distraction, Kaya looked around for the next bit of stocking Paul had left. Spotting it just ahead, she took Marta's arm. As unaccustomed as she was to physical touch, other than Paul's, of course, she hoped it comforted Marta.

"Let's finish this," Kaya whispered, her chest tight with cold and exertion. "Then we can plan the next move."

She really ought to stop using the word "plan" when the only plan she had was to stay alive.

They walked in silence, but Kaya thought Marta's mood seemed lighter. More hopeful, at the very least. Tucking the ends of her hijab beneath her cloak, she wished for something warmer than the linen, which was doing little to stop the cold and wet from seeping down her neck.

She hesitated to ask about Caroline and whether Marta believed her mother would gather the rest of the village and follow them as they'd discussed before they left the inn. Whether they did or not didn't matter—there was no method to communicate with them. She and Marta would have to use what they had, which was only the two of them.

Kaya was utterly certain this was not what Tahir meant when he'd instructed her on strategy.

She didn't know how to tell when they were at the right cave —the mountains were littered with caves, much like the mountains they'd walked through in Egypt. Unsheathing her khanjar, Kaya slowed and hoped the wind would dampen their approach.

She'd memorized Paul's map before giving it to Marta, but he hadn't accounted for snow. Any additional landmark he might've drawn was now obscured.

Then, a piece of stocking fluttered around a branch, a wild, dancing thing caught helplessly in the wind.

Turning to Marta, she held a finger to her lips and motioned for her to draw near.

"We must be close." The storm made it difficult to hear. "We'll start with the first cave, but I believe they're deeper in the mountains. Paul said they were sheltered behind an outcropping."

There wasn't one visible, but that didn't mean they wouldn't stumble upon it accidently and give away their position. It was tedious work, sneaking up on each opening, tense and prepared to fight, only to have it yawn empty and dark before them.

Her shoulders knotted, and her arms ached with waiting, waiting. Kaya looked to Marta, who seemed tired and drained and not at all ready for what lie ahead. Kaya should not have brought her. Granted, she hadn't known about the babe before they set off, but still. She should not have brought Marta.

Marta caught her gaze and must have realized Kaya's thoughts. She straightened and gripped her butcher's knife more tightly despite her heavy gloves.

"I won't let them harm us any longer," she whispered just as they rounded a slight bend in the mountains. "Don't worry about me, Kaya."

Kaya snorted. She worried about everyone today. Paul and his mad scheme who knew how far across the mountains. Marta, who clearly had never held a knife in anger but now walked beside her as they marched into their own battle. Olivia and Vita and the cub, Caroline, and even the villagers of Casa Grigori.

The outcropping loomed large before them. Kaya stopped and studied it, but Paul's hasty drawing made no mention of landmarks—not that she could see any in the swirling snow. Next time she rescued villagers from opium smugglers, she'd do so on a bright summer's day.

Tugging off her gloves, Kaya flexed her fingers and balanced her khanjar. This might not be the outcropping Paul meant. The mountains jutted out in strange places, then suddenly fell away to the valley below. They'd been searching the caves for at least an hour. Maybe more. Time ran differently in the storm.

But she hadn't seen any more pieces of woolen stocking, and her stomach tensed in readiness.

Motioning for Marta to stay back, she crept to the outcropping and leaned around it cautiously. The thick slab of rock made sneaking difficult; she couldn't peer around it without fully exposing herself. Plus, the snow was piled higher here, as if the rocky outcropping stopped it from spreading out.

She didn't need to see into the cave to know they'd found the right one. Lamplight spilled from the entrance, as if the occupants weren't worried about the storm. Behind the rocky slab, it probably didn't affect them, though the cold no doubt did.

She smelled no fire, nor did she feel the heat from one at the entrance.

Marta's hand fell to her shoulder, and Kaya jumped. She jerked her head around and met the other woman's wide gaze. Nodding, she stepped back and leaned against the rock.

She had never been so cold in her life. Her fingers were stiff, and, though she was warm beneath her dress and cloak, the wind battered her face. And she was so tired. Even walking from Cairo to Damietta had not drained her as trudging through the snow up a mountainside had. She needed a moment but was afraid to take any time for herself. So much depended on accuracy.

"No guard at the entrance. They either believe the wagon will arrive later or are lazy and don't want to step foot in the snow." Kaya took off her gloves and rubbed her bare fingers together. The gloves made using her dagger difficult. She'd have to do without for now. "Not that I blame them."

Marta forced a smile and nodded. "What do you want me to do?"

Kaya wanted Marta to return to the village and see if Caroline had managed to rouse the villagers. But that would take far too long, and Marta was her best hope for backup.

"We have the element of surprise," she whispered against Marta's ear. Though she could hear nothing over the storm, she didn't want any sound to carry. "I'll take the lead, draw the guards away, and you make sure your people get out safe."

Kaya closed her eyes and tried to envision what the cave held inside. Had Paul said anything about warm clothing? They'd been taken months ago, and Appleby didn't seem the sort to care about his prisoners' comfort.

"They'll be cold, no doubt. Hungry and weak." Kaya met Marta's gaze. "There's no choice but to make sure they get to the village as quickly as possible."

"We should wait until the storm stops," Marta protested, but it was a weak assertation, and she was already shaking her head in defiance of her own words. "They could become snow blind or wander off. And if they're not properly clothed..."

"I agree, but I don't see an option." Kaya sighed. "If Caroline can't gather anyone to come up the mountain, we're alone with dozens of people who need food and shelter."

Marta looked down for a brief moment then out into the snow. "And if Mama has mustered them, they're at least an hour behind us." She looked over her shoulder. "In this storm, our tracks will be hard to follow. And forgive me." Her lips twisted into a semblance of a smile. "Your husband's map was not the best drawing."

A huff of laughter escaped Kaya. "No, it was not." She sobered and looked to the path they'd forged through the snow. "Hopefully things happen quicker than I imagine they will, but we honestly have no time."

"No, it might be days before the storm stops, and we don't

know what food they have in the cave. We could walk back to the village and up again, but that is a strain."

"This is it, then, Marta." Kaya used her ungloved hands to push off the mountain. "Are you ready?"

"Yes. I am."

Twenty-Five

Paul trudged behind the second wagon, pushing it up a nonexistent path in snow that grew deeper with every passing moment.

This wasn't how he'd envisioned spending his time in Italy. He'd pictured staying close to the coast and the heat of the Tyrrhenian Sea, making love in the warm evenings, enjoying fish on the coast, and never once thinking about his past.

Fate had other ideas.

His bottle long empty, he did his best to ignore the clawing need for more.

The physical exertion through the snow did little to help that need.

What he needed to do was concentrate. He needed to keep his wits about him and not veer from the plan. He snorted, breathing heavily. Kaya was right—plan was too strong a word for this reckless endeavor.

There were five men he needed to deal with: Rogerson and Appleby, and the three nameless guards. The first two men walked ahead, talking together and sharing a bottle of wine.

He'd have to pick them off one at a time.

Luckily, he had just the plan. The donkey, who was by far the smartest of them all, could barely move the carts in the snow. It was a simple matter to stop pushing and call for help. He'd apologize to the donkey later.

Standing upright, Paul called for the guard ahead of him. The wind slapped him in the face and shivered down his neck. "Christ, I hate the snow."

"Stuck?" the guard asked in Marathi. "Snow, it makes everything harder. Like the rains in Bombay."

"Why make this trip, then?" Paul asked, leaning against the wagon. He needed to catch his breath and stall for time. "Is this the last of the season?"

"Aye. Major, he wants another." The man jerked his head toward Rogerson. "But we can't walk over these mountains in the snow."

"Nothing can," Paul agreed. "Come, let's rest against the trees, out of the wind." He stretched and draped an arm over the man's shoulders. "I'm not used to walking in this kind of weather."

The guard, agreeable enough and no doubt as frozen as Paul, laughed. Only a few steps into the tree line, Paul broke the man's neck. It was fast and clean and, more importantly, silent. He couldn't afford anyone to notice, not until the odds were more in his favor.

Four against one now.

He resumed his position against the wagon and pushed hard, startling both himself and the donkey when the wheels lurched ahead. Muttering apologies to the donkey, he planned his next move. Maybe he should've listened to Basu when his friend had tried to teach him chaturanga. But then, he'd always preferred backgammon or...that card game. What was it called?

Damn, he'd loved that game, and now he couldn't even remember it. He'd been superior at it, too.

Struggling for breath, arms aching, legs tired, heart pounding with every push of the cart, Paul vowed to spend the next month as far from the mountains and snow as they could. But first things first. He needed to even the odds.

Calling to the next guard, he asked in Marathi, "What's the name of that card game?"

"Which one?" The man asked as he rounded the wagon.

Paul looked over his shoulder, but no one had bothered to glance in their direction. Too busy trying to stay upright in the wind.

"Ganjifa." Paul looked at the guard and smiled. "Just remembered."

"We should play," he offered. "When we get to the cave. I have cards."

"I'd like that," Paul lied. "Come. Let's rest."

Paul led the laughing man into the woods. Then he waited until a strong gust of wind blew past them, and he neatly broke this man's neck as well. Once he'd returned to the wagon, he looked to the right and saw the guard's lifeless feet sticking out of the snow.

No help for it now, and he refused to feel any remorse over an opium peddler. No, the animals could feast on him.

That left the man with the musket, who was now pulling the stubborn donkey up the snowy trail, and Rogerson and Appleby. He'd leave Appleby for last. He was no match for Paul, who would need all his strength to take on both musket man and Rogerson.

Paul looked ahead but couldn't tell if they approached the cave or not. He'd been there only the once, and certainly not in a snowstorm, so he had no way of recognizing it. He couldn't risk getting there before Kaya. Pushing this cart in the snow had sapped his strength, and he'd no desire to take on even more guards.

Please let Kaya have already cleared out the villagers. Please don't let her be there when we arrive. Paul leaned his head against the cold wood of the wagon. *Most importantly, please let her forgive me for all I've done this last week.*

A week? Didn't seem long enough for the depth he'd fallen.

Kaya took a moment to close her eyes and pray for forgiveness. She had no sympathy for the men guarding the kidnapped villagers. No regrets for what she was about to do.

She still couldn't make out the number of men standing watch over those inside. She'd have to go on Paul's number—three—and hope there were no additional men. As confident as she was in her own abilities, she now had Marta to worry about.

Also, three to her one did not seem the type of odds Gidd would have favored.

"Are you ready, Marta?" Kaya opened her eyes and met the dark, terrified gaze of her friend.

"*Sì.*" Marta nodded, though she trembled—with nerves, with cold, with fear. All of those, Kaya understood.

"I'll go first. Draw them from your people. With luck, you can sneak in and rouse everyone. There's light enough to see by."

Kaya knew the guards had lit the cave not for the storm, but to keep the villagers working. It sickened her.

"And after?" Marta's voice shook. "What of after?"

Kaya swallowed hard. "One step at a time," she reminded her. "First, we need to incapacitate the guards."

By that, Kaya had an uneasy feeling she meant kill. She'd never killed another, had never seriously thought herself capable. Fighting to survive was far, far different than knowingly ambushing a cave full of men who would see each of them dead rather than stop their production.

"Let's move."

Kaya straightened from the mountain face, flexed her fingers, and strode confidently around the outcropping. Almost immediately the wind lessened, and the battering snow all but disappeared. As much as she loathed Appleby and Major Rogerson, as much as she wanted this night finished, she had to admit they'd chosen this cave wisely.

"Ciao!" she called jovially.

Her unexpected presence certainly had the desired effect. Two men whirled from where they played dice and gaped at her. Brandishing her khanjar, Kaya grinned.

Her eyes flicked around the room, but the lamplight only illuminated the front of the cave. Beyond the bouncing shadows, she saw figures huddled together, but she couldn't make out individual faces.

Or, for that matter, any additional guards.

Marta hurried past her, not slowing down as she stepped over the shadows and headed deeper into the cave.

Kaya stepped toward the guards. She'd had a vague idea of disarming them and tying them up, but now she knew that was impractical. She had no rope and little confidence that any of the tormented villagers would be able to help.

"Who are you?" one of the guards asked in English. "What are you doing here?"

She looked at him as if the cold and snow had caused him to lose his mind. "I'm here," she said in crisp, slow English, "to stop you. I'm going to take these people back to their village and make sure you never harm them again. And then I'm going to see to it that your opium smuggling is stopped. Forever."

That last bit might've been a boast she could not follow through with, but fury pounded through Kaya. She might not have known these men's names, but she hated them. Hated what they'd done to the innocents of this village. Hated that they even knew Harry Appleby.

Most of all, she hated that they cared so little for human life and so much for their own profit.

The second guard laughed. "Who's going to stop us?" He sneered. "You?"

"Yes."

Behind her, she felt movement. It wasn't Marta—the sense came from the wrong direction. No, Marta hadn't yet returned from the depths of the cave, and that was fine. It gave Kaya more room to fight.

"Signore, have you ever seen what an Egyptian khanjar can do to a man?"

Truthfully, she had not either. Gidd might not have taught her how to defend herself from opium smugglers, but he did teach her to help those who were weaker than she was.

"I suppose you believe your companion behind me has the surprise."

The man behind her moved, as if compelled by her mockery. Kaya stepped into the mouth of the cave, giving herself more room to attack. She lashed out with her dagger, slicing through the guard's thick coat. She moved again, lightning quick, and slashed his hand.

He screamed and held the bleeding appendage, sobbing and snarling at her as he fell back.

Smiling triumphantly at the other two men, she waited. It was so sudden, she didn't realize at first what, exactly, had happened: the other two guards pulled their daggers and advanced, Marta screamed, and a flying whirl of fur leaped into the cave.

Pandemonium gripped the cave. The previously immobile villagers suddenly scrambled, screaming as loud as the guards. The man she'd cut cowered on the floor as tables and chests went flying around the cave.

Vita, snarling and panting, stood in the middle of the room, commanding it like nothing Kaya had ever seen.

"What are *you* doing here?" she asked, too stunned for anything else.

A smaller shape entered, and Kaya tore her gaze from Vita to her cub, who was guarding the entrance like a true sentry.

Her mind raced. She tried to understand how Vita and her cub had found this cave, found them, when Kaya knew their own den was miles away. She spun toward the opening, already certain she'd find Olivia there.

The girl peeked around the rock face, crouching on the ground, as if hiding. When she met Kaya's gaze, she held up a hand in greeting.

"You followed us?" Kaya asked, incredulous.

"*Sì.*"

Kaya opened her mouth but snapped it closed just as Vita moved. The dog, hurt and angry, attacked one of the guards. The man had moved—foolishly—and clearly Vita did not appreciate it. Kaya looked to where the cub stood in the entrance, then to the third guard.

"I would not move if I were you."

He spat at her but otherwise didn't so much as breathe.

But Vita didn't seem to care and turned on him next. Kaya put her back to them, completely out of her depth on what to say to stop an angry, injured dog and her half-wolf cub. The three men scurried back, scrambling along the floor, away from the snarling dog, as fast as they could. Finally, corralled into a corner and terrified, Vita stood guard over them.

"Marta?" She called into the back of the cave, over the sounds of men whimpering and dogs snarling.

But she didn't move further into the cave, keeping close to the entrance. The caravan would be arriving soon, and she needed to be prepared. Either Paul would walk in having stopped Appleby and Rogerson, or she'd need to defend these people against both men.

And avenge Paul.

Either way, at least now she had Vita and her precious cub. Reaching down to pet the cub, she grinned. The cub looked at her with beautiful golden eyes but didn't move. Yes, having these two with them proved a far better plan.

"Azizi," she whispered in Egyptian. "It means precious."

Those yellow-gold eyes flickered, and Kaya thought maybe the young pup approved.

They'd stopped again. The donkey brayed, and Rogerson shouted and spat when two of his guards didn't reappear. Paul blew on his hands and moved closer to Appleby while Rogerson and the third guard called for their missing brethren.

"How much farther?" he asked Appleby. Paul was alternately shivering and sweating. He'd never worked so hard in freezing temperatures; he'd never been both sweaty and freezing. Frankly, he never wanted to be again.

"Just over that rise." Appleby kicked the snow, stomping his feet in what had to be a vain attempt to get warm. "If this damn donkey would move." He looked around. The wildness hadn't abated.

"I wouldn't move in this weather, either," Paul muttered. Appleby didn't seem to hear. "How trustworthy are these guards?" he asked instead. "Two of them seemed to have run off."

"Aye." Appleby frowned and looked at his hands.

They were empty, but Paul knew he was thinking of a bottle of wine. He looked nauseous, unsteady on his feet. Paul frowned. He'd thought Appleby's erratic nature was because the man kept himself drunk the entire time they'd been in Casa Grigori. Now, he wasn't so certain.

Perhaps Appleby's paranoia, the hallucinations, were caused by something else? Paul suddenly felt it was more than just overindulgence.

Frowning, he looked to see Rogerson and the final guard emerge from the trees. "Find them?" he called conversationally. "It's too cold to wait any longer." He walked to the donkey, who eyed him as if ready to bite. "Shh, shh," he cooed, reaching out to stroke the donkey's nose. "I know."

"They damn well disappeared," Rogerson roared.

"Probably got lost." Paul shrugged, still stroking the donkey, who seemed almost amenable to his touch—almost. "Bite Rogerson for me, eh?" he whispered and stepped away.

If the cave was just over the rise, the time was now. Since he couldn't expect the donkey to do as he'd asked, he needed to act, and quickly. Slipping one knife free, he pictured Kaya as he'd last seen her in bed this morning.

I love you, he thought and hoped she knew just how much.

All right, then. Now or never. Paul walked around the cart, as if to check the wheels. He ignored Appleby, who continued to look around the area, probably still expecting a wolf attack. Slipping behind the final guard, Paul gauged the thickness of his clothing and the force he'd need in order to penetrate that and the man's back.

The guard still carried his musket but had grown lazy with it. With the cold and the distance, he'd forgotten he didn't trust Paul, and he didn't even raise it when Paul slipped around him and quickly slit his throat.

Dropping the body to the ground, he turned to Rogerson, who was staring at him in open-mouthed shock.

"What in bloody hell—"

Appleby shouted something, but Paul didn't turn his attention from Rogerson. "I won't let you hurt any more people, you damn bastard. This ends tonight."

"Paul." Rogerson laughed, a short ugly sound. "You always were too noble for your own good."

The three bodies he'd left in the mountains could attest to quite the opposite. Noble? He almost laughed. What man did Rogerson think he knew?

"It's over, Major."

Rogerson lurched, but Paul anticipated it and pivoted out of the way, letting the wind and snow slide Rogerson down the small hill. Paul followed. He wanted to follow Appleby, didn't want him anywhere near Kaya. But if he didn't stop Rogerson now, the man would only recruit more people to peddle his opium.

Paul couldn't allow that.

Rogerson scrambled to his feet, his coat swirling around him in a tangle of fabric and cursing. Paul didn't wait but attacked.

The dagger, an extension of his hand, moved gracefully through the air, slicing Rogerson's hand. Shouting in pain and rage as his knife fell to the snow, Rogerson leaped at Paul.

Expecting the sloppy move, Paul merely moved out of the way. It was not graceful, and he slipped in the snow, sliding inelegantly several feet. Cold, wet, and angry, he scrambled to his feet and whirled to face Rogerson again.

"You have two choices." Paul held the low ground against the other man, but he was far more confident in this fight than Rogerson seemed to be. He'd turned wild, clumsy, too angry to fight and win. "I can take you to the local magistrate, or we can finish this here."

"Magistrate?" Rogerson snorted. "There is no law here. That's why it's so perfect! Even the damn priests take whatever they can from the rich landowners. Nobody would care if you brought me in chains, carrying the chests."

Something in those words rang true, but Paul merely shrugged. His coat, already too small for him, had torn to shreds, and the wind sneaked into the uncovered gaps. Snow slithered down his neck and back. His knees were wet, and that slipped down to his feet.

"Then I guess we end this here."

Rogerson laughed again and, weaponless, leaped at Paul. On unsteady ground and downhill from his opponent, Paul was at a distinct disadvantage. He tried moving again but wasn't fast enough this time, and he caught Rogerson's full weight.

His knife also caught Rogerson's belly.

Scrambling from under the man, Paul knelt beside him and met his gaze. "You deserve worse than this for what you've done here. What you did in Bombay. You deserve to roast in hell."

"I'll see you there," Rogerson spat, his lips bloodied.

"I've no doubt." Paul stood and stepped back.

He didn't look at the blood on his hands or the red staining the snow. He did, however, look at the donkey. Unhitching him from the carts, Paul pointed at him and said, as if the donkey understood English, "Stay here."

He couldn't leave the donkey here among the cold and whatever animals were drawn to the scent of blood. Turning for the cave, he ran after Appleby.

Twenty-Six

Kaya stood watch at the cave entrance. Her heart tripped over itself, and she couldn't catch her breath. She didn't know if that was because of fear, cold, or a combination of everything that had happened.

Time had no meaning as the snow continued to fall. Had mere moments passed, or had it been an hour? She gripped her khanjar, flexing her fingers to keep them warm and ready. The heavy white obscured everything and yet amplified every sound.

Behind her, Vita and Azizi stood guard over the men who'd kept these people trapped here. They did a far better job than Kaya could, snapping at them every time they so much as shifted on the floor. She was grateful for that. She didn't wish to split her attention between those men and the outside.

She hadn't checked on Marta, but she heard her voice occasionally echo from within the cave. Assurances to those who'd been trapped here for months and months, promises they'd be back at the village before nightfall.

Marta's reunion with her father had not gone as Kaya had expected. He blamed his daughter for his being taken, for what Appleby had done to the village, for Appleby's mere presence—

for the snow, as far as Kaya could tell. And all in front of Olivia, who had been so happy to see her grandfather.

Kaya wanted to turn and rail at him, scream at him about how brave Marta was. The words welled within her, hot and angry and ready to burst free. She wanted to scream that he'd done nothing while Appleby hurt and abused his daughter. That Olivia was a far braver person than he.

But she didn't say anything. This wasn't over yet.

In the snow, a shadow caught her attention, and she readied— it wasn't Paul. She knew his body as well as her own. His long gait, the graceful movement of his arms as he wielded a knife. The way he moved when he ran, with such economy of movement.

This man was running clumsily through the snow, falling and screaming into the wild. Harry Appleby.

"Marta!" Kaya called back, stepping from whatever shelter the cave entrance offered. "Keep everyone inside. Vita, Azizi." She spared a glance to her newfound friends. Could animals be called friends? She had absolutely no idea. "Don't let those men move."

"Appleby!" she called into the wind.

Kaya wanted no mistake when he turned to her. She wanted him to know who stood before him, khanjar at the ready. He turned toward her, slipping on the ground, his eyes wild even from this distance.

What had he seen to make him mad with fear? Or was it deeper than that, an ingrained madness that had always been present? Paul had not mentioned anything, and he'd known Appleby for decades.

"You!" Appleby snarled and drew his knife. It had a smaller blade than her khanjar, and he tossed it from hand to hand, as if to boast of his prowess. "This is all your fault."

"I fail to see how." Kaya stopped just at the edge of the flat ground and waited for him to come to her.

Never give up the advantage. Never rush an enemy when they can make the first move and come to you. Patience is behind you, Kaya. Let them make the first mistake.

Gidd's words echoed in her ears. A lifetime's worth of lessons now merged into a single action: stay alive. Kill Appleby so he never harms another living soul again. End this today.

"Paul would've never betrayed me like this before you!" He looked wildly around the area, spittle flying from his lips.

"Paul is his own man. I have not changed what's within him. Who he is today is who he has always been."

Where had those words been when she tried to tell Paul the same thing? When she stumbled over them last night, this is exactly what she meant. Ten years ago, he'd saved her grandfather's life. He didn't have to; he needn't have done anything for the Egyptian general, who Paul had known nothing about. But he had.

Kaya believed, deep in her soul, that that man was who Paul truly was. Acting without thinking, yes, most definitely. To save others. Gidd, the slave woman in the desert mountains.

"Bitch whore!"

She had a brief thought about men using that term to refer to women the world over, but then Appleby was rushing to her, and she braced for the attack. He clearly had some training, but he was unsteady on his feet. Drink had made him sloppy—*sloppier*, she supposed, as she easily sidestepped his knife.

One quick flick of her wrist, and he dropped it.

"I'm going to kill you!" he screamed.

"Not today." She whirled from his grasp, an inept attempt to grab her. "Today is the last day you harm anyone." Kaya arched her knife through the air, slicing Appleby longways across the stomach. "Today is the last day, Harry Appleby."

He was sobbing now, clenching his stomach but somehow still upright. With one more flick of her wrist, Kaya slit Appleby's throat.

"You've brought nothing but harm. Death and grief and greed." She stood over him and watched dispassionately as he bled onto the snow. "I doubt anyone will mourn you."

"Kaya!"

Paul's voice echoed over the mountains. Tearing her gaze from Appleby, she turned for her husband. He ran over the last incline, hatless, gloveless, his long strides eating up the distance. Kaya didn't think. Just ran to him.

"Kaya." He held her tight, breathing hard. Frantic, frozen fingers brushed over her cheeks, tangling in her hijab. "Are you all right?"

"I am." She grabbed his hands and discovered hers were shaking. She'd never killed a man before, though she'd known she could. Gidd always said that defending her own life might mean taking another.

She didn't look behind her at Appleby. Though the rush of the fight was still racing through her, she felt no remorse at killing him.

"You?" Blood stained his cheeks and hands. Alarmed, she stepped back and looked him over.

"I'm unharmed." He pulled her back into him, kissing her roughly. "You're safe." His hands cupped the back of her head, keeping her close. His lips tasted hers again and again. "You're safe. Kaya." He kissed her. "Kaya."

"Kaya?" Marta's voice called from the cave. "What are you..."

Her voice trailed off, and only then did Paul release Kaya. His hand clasped hers.

Words bubbled on the tip of her tongue, love and happiness and understanding. She wanted to tell Paul what she'd told Appleby, that he was more, so much more than what these people were. There wasn't time, but Kaya didn't want to lose the moment.

"I love you," she said simply. "Nothing can change that."

He looked at her. He was battered, tired, wet, and clearly lost. "Why?"

"Because the man I married fights for what is right."

"Kaya!" Marta raced across the small clearing. She stumbled when she saw Appleby's body and skirted around it, leaving a wide path. "You are not hurt? Signore Paul?"

"There's a donkey down the path." Paul didn't release Kaya's hand, didn't look from her to Marta. "And a pair of small carts. If the donkey hasn't wandered off, we can use him and the carts to take these people back to the village."

"Olivia!" Marta called. "Come help with the donkey!"

"Olivia?" Paul shook his head, eyes wide. "What's she doing here?"

"Come into the cave, *ya rouhi*, out of the snow."

"You've said that before." He followed her up the small incline, past Appleby's body and into the shelter of the cave. "What does it mean?"

"My soul."

He glanced to where Vita and Azizi stood guard and shook his head. Turning back to her, he leaned against the rocky wall and pressed his forehead to hers. "And you are mine."

———

"What do you want to do now?" Kaya asked in the quiet darkness of their room.

Outside, the wind had all but stopped, though the snow continued to fall. Paul had taken a blanket and tucked it around the window's shutters to keep out what he could of the wind and cold. Their small brazier burned hot and bright, but it was a small fire to combat the outside temperature.

It'd taken hours for them to transport the villagers from the mountain cave to Casa Grigori, even with Caroline and several villagers to help. Bravo, the donkey Olivia named, had been less than helpful, graciously agreeing to pull a single cart downhill only once.

Kaya didn't blame the donkey. Given what she knew of Appleby and Rogerson, she doubted they'd treated him kindly.

"*Do?*" Paul shrugged but didn't move his arms from around her. "We can't walk anywhere in this snow." He blew out a small breath. When he spoke again, it was soft and halting. "I don't want to stay here."

"No," Kaya agreed, but she hesitated.

"You want to stay?" Paul shifted to look down at her. His hair, clean of blood and snow, curled over his shoulders, and she ran her fingers through it. The simple act settled in her, and she vowed never to take anything in their life for granted.

"No, not here. I don't—as lovely as the village looks, they are not kind people." She hadn't told him what happened, hadn't mentioned Marta's father's harsh words in the cave nor the baby she was expecting.

She'd been rushed tying up the guards, though she still had no idea what they were to do with them. And then she had to tend to Vita, who even now struggled to breathe. The dog was in Marta's small cottage, looked over by a worried Olivia and an exhausted Marta. They'd ensured that the villagers returned home, and they'd seen to it that the opium burned—a fire worthy of the pits of hell.

"What happened?" He stilled, as if preparing for a fight.

"Marta is carrying Appleby's child."

Even in the darkness, Kaya saw his face drain. He closed his eyes and pressed his fingers against them. "Christ. I'm sorry."

"Aye. She can't stay here. Her father—when she found him in the cave, he did not seem happy to see her. I believe he blames her for..." Kaya waved a hand, uncertain how to encompass everything that had happened to Casa Grigori in the last several months.

"Not everyone is like Tahir," Paul whispered into the darkness.

"No," Kaya agreed. "Not everyone would take in a pregnant woman and her *odalik* on the basis of a letter, defy the Turkish sultan, and spend the next twenty-two years hiding his granddaughter to keep her safe."

Paul snorted. "Is that how old you are?" He kissed her shoulder, his lips cool against her chemise. "I didn't know."

She hugged him closer. "There is much neither of us knows about the other, I think."

His smile fell away, but he nodded. "I never wanted you to know that side of me. It's going to be a difficult few weeks, Kaya. Even now, I can smell the opium. It burns through me, and I want to race back to that cave and root through the ashes for more."

She had not thought of that. "Do you think those who were forced to sort the opium will have that same reaction? They've touched it constantly, they've transported it. Will they now feel the craving?"

"Yes." His voice dropped, and his hands tightened around her. "Just as Marco will always want the taste of it, just as I still struggle, so will they."

"I fear we did not help them as much as I had hoped."

"You did." His words were hot and harsh. "You did. We stopped the caravan from coming over the mountains. Forever?" He shrugged. "Nothing is forever. But you gave them their lives back. What happens now is up to them. Will those who knew accept that they were complacent in what happened to Marta?" He moved restlessly and shook his head. "Probably not. She'll never have a place here again."

"Perhaps she and Olivia should travel to Villa San Giovanni." Kaya frowned as she pieced that together. "Antoinette would welcome her."

"Aye, that's true." Paul hesitated. "But with Marco, I'm not so certain."

Teresa would be happy to have a friend in Olivia. And Marta needed to get away from here, but Paul had a point. "Marta does not need the reminder of all the harm opium does, and Antoinette might not be able to take on Marta, Olivia, the babe, *and* Marco."

"We'll find a place for her. Once the storm abates and we can walk out of this town, we'll head for the coast. Perhaps set Marta and Olivia up in a nice cottage so they don't need to worry about money ever again."

"And Azizi," she reminded him. "Vita, too, though I do not believe she will make it through the night."

"No, poor thing. But she took revenge on the men who harmed her." Paul let out a short laugh. "And I'm certain she would've attacked Appleby had you needed her to."

"Yes, she is a very smart dog." Kaya closed her eyes and snuggled deeper into his embrace. "But what about Bravo? We cannot leave him here."

He snorted. "Regular menagerie you have here."

"I do not," she protested and kissed him. "But they can't stay here."

"We'll leave by week's end, with luck." He stopped, and she waited for him to continue.

When he did not, she pulled back and looked up at him, frowning at the dark look on his face. "What's wrong?" She traced a finger between his brows, her heart leaping with nerves.

"I—I don't know what's going to happen," he whispered, his words halting and uneven. "When we walked from Bombay to Cairo, my sobriety was forced. I don't want to go back—I don't want to be that man again. The one I am when I drink. I want—"

He stopped and held her tighter, tucking her head beneath his chin, clenching handfuls of her chemise.

"Do you think I will leave you?" Kaya asked quietly. A shiver raced down her spine once the words held life, as if saying them had sparked some sort of truth.

"I—I don't know," he finally said. "What I do know is that I can't do this without you."

Kaya didn't know what "this" entailed, but she pressed her lips to the underside of his jaw and held him as tightly as he did her. She tried to think of something to say, but she honestly had no idea what Paul was going through. What he was about to go through.

"We promised to be together," she whispered. "As long as we work on keeping that promise, I think we'll be all right."

"Oh?" he asked, leaning back to meet her gaze. "As simple as that?"

"No, not simple." She frowned and reached for the words that would convey what she meant. "I am discovering that this world is not as simple as I believed. Not even my love for you." His hands flexed on her back at that, but he remained silent. "But we agreed to commit to this marriage. And that is a commitment I intend to keep."

He kissed her forehead, and she felt his smile. Her answering one widened on her lips, and she settled her head on his chest.

"I suppose I'm stuck with you, then," Paul teased. But his hands hadn't loosened from around her, and his voice caught.

"There are worse wives, I am certain." Kaya giggled. "Everyone should be so lucky to have me."

"Sorry, you're mine." He kissed the top of her head. "I'm not letting you go."

"Good, because I love you."

"And I you, my Kaya."

Want more?

Never miss a story update! https://bit.ly/3kSzMjI
Kaya and Paul's adventures will be continued in *A Lover's Promise*. Also look for *Smuggler's Captain...*

Nadia Koltsova escaped St. Petersburg in the dead of night, young, injured, and terrified. Ten years later, she's determined to protect the family that saved her. Even if it means sneaking into a human smuggler's warehouse in the middle of the night with only a dagger for protection.

Captain James St. Clair is searching for the same group of smugglers. They've killed one of his men and he's determined to bring the murderers to justice. He does not expect the witty, capable woman with the wicked dagger who insists she's more than capable of taking care of herself. He also doesn't expect to want her as fiercely as he does.

They both need help discovering where the missing people are located. Just perhaps not each other's help.

Sign up to my VIP list to learn more! https://bit.ly/3kSzMjI

Get a free short story!

I occasionally send newsletters with things like new releases, special offers, pictures of my dog, recipes, and other exciting news about my stories I hope you'll enjoy as much as I do.

If you sign up for my VIP list, I'll send you my short story series starting with *One Day with You*. This series is only available to my list.

https://bit.ly/3kSzMjI

Escorting a widow and her six children away from London and her husband's shady activities didn't fit Lieutenant Malcolm Sawyer's plan of infiltrating the seedier side of Dover. Tea with the lovely Lady Hélène, did. However, it was only a brief stop on his way to find proof of a suspected French invasion.

He had not imagined the lovely Louise Ardenne opening the door with a modified walking stick, ready to bludgeon him.

Louise had no time for dashing English officers. A refugee from France who traded all her possessions for safe passage across the Channel, she owed her life to Lady Hélène and had more serious business than blushing at pretty compliments. The tall, sapphire-eyed officer posed an intriguing mix of threat from arrest and an opportunity for help finding her missing father. If she didn't melt at his searing looks first.

Revolution had burned her world to the ground. Malcolm, with his honor and kisses that stole her breath, may finish the job. She's not a French spy. He doesn't trust her. An alliance is built not on trust but need, for the heat building between them and the answers they both seek amidst a world in chaos where even the closest friend could be an enemy.

Will their tentative alliance in the face of intrigue and spies be enough to convince him she is who she says? Or will her questions lead to her own death?

If you enjoyed this book

If you enjoyed this book, I'd really appreciate it if you helped others enjoy it, too. Reviews are precious and help persuade other readers to give my romances a try. More readers equals more incentive for me to write! And so many more stories for you to read!

About the Author

C.K. Mackenzie is the author of a series of Georgian and Regency Romances following a family as they navigate life, love, and war. Find out more at her blog: ckmackenzie.com. If you want to email her, please do so at ckmackenzieauthor@gmail.com.

By Christine Mackenzie

Conrad Chronicles

Husband of Convenience

Sins of a Rogue

Smuggler's Captain